CONCERTO

IN

CHROMA

MAJOR

NAOMI
TAJEDLER

interlude 🧩 **press**. • new york

This book is dedicated to the loving and aching memory of Alain Aaron Abraham Tajszeydler, who instilled in me a love for music before I could even draw my first breath, who taught me that learning is a never-ending process. Every passing day makes your absence more present.

לוּ יְהִי ...

The piano keys are black and white but they sound like a million colors in your mind.

—Maria Cristina Mena

AUTHOR'S NOTE

The characters in the story are human, with their flaws and imperfections, but they grow and learn—as we all do.

At the beginning of the story, a main romantic lead is someone who has been so completely sheltered from the "real world," that she talks without thinking and seems insensitive. The whole point of the story is to show that she, like all of us, can learn and grow to become the best version of herself.

Her biphobia is something that I, a bisexual Jewish woman, have experienced ever since I came out, and I wanted to show that it happens and can be changed through love and patience.

While this story is a contemporary romance first and foremost, it contains some elements that could be disturbing for readers.

These elements include:

Biphobia, fatphobia, insensitivity, miscommunication, graphic sex scenes, intrusive thoughts, and anxiety; prior to the story but mentioned—homophobia.

(www.interludepress.com/content-warnings)

Because this story involves citizens of the world, several languages are used. A glossary is available at the end of the book.

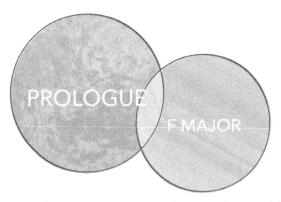

PROLOGUE
F MAJOR

Persian Green, Turquoise, and Spots of Marigold

CHIN IN HER MILLION-DOLLAR-INSURED HANDS, Halina Piotrowski must admit it: She has grown bored with her wandering life, with never settling down, with not having a home, with not even keeping track of where her manager has booked her. Just for once, Halina would appreciate the chance to explore the city where she performs. She doesn't think it's that unreasonable to want to know where she is and what makes the city, beyond its airport, fancy hotel, and concert hall. It takes her a moment to remember which American city is hosting her now.

"*Psiakrew!*"

She slams her fists against the piano keys and swears; the Polish consonants are sharp under her breath. The discordant notes echo through the empty auditorium and sharpen her frustration. They also bring to a sudden halt her assistant, who has been droning a recitation of her program for the next days. With a question in their eyes, Ari cocks their head. Halina waves at them to go on.

Ari Fowler is more than her assistant. They're her best friend, and she trusts them with her life, quite literally on a daily basis.

"Rehearsal with the orchestra at three, followed by an interview with *The Guardian* and a light dinner. Do you prefer to eat alone or—" Ari goes back to their bullet points. Their long frame is stretched against the grand piano.

Halina jumps into the window of opportunity. "No."

"No? No dinner?"

"No dinner for me," Halina clarifies. She stands and gathers the sheet music strewn over the lid of the piano. "I want to walk around the city, get some fresh air."

Ari closes the notebook. "Is there something you need me to do?"

Halina shakes her head. "I want to... Ari, I need to do more than just perform."

"You do more than just perform," Ari replies softly as they put their hand on her elbow to make her face them. "Do you want me to come with you?"

Halina shrugs off their hand and puts on her leather jacket. Its wide collar shields her face, giving her time to consider the offer, and she furtively glances at Ari.

Ari Fowler has been her constant companion for the last five years. Their carefully designed, androgynous style is a recent development; the sharp angles of the outfit they wear do wonders for their figure as it highlights their narrow waist and the curves of their hips. Their bangs—this month a platinum blond—and minimalist color theme match the severe set of their face and age them just enough to give them authority.

"Only if you lighten up a bit," Halina finally replies.

"I'll get changed before we go to the symphony hall." Ari's face is illuminated by a rare smile.

They're smiling now, a treacherous voice whispers in the back of Halina's mind, *until they leave for someone better, someone who will be nicer to them and is more talented than you...*

Halina wills the venom out of her head with a roll of her shoulders and a quick wince. It has been three years; her mother shouldn't have such a presence, such power over her and her thoughts.

"We can go to the Space Needle and *the* library, the one with the yellow stairs, and we'll eat some teriyaki salmon. Let me find a good place..."

"We have to get a coffee at the original Starbucks," Halina adds, silencing the voice of doubt to try to enjoy the present.

Ari graces her with a judgmental expression. Halina is tempted to take a picture and make it Ari's profile picture in her contacts list. She's tempted, but her sense of self-preservation is stronger.

"Duh." Ari returns their attention to their phone. "And some motherfucking doughnuts."

"And some motherfucking doughnuts," Halina repeats with a snort of laughter. Ari's rare curses are one treat she has learned to enjoy.

"But first, rehearsal and the interview; there's no way around it."

"No, indeed," Halina whispers as she drops onto the piano bench. Her fingers tap a gentle, bittersweet melody against the fallboard—Mark Knopfler's tribute to Seattle suits her just fine.

"Halina, are you…" Ari's voice is uncharacteristically gentle. "Are you okay?"

Halina closes her eyes as she rests her forehead against the cool, varnished wood. Her fingers are still on the keys. "I think I'm tired of this, Ari."

"This?"

"All of this: the travels, the hotels, the uncertainty of the tomorrows. I—I need to stop moving for a while."

Ari stays silent behind her. Halina can practically hear their mind's cogs turning at full speed, making a list of pros and cons.

"On it. I'll call Bhasin and ask him to find more permanent engagements."

Ari Fowler and Saral Bhasin—her very own dynamic duo. What change her life has been through since they entered it! Now she hopes they'll be able to help her regain balance.

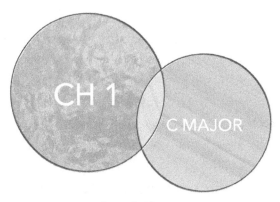

Reds and Chartreuse

THE METALLIC STRUCTURE STANDS BEFORE them, an alien ziggurat in the middle of Parisian suburbs. On one side, its sharp angles contrast with the 1970s buildings in the background. The other side, curvier and more complex, is still under construction. Metallic elements glint in the August morning. Whichever sides she chooses to look at, Alexandra Graff has to crane her neck to get a good view.

She was quite fond of the former Philharmonie, all wood, velvet, and history. This new building has none of the previous incarnation's aesthetic or appeal. That assessment will stay within the confines of her mind, though. The people in power have spent a crazy amount of money, millions upon millions, on this project, and adding the Philharmonie to her résumé would be fantastic. Voicing her opinion would only put her big break in jeopardy.

All her work, since she arrived in Paris and opened her studio, building its reputation from the ground up, has led to this opportunity. It's not her success alone, naturally. The studio has thrived because of her talent and her partner's creativity. And Leo can't seem to hide his glee any more than Alexandra can. They stand at the bottom of the metal and stone ramp leading to the entrance of the Philharmonie. The photobooks in his hands limit Leo's natural exuberance; he would clap his hands if he could.

"Showtime, bud."

Leo straightens and squares his shoulders as they walk along the ramp up to the construction site where Paris's new concert hall will open soon.

"The freakin' Philharmonie," Leo says under his breath for perhaps the hundredth time since two days ago, when they got the appointment for their meeting. "Our work is going to be exhibited in the freakin' Philharmonie."

"Hold your horses." Alexandra walks faster to match his speed despite their height difference. "It's not a done deal yet. Can you imagine how many artists must be competing for this?"

"Ay, *carissima*, don't be so negative," Leo retorts, bumping into her. "Our work speaks for itself. It's brilliant, and everybody worth their salt will have to admit it." He pauses, and a cocky grin stretches his lips. "And we come highly recommended, don't we?"

Not too long ago, his smile and the russet quality of his voice would have turned Alexandra's legs to jelly and made her accept anything he said. Those days are over, and Mr. Neri doesn't have the same influence on her, but she can still appreciate the calm his presence grants her.

"Indeed, we do," she replies with a new spring in her step as the entrance to the strange structure comes into view. "I never imagined my glassblowing master would suggest my name for a job of this magnitude."

Leo barks a laugh, and the sound echoes against the stone and the metal. It evokes swirls of copper at the forefront of Alexandra's synesthetic mind. "Pretty sure your apprenticeship left an impression in Sue-Ji's bed too—must have helped jog her memory."

Alexandra elbows him. He misses a step but manages not to drop the portfolio. "Do you imply I fucked my way to where I am?" She squints at him, tongue sharp and ready to lash out. "'Cause the last time I checked, I didn't sleep with any of our patrons to seal any deal."

"Neither did I," Leo replies, his most angelic mask on. "Not implying anything, boss."

"Right, because we are professional." She softens as she refocuses on the task ahead. "And I prefer to believe Sue-Ji's recommendation is based on the quality of my work rather than on my sexual prowess."

Leo's brown eyes seem to darken. "Once this is over, you want to remind me of that or...?"

"Psh, be serious."

Leo shrugs off her rejection. "*Certo.* That's our contact?"

Alexandra sees a woman at the entrance of the building. Her short white hair and pantsuit match the building and contrast with the rich brown of her skin.

"I told you they were allergic to colors," Leo whispers, and Alexandra takes a deep breath to control her laugh before she introduces herself.

"Madame Loupan, I suppose?" Alexandra says.

The woman shakes her hand. "Mademoiselle Graff, Monsieur Neri, *bienvenus.*"

"I'd shake your hand, *signora,*" Leo says, "but mine are a bit full."

"So it seems," Mme. Loupan replies with a raised eyebrow as she surveys the stack in his hands. "Color me curious."

Alexandra is very careful not to glance at Leo, lest they both start giggling at the executive director's choice of words. "These are our portfolios, to show you what we achieved in the past and what we propose in general, based on the information you sent us." She falls into step with the director as they enter the shell of the structure. "Adjustments might be necessary, but we are always flexible; it all depends on the budget."

Michèle Loupan takes three helmets from a metal basket and hands one to each of them. "Mademoiselle Yong was adamant you were precisely the answer to our quest." She guides them to a series of naked rooms of white curvy walls where two men wait for them. "Hence this hastily scheduled interview. The floor is yours."

The two men introduce themselves as Monsieur Padirac and Monsieur Rochard, members of the board of directors for the Philharmonie and in charge of relationships with patrons and sponsors.

Alexandra opens the largest portfolio. As Leo slowly turns the pages, she points out the finer details. "As you can see, we specialize in creating stained glass for pre-existing spaces and blending them into their environments." Her voice is more confident as she presents her creations. "Our patterns are abstract. They highlight the lines of the architecture that will surround the panels. I believe we could create an ensemble of stained glass panels to match the Philharmonie's energy and versatility." She pauses, keeping a firm rein on her words before they can tumble out of her mouth. "Through the different colors and thicknesses of the glass and the use of a variety of widths of lead, we give light a physicality to inhabit the room it's presented in."

"What about windows not exposed to natural light?" Padirac asks. His high voice grates on Alexandra's nerves. She blinks to remove the sharp greens and yellows his voice brings to her mind.

"How do you mean?" she asks.

Loupan glares at Padirac, a confirmation that Alexandra is not the only one irritated by his interruption. Padirac shrinks into himself and mutters an apology.

"Our first foyer is the room where the chosen work will stand. It will be completely closed off from the outside," Loupan says, "which means the art will have to be self-sufficient, lighting-wise."

"Given this room's arrangement, I assume the foyer is somewhere else," Leo intervenes, his head tilted to the curved, floor-to-ceiling windows. "Perhaps we should continue this conversation in the foyer itself?"

"Indeed, Monsieur Neri," Rochard replies. His baritone booms in the empty space in the form of deep sapphire blue spheres through which paple pink lines appear. "But it's undergoing construction as we speak. We'll have to use the architectural model to show you what we expect from you. Monsieur Padirac, if you don't mind helping me?"

"Not at all, Monsieur Rochard." Padirac rushes out of the room.

While they wait for him to return, Alexandra lets the sounds around them come to the forefront of her mind. The echo of the construction appears as green ripples across the fluidity of the beltway noises on the canvas of her mind. The clangs of metal become orange lines raining over it, crisscrossing and splitting the space. The footsteps on cement that echo against the bare walls turn into ephemeral white and gold circles.

Alexandra tries to picture the finished building. Do the plans include rich materials to make this colossus of cement and wood more comfortable and approachable? Will it remain bare and minimalist, composed of raw materials the audience will be able to ignore to focus on the music and nothing else?

As if cued by her inner questions, Rochard and Padirac return with a squeaky trolley bearing a model. Designed as a man-made hill, the building is divided into offices, small concert rooms, and the big auditorium. While the auditorium seating curves around the stage, some balcony seats appear almost to hang in the air, as if clouds or satellites. The design is more poetic than Alexandra would have guessed from the building's exterior.

"Here," Loupan points, and they all come closer to study the miniature room. "Within the folds of the roof, right above the stage."

In one swift move, Alexandra takes off her jacket and pulls her notebook from her pocket. She holds it up for Loupan's authorization to sketch the room and the position of the installation they may be commissioned to create for the only spot left blank in the detailed model.

Padirac had a point; the space cannot welcome windows. It can host decorative pieces, though, perhaps a folding screen. Leo comes to her side to point out some of the differences in shape and shadows created by the architecture, elements they will need to take into account if they do get the contract.

"What we want is a work of art to fill the whole wall." Loupan's eyes dart between the model and Alexandra's notebook. "A bold, spectacular piece. A work with the strength to complement Monsieur Novel's vision for the Philharmonie without being overshadowed by it."

Alexandra and Leo nod as she writes this down.

"How could we illuminate it?" Leo mumbles.

"What about LED lighting?" Alexandra whispers back.

"It will be easy to incorporate that into the structure, even if we have to do it within the frame," Leo agrees. "Economic, consistent light throughout and green energy. We'll have to experiment a little to secure the wires to the structure, but it's perfectly manageable."

"Good point," Alexandra says, gazing into space as she makes a mental projection of what could be. The possibilities her inspiration and experience create become notes and sketches. She returns her attention to Loupan and her sidekicks. "As our portfolio shows, we use color freely. Would it be a problem for the homogeneity of the structure, or the architect's aesthetic?"

"Quite the contrary," Padirac replies. "Since the room will host mostly receptions and parties, we want to create a pocket of space with a different aesthetic from the rest of the building."

Alexandra adds that information to her notes and sketches. Silence stretches between them, only highlighted by the green ripples of the distant sounds of the construction site around them. They dissolve into silvery tendrils when Michèle Loupan clears her throat and pulls Alexandra back into the interview.

"We still need to decide where we want to take this little project," she says, brushing invisible lint from her sleeve, "but I have a hunch it would be interesting to work with you, Mademoiselle Graff, Monsieur Neri." She shakes their hands once more; the ghost of her smile remains on her lips. "As discussed over the phone, I will deliver your photobooks for the entire board to review, and we'll keep in touch."

Everybody shakes hands, and as the pair is escorted to the door, they give a last glance over their shoulders at the books holding all their chances.

THE WALK OUT OF THE building and back to the car is a silent affair. Once seated, eyes on the steering wheel, Alexandra takes a deep breath.

"Do we have what it takes?" Leo asks, voice muffled as he bites his thumbnail.

"We do."

"All right, what you say goes, boss. What now?"

"We start planning," Alexandra replies before she starts the engine. "If you don't mind, I'll drop you at the studio to let you run some tests with LEDs."

"Roger that. Where are *you* going?" Leo asks, his eyes on his phone.

"I need to work on the templates for the different panels; I counted the possibility of a dozen in the frame they showed us."

"Add one just to be safe," Leo corrects. "The central one needs to be divided into at least two parts, with the curve at the center. I mean," he amends, "we could do it as one, but it would be enormous, and far too risky."

"*Merde*, you're right," Alexandra mumbles. She mentally adds it to her plans. "I'll paint the templates for each panel. Tomorrow I can bring the canvases to the studio, and we'll take it from there, all right?"

"*Comme d'habitude*, boss," Leo says with a mock-military salute. "Drop me off near Place de la Nation though; inventory says I need to get some bulbs and wires. And we're short on lead."

"When are we not?"

AFTER SHE DROPS LEO AT the store, Alexandra takes her time to drive back to her apartment, and the small room above it that she rents from her neighbor solely for her painting. She needs the silence in the car to consider her plan of action.

She has two options: she could turn the different synesthetic experiences she has sketched in her notebooks—from the songs she caught on the radio while drafting the presentation to today's photisms—into glass panels. They are so varied in color and dynamic, though, it may be too complicated to find a harmony.

Or, she could leave the synesthesia aside and compose a piece guided only by color harmonies and generic shapes. This would give Leonardo a bigger role in the creative part of their association, as he has turned color theory into a lifestyle—which is why he is the one turning her sketches and paintings into panels. The downside of this option is the obvious frustration it would generate for her; since the first phone call from Loupan's assistant, her synesthesia has been particularly active, catching every sound and demanding to be used.

It's not an easy decision, and Alexandra carefully weighs every aspect. As she drives, each turn and stop reflects the choice she needs to make. In her studio, with her Corgi by her side, one hand around her phone and the other tight on her mug of hot tea, she nails down the final decision: The way she has reacted to auditory stimuli these past weeks, especially in the Philharmonie, is far too memorable and inspirational to be set aside. She will carefully choose which photisms to visually represent, though, in order to reach harmony.

When she arrived in Paris, she needed to find a therapist to deal with her anxiety attacks. The therapist she matched with recommended she focus on her breathing to clear the cloud of anxiety and use her "creative outlets" as a lifeline to find her balance again. Given what is at stake, her cloud threatens to turn into a thunderstorm and overwhelm her.

Sitting in front of her easel while Punshki finds his allotted spot on top of her feet with a satisfied sigh, Alexandra sips her tea with her eyes closed; the rosehip and hibiscus fill her senses over the lingering smell of paint. She counts her breath, seven seconds in and nine seconds out, and repeats the cycle until her heartbeat is slow and regular. Now the colors and shapes she has recently heard come back to her, along with their inspirations, in her very own private creative soundtrack. The song she's often heard in the Metro's halls on her way to the studio in the past weeks turns into papaya, cream and cinnabar swirls overlaid with soft, ephemeral spots of chartreuse.

"*Tire, tire, tire l'aiguille, ma fille…*"

The composition is summery, bouncy, and energetic. It could be divided into two windows on each side of the wall at the Philharmonie: bookends for the whole installation.

Alexandra loads her brush with tepid water to dilute the pigments. She delicately layers the warm colors, translating onto canvas the music her mind translated into swirls.

While it dries, she takes the canvas off the easel to start another one. Simultaneously inspired by Loupan's voice and presence and the clangorous quality of the building where the work will live, she picks whites, black, and silver and creates a metallic vortex as a background. This time the paint on her brush is thick and her brushstrokes heavy, indicating the depth of the synesthetic episode.

The pattern could be used for narrow separation windows, which could appear, like pauses, before each wider one. It would establish a rhythm and advantageously diminish the size of each glass panel. It would also allow her and Leo to adapt to the curve of the structure.

In her sketchbook, Alexandra adds some notes over the sharp angles of the outer shell of the building and the soft curves of the main room. The sketch's lines get thicker, more defined, with arrows pointing at the allocated spots for the panels she envisions. Alexandra goes back and forth between sketch and canvas, focusing on the pattern. Only then does she put aside the synesthetic part of her inspiration and highlight it with conscious, artistic brushstrokes to bring whites into the composition.

How long she spends at her easel she cannot say—more than a couple of hours, certainly—but the strain in her neck when she rolls her chair back is a good indication it may have been too long.

With the tip of her foot, Alexandra gently pushes her dog, who is asleep and snoring at her feet, and stands. She rolls her shoulders to get rid of the stiffness and observes the two canvases drying. It's a good start. Now, what to do for the center? It will be a challenge; Leo was right on the money there. Being able to divide it into multiple parts takes off some of the pressure, but each panel still has to be perfect by itself.

Alexandra takes another canvas and taps the wooden end of the paintbrush against her lips. The moment of stillness stretches, and she takes in the smell of pigments, paint thinner, and varnish that permeates her little studio. Once again, she counts her breath, seven in, nine out, and...

Nothing.

Nothing comes to her: no color, no shapes, no idea. She gingerly puts the brush on the easel's resting shelf. Past experiences have taught her not to force herself to paint without inspiration.

Ten years ago, when she was Sue-Ji Yong's apprentice, she sometimes forced her inspiration and pushed past barriers, only to get the result smashed to the ground by Sue-Ji or herself, along with her hopes. She'd wanted to learn everything about the technique of glassblowing before she could allow herself to move onto stained glass—who better to learn from than an artist such as Sue-Ji, whose work Alexandra had admired from the very first glance.

The attraction between the two women had not altered the relationship between master and student. It only came to fruition when Sue-Ji admitted it was time for Alexandra to work on her own—and what a night it had been. When Alexandra pulled a long, teardrop-shaped vase-to-be from the fire of the lehr, the sparks between them had turned into a different fire and burned away any reluctance.

Sue-Ji had provided a precious piece of advice Alexandra has kept close to her heart, in her work and in her relationships: *Patience yields focus; focus yields perfection.*

Rather than force inspiration now, she takes Polaroid pictures of the completed paintings so she'll have some materials to start working on with Leo. He's the best at finding rhythm and pattern in her work, and she trusts his instincts. They work symbiotically, whether they are a couple or just friends.

For now, she will go to the authentic British pub down the street to treat herself with a comforting shepherd's pie. Its richness is bound to soothe her. The quiet environment this restaurant provides will allow her to work on her administrative responsibilities, to draft a budget to go with the artistic proposal. She can't predict what the Philharmonie will decide, but whatever they choose, Alexandra and Leo will be ready for it.

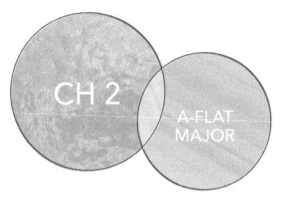

Thulian Pink, Carolina Blue, and Copper

HALINA AND ARI ARRIVE IN Paris alongside a heatwave announcing an Indian summer. Her first interview with the musical director of the Paris Philharmonie leaves her simultaneously worried and ecstatic. A long cycle of tribute to Hungarian composers is a challenge she is ready to tackle with gusto, even if it means she'll have to cut her nails short and stock up on Band-Aids and arnica to deal with the brutal dynamic designed by those composers. From a young age, Halina learned sacrifices were to be made at the altar of music—physical ones were the easiest. For the second program, names of great modern composers such as Antheil or Bernstein were mentioned, with the certainty of no less than two cycles dedicated to the Gershwin brothers. Halina cannot wait to get her hands on those modern melodies.

Jazz has always fascinated her, but her mother, who was once also her manager, thought it not elevated enough to be worthy of their attention. She never let Halina play any form of music related to jazz; no such composer, not Gershwin nor Gould nor whomever, found favor in her eyes. What else was Halina supposed to do but play it as her personal rebellion against the prison her mother built around her?

She spent many nights at the family piano with her foot on the damper pedal and her ear pressed to the lacquered wood as she played melodies from memory. These were the best memories of her teenage years, of her "before." The fact that she'll be able to play at full volume with the support of the orchestra and share such an intense energy with an audience fills her with glee.

The challenge of both programs is certain, but they're not the reason for her concern. She worries because, for the first time, Halina is going to be part of the ensemble, not a temporary guest exempt from the group's rules. Her manager may believe she has been blind to everything around her, but Halina has heard some of what the gossip mill of the musical world has been saying about her. If she has been sheltered from the brunt of the media backlash and most of the hate mail, it's because of his decisions, not hers. She can't blame him for protecting her.

The program gives her the lion's share of the season and thus focuses most of the media attention on her and her reputation. Halina is not about to complain though; she can count on one hand the musicians who can say a whole season was built around them, and to be among them is a badge of honor.

It's not much of a stretch to picture how the orchestra will react, from the concertmaster to the various corps of instrumental sections. Musicians are focused animals, hungry for the spotlight, and any newcomer stealing it instantly becomes a target. As much as she tries to shrug it off, Halina is not thrilled at the prospect of another bullseye painted on her back. Her first interview in Paris gave her a taste, and she still has to work around the bitter tang of it. The pianist and host of the radio show, Jean-François Zygel, was nice enough about it, she'll admit. He didn't tiptoe around the big scandal of her career, but seemed curious to know if she had plans for an encore.

Three years ago, kissing her maestra while bowing to their audience had seemed the only way to come out in a way Mariola Piotrowska wouldn't be able to brush under the carpet. Her mother, unrelenting and unforgiving, was her first manager. Her voice covered all other sound, all other comment, drowning every compliment with her own reprobation—until that kiss.

For the public, it had been a statement, a message sent to everybody who had followed her career since her début. Halina Piotrowska became

Halina Piotrowski, using the masculine gender of her surname as a way to sever herself from her mother, to show that she was a grown woman controlling her sexuality and her career. In private, it had been a more complicated matter. The conversation behind closed doors featured insults and old resentments that had festered over the years. Firing her mother gave Halina the strength and the pride to burn all the bridges between her younger self and who she aimed to be.

Now, accompanied by Ari, Halina loudly claps her hands in the empty concert hall that formerly housed the Philharmonie. She bows as low as she can, then holds the position. The gesture is beneficial on two counts: It dissipates the ghosts of her past and honors the room and the myriad of artists who filled every crook and corner of it with their own musical energy. She will honor it before she moves on to the new space.

The news about the construction of a new concert hall, a new Philharmonie, was enough to get her attention. She would have followed the development if only to keep herself up-to-date with the music world as a global entity. The choice of architect and the choice of location—at the north end of the city—are delicious cherries on the gossip sundae.

The building is no longer merely a source of rumors: it will be Halina's home for the next year, for the longest commitment of her career. She needs to stand before it.

A question in their brown eyes, Ari peers at her, and she nods. "Let's go."

The Philharmonie is not what she expected, and, from the expression on Ari's face, she's not the only one surprised. The building, with its chrome and sharp curves, is more reminiscent of a spaceship than a concert hall.

Once they step indoors, the idea of science fiction flies out the window. All round shapes and honey-toned wood panels and white-to-yellow walls, the Philharmonie's interior is an invitation to relax and enjoy the moment, a cradle for an audience as well as for the musicians. The stage is made of darker wood. Nestled within the largest curve in the building, it reminds Halina of a womb. That's fitting, in her opinion, for a space dedicated to bringing music to life.

They have been authorized to walk around the stage, even if construction workers are still busy throughout the structure. Halina walks with her head up, and her eyes follow the line of balconies. Ari clears their throat and moves the harmonica in their hand in a silent question.

"Go ahead, Ari," Halina replies as she sits on the stairs and closes her eyes.

Ari plays a melody both familiar and foreign. It speaks of nostalgia in the first language Halina learned to speak, the only one she's truly mastered. Music conveys emotions so much more easily than heavy, complicated words. She lets the notes wash over her, lets them bounce over the walls of the room.

Smoothly, Ari modulates the notes until they play "La Vie en Rose." Halina lets out a surprised laugh, then sings along under her breath. Something tugs at her heartstrings as the lyrics register, something foreign and forbidden. Halina never learned to let someone in; how could she demand someone's "heart and soul" to find her own happiness? She draws a blank when she tries to find something in herself to offer beyond her body, her money, and her music; how could she ever build a relationship with another woman?

She tries to keep her voice under a whisper, but it's still loud enough for Ari to catch it. They stop playing with a wince. "Gosh," they say, "for someone so talented behind an instrument, you are the worst singer I've ever had the misfortune of hearing."

"The worst, really?"

"The absolute worst."

Halina cackles, her fingers raised in a V. "It means I'm still numero uno! Woohoo!"

Ari twists their mouth into a grimace. "At being bad at something. Congratulations," they say, deadpan, and Halina's victory crow turns into a soft chuckle.

The epitome of overgrown children, the two of them sit at the edge of the stage and kick their feet. Halina rests her head on Ari's shoulder.

"I guess we could stand a year in this place," Ari says. "Want me to find us an apartment for the season, or should we stay in a hotel?"

"Hotel," Halina replies immediately, letting go of the comfort of Ari's strong shoulder. "I'm not ready for a bigger commitment."

"Gotcha, boss."

"But," she adds, biting her lip, "can it be a homey one? Something in the heart of Paris, maybe, but not too crowded with tourists?"

"You got it."

Halina lets the silence stretch over them like a blanket before clearing her throat. "Come on," she says, "there's a whole city waiting for us."

"Pah-ree," Ari replies in a terrible French accent.

Halina takes hold of Ari's hand once they're both on their feet. "The gay Pahree!" she exclaims in the same accent, and savors the sparkle of interest in their eyes.

"Speaking of which, want to get the full experience tonight?" they ask with a crooked smile, and Halina nods.

She shakes her shoulders in an approximation of a shimmy. "Let's go dancing."

Ari snorts when they jump off the stage to follow her. "Come on, boss, let's get you settled while I find us a bar to go to tonight."

HALINA CLOSES HER EYES AS she lets her instincts take over. Her body follows the beat of the music, and Ari's presence is a nice shield against the dance floor crowd. This bar is the right choice for her mood, and the sapphic clientele is the right choice for the purpose of the night.

They dressed similarly, she and Ari, in tight, dark tank tops and black linen pants. Until her assistant changes their hair color yet again, they could be mistaken for twins, or at least siblings. They have the same willowy, slender body type and the same fair hair.

Halina lifts her arms above her head. Her long braid moves from side to side on her back. Ari puts one hand on her waist.

"You need to drink, Lina," they say in her ear to cover the volume of the music.

"Not thirsty." She opens one eye when they lightly pinch her arm, only to find them smirking.

"You need to drink," they insist while they make Halina turn toward the bar, "and I need to get to the bar pronto."

Halina glances at the bar. Ari's sudden and unquenchable thirst is due to the man behind the bar. Sleeves of tattoos cover his impressive muscles and dark skin; eyeliner circles his eyes, their green shade catching the light of the lamp over the bar. The other bartender is much more to Halina's taste. Her dark skin is almost blue in the bar's lights, and her small breasts and tight abs are artfully hinted at under a pastel pink top. She has the most dignified posture Halina has seen in such an establishment. She would love to make her less dignified, take her apart with her fingers as though she's a complicated piece of music to bring to life.

"Maybe I am thirsty," Halina says. She stands with her forehead against Ari's temple, never taking her eyes off the bar. Ari laughs and plays along until more eyes are on them.

At the counter, Ari bends over the metal bar top, arching their back and twirling the one long strand of hair on the left side of their head between their fingers until the barman finally approaches them. From the dark-eyed leer he gives Ari, Halina is confident of two things: It's a good thing she doesn't care to fight Ari for the man's attention–she would lose—and she needs to find herself a companion for the night.

As she waits for a potential companion to come her way, Halina keeps her back against the bar to show off the long line of her body in the best light possible. She sips the drink Ari slid her way and watches the crowd. From the corner of her eye, she spots the dignified bartender gazing at her, a dark sunflower drawn to Halina's starlight. Halina doesn't react. It's better to let her come to her at her own pace, which gives Halina the upper hand, so she keeps her eyes away from her.

Her eyes land on a short woman who dances by herself. She's not spectacular in any way: short, dark hair stuck in curls against darkish skin, compact and curvy body wrapped in a black dress with no regard for the fashion rules for her body type. But her attitude is enough to catch Halina's attention. She moves as if she's alone, as if she doesn't care about being the subject of more than one conversation. It's not an act of seduction, her dance. It's pure, unadulterated self-pleasure, right there in the middle of the group.

Halina keeps her eyes on her, and the bar's lights help her catch gray eyes and a wide smile. While she's not usually attracted to that body type, she could be tempted by the dancing woman if she doesn't manage to seduce the bartender.

"*Bonsoir.*" A deep voice behind her pulls her from the hypnosis of the plump woman's hips. Her eyes find black ones surrounded with sparkly eyeliner.

Bingo.

"Hello," she replies, draping herself against the counter as she deepens her accent for the "exotic" factor. The way the bartender's expression turns predatory before she slides a glass toward Halina means it's certain she'll get to unravel Miss Regal's impeccable posture before the end of the night.

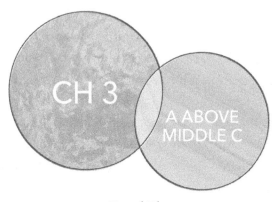

Royal Blue

MORE THAN ANYTHING, GOING OUT dancing tonight was a celebration, a way to let out her enthusiasm lest it overwhelm her. The email from Loupan is still fresh in her mind; for something so important to their future, it was surprisingly short: two lines to tell them their work convinced the board. Their proposed budget was deemed satisfactory "if you can meet the time limit," and they are to come to her office in two days' time to get their proofs of accreditation. Leo and she needed to read it a couple of times to let the message seep in: work was entirely impossible.

She decides to connect with the life she left behind across the Atlantic and across North America too. *Christ, the West Coast is far away.*

The lilac of the Skype ringtone can bring excitement or dread, depending on who is on the other end. Alexandra bites her little finger's nail while she waits, but she stops when her mother's face fills the screen.

"Alexandra!" Pauline exclaims, Independence blue filling Alexandra's mind. Alexandra can see her eyes going soft despite the pixelated image.

"*Mamuschka*," Alexandra replies with a wave.

"How are you, *bubbeleh*?"

The Yiddish term of endearment makes her grin, and she sighs happily. "I'm good, Mom," she replies. "Lots of work, but it's exciting."

"Good, good." Pauline pauses. She runs her hand through dark hair streaked with white, and her eyes avoid Alexandra's gaze. Alexandra's heart squeezes in her chest.

Not today, please, Mom, not today...

"And how are things with Jeannette and Georges?" Pauline asks happily, ultramarine blue now.

Now, Alexandra's heart is beyond squeezing, it's breaking. "Mom," she starts slowly, "Aunt Jeannette is dead, she... she has been dead for eight years now."

A frown appears on Pauline's face; doubt and confusion are clear in her gray eyes, so similar to Alexandra's own. "Has she?" she asks. Her voice is small and childlike; blue veers into green.

Alexandra nods, and it takes a lot to keep her tears away. "I'm sorry."

Pauline shakes her head. "No, bubbeleh, I am the one who's sorry," she says, in a stronger voice.

"Mom, do you take the pills the doctors prescribed?" Alexandra asks, anxious to take advantage of this moment of lucidity.

"I do," she replies, "but..."

"But?"

"But," Pauline says with a sigh, "it's been a while since I went to the doctor."

"Mom!"

"I know, I know." Pauline's defiant pout is too far out of character for Alexandra's liking. "I just didn't want to go."

"And Dad just let it happen?" Alexandra asks, fighting the pain in her chest at the mention of her father. Her pain must appear on her face nevertheless, if her mother's softened gaze is any indication.

"Your father..." she starts, wiping the side of her face, "...he's a good man. He doesn't want to hurt me so he just—"

"Does nothing." Alexandra groans. "Mom, all Henry needs to do is take you to your appointments, whether you want to go or not."

"I know, bubbeleh."

"I don't—I don't suppose he'll agree to talk to me?" Alexandra asks. She has to ask, although there is no reason for any different outcome than in all her previous calls.

"Bub…"

"No, it's—it's okay," Alexandra says. A dismissive wave of her hand ends the discussion. "No point in forcing it."

Alexandra inherited her stubbornness from the Graff side of the family. She and her father were cut from the same cloth: loyal to their opinions and beliefs and as headstrong as wild horses.

Ten years have passed since their falling-out, since her coming out. Ten years, and her father still doesn't want to mend the bridge he burned. Alexandra won't apologize for this part of her, and, if Henry wants them to stay on the worst of terms, so be it.

"And how is your Leo?"

Alexandra squints at the screen and fiddles with the brightness to properly examine her mother's face. *Is it a joke or another episode?*

"Um, we work well together." She is still on edge. The moment her mother's deep laugh booms in her speakers, though, as sweet and amber as date honey, relief floods through her.

"Just kidding," Pauline says, dark eyes sparkling in the light of the California morning.

Alexandra pokes out her tongue, and her mother only laughs harder. "Go and see your doctor today, Mom? Please? For me?"

"Scout's honor," Pauline replies, lifting three fingers in a jaunty salute.

"I love you, Mamuschka."

"Love you too, bubbeleh."

The screen goes dark when her mother hangs up, and Alexandra buries her face in her hands. Telling her parents, her mother at least, about her professional success was the whole point of her call. Instead, Alexandra just piled more worry on her shoulders.

She needs to collect herself before she calls her twin sister. She has no doubt about Elisabeth's ability to read right through her as if she's made of glass, but she can hope. She lets the dark colors of the nightlife wash over her and replace the worrisome variations in her mother's voice, then makes the call.

"Sasha!"

"Hey, Liz." Alexandra's mouth stretches into a wide smile at the sight of her sister.

During their childhood, their parents encouraged them to dress and behave as identically as possible. Time has passed, and their paths have created differences: They wear their hair differently; they have put on weight in different areas. Now they are mirrors for each other's inner selves, which are still intimately connected, no matter how far from each other they may be.

Elisabeth is usually immaculate, the perfect Jewish princess, not a hair out of place and wearing a pristine outfit. Who is the woman filling her screen with bags under her eyes? She wears a messy braid, and Alexandra notices creases and stains on her videogame-themed T-shirt. Elisabeth Yael Graff-Abernathy does not own T-shirts, much less geeky, dirty ones.

"What's wrong?" Alexandra asks.

Elisabeth twists her mouth into a grimace. "Am I so obvious?"

"I wasn't aware you could do casual, Sis," Alexandra points out.

Elisabeth examines herself, puzzlement written over her face. "Oh."

"Seriously, Liz, what's going on?"

Elisabeth attempts a smile, but her chin quivers. "I petitioned for a *gett* this morning."

Alexandra's eyes open wide, and she scoots closer to her screen. "You're getting a divorce? For reals?"

"Oh, yeah." Elisabeth pushes a stray strand of hair away from her face. "I kicked Matthew out of the house last night."

"Fuck."

"Yep." Elisabeth clenches her jaw and sits back in her chair. "Fucker took me for an idiot one time too many. Or maybe banged one. I don't want the sordid details."

"He cheated on you?"

"He didn't even try to hide or deny it, Sasha." She bites her lower lip as a couple of tears roll down her cheeks. "He had lipstick on the zipper of his pants! The idiot just put the pants in the laundry basket, like I—as if it didn't matter what it did to me."

Alexandra's jaw drops. She's so angry she could take a plane, find her piece-of-shit, soon-to-to-be-ex-brother-in-law, and kick his sorry ass. "The fucking garbage reject."

Elisabeth nods through her sniffles. "Should be settled fairly quickly," she says, wiping a stray tear.

"And how did the munchkin react to the whole mess?" Alexandra asks, and Elisabeth brightens.

"The munchkin is fourteen, Sash."

"My nephew is still very much a baby and will always be, thank you very much."

"And to answer your question, Zach helped me pack his father's stuff."

"Oh?"

"As in, he threw the opened suitcase down the stairs."

"How very helpful."

"I know, right?" Elisabeth exclaims, with more enthusiasm in her voice than in her eyes. "You should have seen the way he signed his insults. I was so proud."

"Me too." Alexandra mirrors her sister's posture and rests her chin on her closed fist. "Will you be okay?"

Elisabeth shrugs, in a perfect imitation of her teenage self. Her braid is visible as it swishes side to side. "I'll get over it. Perhaps I'll spend our birthday with a bottle of Shiraz for company, but it will still be better company."

"You're more than welcome to my couch. I'm sure Punshki misses you," Alexandra insists.

"You know what, it's a great idea." Elisabeth smiles, her happiness now clear in her eyes. "Maybe not for our birthday though; it's too soon, isn't it…"

"We can take care of the logistics whenever you choose to come, Liz. Put those frequent-flyer miles to good use. God knows Matthew doesn't have a say in how you live your life anymore." Alexandra pauses. "As if he ever had any. He never deserved you, and you're too smart not to be aware of it too."

"You always told me so."

"Always thought so."

"Hmm."

"I also always said the world was yours for the taking, and your recent loss of two hundred pounds or so of unhelpful flesh should help."

Alexandra and Elisabeth share a smile and both reach for the screen in a virtual joining of hands.

"Keep me posted," Alexandra says before blowing her a kiss. "Paris and I will welcome you with our arms wide open."

"Will do." Elisabeth's lips are puckered in a kiss, far too close to the camera, but just what Alexandra needed in order to laugh. "And we need to talk about your side of the pond, Frenchie."

"Will do."

She wants to talk with her sister about their mother, the recent development in her mental illness, and how they need to be more watchful of her decline, but this is not the time. Next week—next week for sure, she'll talk with her sister to make sure the burden of the situation doesn't fall on only one set of shoulders. She also wants to share the good news about the Philharmonie's commission and how she won the contract, but this, too, can wait. Clearly, sharing her big step was not in the cards for tonight.

The energy from the club is not entirely dissipated, not enough to let her find sleep. Worse, it now walks hand in hand with anxiety over her loved ones, too far away for her to protect them.

Alexandra puts on her jacket and goes out. Who cares if the clock is striking morning hours? When one walks the streets of Paris, there is always somewhere to go, something to see and, given her neighborhood, something sweet for comfort.

* * *

WITH ALL THE DELAYS DUE to weather and construction, they need to work more quickly than usual to respect the approved timeframe. Completion before the start of the next year seems to be an impossible task, and yet it is the timeframe they agreed on.

They set up their work stations in the space allotted to them; they have two large tables on which to pin the blueprints of the windows so they can cut each piece of glass without fuss. At a safe distance, they set up a sturdier table to pull the lead without hitting a piece of glass or each other. They also install a welding table to work on the LED system Leo will put behind the panels. And then they begin work on the simpler panels while the orchestra starts rehearsing.

It seems everybody has been set back, Alexandra muses as she rolls the bubble wrap from one of the orange panels that will frame the whole structure and give it its dynamic. From the concert room below them comes the muted, indistinct noise of instruments being tuned and people shouting at each other in various languages. Far from an annoyance, it makes Alexandra relax. This Tower of Babel suits her and her mindset just fine.

As Leo slides one of the biggest pieces out of the crate, Alexandra freezes. She catches a change in the chaos reigning over the orchestra. It's much more harmonious; all the instruments come together around a single note, staggering in its clarity, in its purity. The note, a tuning A if she isn't mistaken, lasts, hangs in the air, and even gains momentum. Alexandra can't for the life of her move away from it. She's captured in the perfect space of royal blue euphony.

It stops, abruptly, and Alexandra brings herself back to the world around her. She gets dizzy and shakes her head. Be it in the central panel or as a recurring detail, she has to incorporate this particular royal blue in the composition. Now if she could only—

"Ahem."

Leo leans against a wooden crate. "Welcome back," he teases gently, and points at the crate. "Now, I could use a hand with this."

Alexandra rushes to help him. She is always embarrassed when her synesthesia gets the best of her at inopportune moments. "Of course. Here, sorry."

They carefully hold the fragile edge of an intermediate panel. She focuses her strength on keeping it steady while Leon pulls it out of its box.

Once the glass is safely on its table, Leo laughs off her inattention. "If I wasn't used to you going away into the music or into your head by now," he says with a wink, "we would have a serious communication problem, carissima."

More music comes from the concert room, but, this time, Alexandra is in control. The notes and their matching colors float around her without affecting her. They have too much to do in too little time to pay attention to rehearsals. She'll have plenty of other opportunities to lose herself in the music.

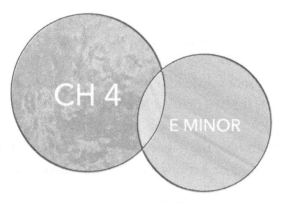

CH 4

E MINOR

Bordeaux and Blues

HALINA HESITATES IN THE WINGS as the tuning A-note echoes through the auditorium. Hidden in the shadows, she observes the orchestra members tease each other while they tune their instruments and settle in. She should sit at the piano and chat, that's what she needs to do. If she is to spend at least a full season with them, she ought to fit in, be friendly—make herself at home within the group.

Easier said than done, her mother's voice taunts, *it's not as if you're the friendliest person to begin with.*

In the past, her mother did everything in her power to keep Halina away from the orchestras she was invited to perform with. Mariola poisoned Halina's mind with lies about the other musicians, painting them all as snakes ready to strike her in their jealousy. Her younger self, firmly under Mariola's thumb, was too afraid to check for herself what would happen if she answered the smiles and friendly attitudes.

Three years away from Mariola have not helped Halina shake the instinct to put a wall between herself and others. Her position as soloist, set apart from the group, supported such a distance, but her reputation as the cold diva precedes her everywhere now. Maybe there is some truth in what Mariola said.

"Shut up," Halina says under her breath. She takes a deep breath with her eyes closed and hands tightened into fists to help her focus on one long inhalation and one longer exhalation.

And then she steps out of the shadows. Eerie quiet falls on the group, and that makes her stand taller. She can feel her face set in a mask of arrogance.

As she walks between four rows of cellists and violinists, Halina can feel their eyes on her as surely as the wooden stage that vibrates under her feet. She can hear the whispers rising across the stage, above the various tunings and amidst the different corps.

"What is she doing here?"

"The Ice Queen came down from her castle?"

"Nah, the Ice Treble."

"The Les-Wein?"

"Ah, good one, Philippe."

"Seriously, we don't need her; can't they find someone else?"

"She brings the spotlight on us, *crétins*."

The last remark comes from a short, older woman with neatly cut hair and a severe bearing who raises her head from her violin to glare at the orchestra from behind the red rims of her glasses. Since her chair is right behind the piano bench, it's clear who's come to Halina's defense: the alpha of the whole group, the concertmaster, who was undoubtedly consulted before Halina was hired. Whether she approved of the board's choice or not, she seems sensible enough to understand how beneficial Halina's presence is for the group, in terms of publicity.

Some musicians whisper unhappily, but the concertmaster stands, her hand extended toward Halina. "Welcome to Paris, Piotrowski," she says, her voice carrying through the group. A small smile softens her features. "Odile Moineau, *premier violon*."

Halina shakes Odile's callused hand and then sits at the piano. She puts her hands on the closed instrument and finds strength in the lacquered wood. "When I arrived, I thought my driver had taken me back to the airport," she says in jest. Internally, she berates herself for her strongly accented French.

However, her little joke breaks some of the tension, and the group returns to their tuning with more jokes and guffaws.

Joining the group, check. Now she just needs to make it last a whole season.

Can I make it work that long?

LEO MUST HAVE SAID HIS goodbyes to Alexandra when he left, but when she does shake herself back into reality, she is surprised to find the room empty. The echo of rehearsal is a faint, distant sound.

Putain de merde.

Alexandra wipes her hands on her apron and puts it in a bundle on her workspace. She has done a lot. Her piece of chalk was put to good use, drawing Leo the shapes she needs to "carve the light" to her liking. Her first teacher compared creating a stained glass window to sculpting light rays, and the metaphor stuck with her. She used that phrase whenever Leo's self-doubt threatened to suffocate his talent and would whisper that he should leave that chimera. The idea that their material was the light, not the glass, quieted his worries to allow his reason to catch up with the intrusive thoughts. After all, a light-carver sounds more prestigious than a window-maker, no matter how beautiful said windows may be.

Alexandra sighs and stores the memories for a later time, when she's able to linger on the nostalgia and its inherent bittersweetness. For now, she needs to wrap it up, in both senses of the word, and leave notes for Leo, since he'll arrive before her tomorrow. She details what color they need to produce and which panels should be taken back to the workshop to remove some layers of enamel. Some colors need to be softer, deeper, more in tune with the rest of the composition.

Turning off the lights, she is forced to focus on her spatial memory and her other senses to find her way out. In retrospect, that will be the reason for the way she catches it—more accurately, for the way it catches her.

It is a soft, melancholic melody: just a handful of high notes on a piano over a repeated theme in a lower register. The theme serves as a background for the flutter of gradually higher notes. The music makes

Alexandra freeze on the spot, and she has to support herself against the wall.

She closes her eyes to let the music and the colors swirl around her head and rise to their full potential: deep red, as rich and enthralling as the finest wine for the background, the repeated melody; curvy lines in the whole palette of blues from sky to the darkest royal crisscross in time with the highest notes. To seize the whole concept, Alexandra must mentally add the LED system Leo developed. This is what she's been waiting for, desperately: the inspiration for the main panel, the centerpiece of the composition.

She opens her eyes and lifts her hands to help her visualize it: The two orange panels on each side, yes, they will bring more focus to the deep red, making it luminous and passionate. They'll need to be careful with the enamel to give it depth and emphasis, since red pigments can be so contradictory and fleeting...

Alexandra frantically searches in her pockets for her notebook in order to write it all down before the music stops and the colors fade. Creative energy thrums through her body. Now, if she could just put a face with the music...

She's well aware of the old maxim about curiosity, felines, and doom, but she is more canine, all things considered. Besides, it's not just curiosity. Something in her needs, wants, to thank the person who is playing the main theme from *Amélie*.

As QUIETLY AS SHE CAN, Alexandra finds her way to the concert hall. The pianist plays around with the melody to create new pieces one after the other, each of them a bubble of colors popping in Alexandra's mind. From Alexandra's perspective, at the top of the stairs leading down to the stage, the lone figure in the spotlight takes on a mystical appearance. The only mundane thing about it is a denim shirt, which covers a slim, yet undeniably feminine, body. Her long hair is a vivid contrast to the dark shine of the piano lid.

Impulsively, Alexandra descends the stairs and walks closer to the stage. The woman doesn't appear to have noticed her, or, if she did, she hides it very well.

As Alexandra gets closer, the woman's features come into focus: pale skin, blonde hair glowing silver in the spotlight. Now, Alexandra can fully appreciate how the woman seems to be made entirely of long, elegant lines, a Modigliani in motion.

Alexandra's lips stretch into a smile as she stops her descent midway and sits quietly. She wants to ask the pianist on a date or two, or a hundred, but she also wants to talk about her music, about her interpretations, about how she herself perceives the notes tumbling from the instrument into splashes of color. For now, she's more than happy to listen and quietly bask—

"Hey!"

The voice startles Alexandra and the musician, and the melody ends in a cacophony of notes pressed onto the keys with way too much strength. The burgundy is washed away by an awful combination of moss green, magenta, and yellow.

"Who are you, and what are you doing here?" asks the person who has just come out of the shadows. The musician squints at Alexandra, who watches a tall person march toward her.

Alexandra stands, her hackles raised at the open aggressiveness of the young—well, the young person. She can't tell for sure what gender they are, and she can't bring herself to care. "I work on the foyer," she replies curtly. "I just heard the lady playing, and it was so pretty I stopped for a moment on my way out."

"Pretty?" they repeat, their voice dripping with contempt, wrapped in a strong East Coast, cerulean accent. From the corner of her eye, Alexandra sees the musician tilt her head, still looking in their direction with a Mona Lisa expression. "Miss Piotrowski's craft is not merely pretty. It's pure talent and has been acclaimed as such all around the world, its perfection praised by the harshest of critics. She has no time for groupies and sycophants, so may I suggest you—"

"Ari, enough."

Alexandra and Ari turn to face the musician now standing near the piano with one hand on her hip, the other over her eyes to shelter them from the glare of the spotlight still aimed at her. Her voice is just as attractive as her music, high without being shrill, the photisms a rich combination of peach and light orange. Her English is accented with a foreignness that echoes in Alexandra's very DNA.

"I didn't mean to disturb you," Alexandra says loudly to make sure she is heard. Ari rolls their eyes at her and crosses their arms over their chest. "I heard the music, and it captivated me." She throws Ari a glare before she turns to the musician. "I'll leave you to it."

Still squinting against the spotlight, the woman looks at her. Alexandra would love to stay and talk with her if it weren't for the almost-visible storm cloud gathered over Ari's head as they glare back at her.

"I'll... leave you to it," she repeats, nodding nervously toward the musician's Cerberus. Then she turns to climb the stairs and practically runs to her car.

Before starting the car, Alexandra gives herself a few minutes to calm down. The day weighs on her at full force: the inception of the commission; the bout of synesthesia, which took her by surprise; the remarkable, out-of-this-world woman who triggered it. All of it is more than Alexandra can handle in one day.

"WHAT WAS THAT ABOUT?" HALINA asks when they are seated in the back of the car supplied by the Philharmonie; their chauffeur navigates traffic with ease.

Ari keeps their eyes glued to their phone in a show of innocent disinterest. "What was what?"

"Cut the BS with me, Ari," Halina says firmly, annoyance building in her voice. She reaches across the armrest and lays her hand on their forearm, forcing them to look at her. "Since when are you so mean to spectators? To people who have every right to be around the concert hall, might I add?"

Ari opens their mouth and closes it in a petulant fashion. Their twenty years of age is more obvious than ever. "She disturbed your creative flow."

Halina shakes her head, huffing in annoyance when the move sends a few stray strands of hair into her eyes. "I didn't notice she was there until you barged in like a *buhaj.*"

Ari's eyes bulge out of their head. "Like a what?"

"A bull," Halina corrects, as she mentally berates herself for letting a Polish word slip out.

"Oh. Well, I'm sorry."

This is a moment for Halina to step up and be their boss, isn't it? After all, Ari's behavior reflects on her, and she can't afford to have anyone in the Philharmonie, musicians or people who work on the building, against her. But it's late, and the day has been long enough.

A moment of silence stretches between them. The music on the radio fills the uncomfortable gaps. *Never mind,* Halina decides. The short woman didn't sound too insulted when she walked out.

A smirk finds its way to her lips. "Was she cute? I couldn't see with that light in my eyes."

"Not your type."

Halina barks out a short laugh and rests her head against the window, her eyes lost in nocturnal Paris outside. "What's not my type?"

"American. And chubby." They laugh derisively. "Like I said, not your type."

"If you say so."

"She was cute, though."

"We'll see."

*   *   *

THE ROOM IS NOT NEARLY ready to welcome tonight's fundraising gala, and Madame Loupan has made it very clear that they need to work faster. Alexandra tries not to let this affect her, but she cannot silence the bothersome voice in the back of her head relentlessly telling her what a failure she'll be. They'll have to work around the clock. They'll start this brutal schedule tomorrow.

She shakes her head and blows a curl away from her face as she walks up the ramp to the building. Winter is already here, and her breath creates a tiny swirl of fog. In the darkness, the building looks even more like a spacecraft. On a professional level and as a sci-fi fan, Alexandra is elated to have permission to come aboard.

Leo will join her later, after a quick visit to his latest "bed warmer," his words, not hers. Alexandra observes the crowd around her.

Members of the board are easily recognizable by their stiff postures and the expensive, but subtle, jewelry their spouses wear. Musicians, members of the *corps d'orchestre* and choristers, are also easily recognizable. They move in groups and seem out of their comfort zones. Soloists strut, peacocks in color and demeanor, and charm the pants and wallets off the board members. Investors, special guests, plus-ones all look supremely bored or extremely high.

Alexandra doesn't care to find out who is which. She navigates the uninspiring whirlwind photisms of beige and gray to get to the bar. To summon her mother and sister's uncanny ability to change the tide in their favor, she needs to increase the amount of alcohol in her body.

She orders a Continental Sour and subtly checks to make sure the kimono fold of her dress is not too revealing. Just the top of her cleavage is showing. *Good.* Her outfit marks her as the quirky American artist who can bring color to the lives of these people.

She smiles at the barman as he slides the glass toward her. Eyes closed, she takes a sip. The bitters and orange come together in perfect harmony, spicy and tangy and just sharp enough to keep her from getting drunk too fast.

Humming in satisfaction, Alexandra shifts some of her weight onto her forearms, which are resting on top of the bar, to get some relief from her spike heels. She rotates her ankles.

"Not comfortable on heels?" The voice is lightly accented. Its tone reminds Alexandra of her grandmother. Peach fills her mind. She immediately looks up to face the voice's owner, who continues, "or do you want to attract everyone's attention, because in that case you succeeded."

Alexandra can't hide her excitement when she recognizes the pianist. Her blonde hair is arranged into a loose, tousled, side updo that highlights the natural elegance of her face and draws attention to the slope of her neck. Her outfit, a black and white jumpsuit with coordinated stilettos, strengthens the long lines of her body. Overall, the image reinforces everything Alexandra noticed when she saw her the first time.

"It wasn't my intention, but thank you," she replies. Her heart beats faster as the woman comes closer. "I'm uncomfortable in these shoes, but heels are an essential component of a party outfit, or so I hear." She tips her head toward the woman's high heels. "You abide by that rule too, don't you?"

"You get used to it, when you don't have a choice."

"My kingdom for a pair of flats." Alexandra raises her glass in a toast. Her smile only grows when the pianist clinks her glass, filled with crushed ice, against hers. "I'm Alexandra."

"Halina."

Alexandra repeats the name in her mind; it fits the mystical-creature aura the musician projects.

"You're a pianist, aren't you?" Alexandra asks—anything to prolong this moment.

Halina nods as she cocks her hip against the bar and lets her glass hang from the tip of her fingers. "And who are you?" she asks back. Her focus on Alexandra makes her feel like the most important person in the room. "You look familiar."

Alexandra rests her back against the bar; not only does this provide relief, it allows her to show off her curves. "I'm in the building," she replies, vague on purpose.

She may not be the best at the game of seduction, but one thing is certain: she has to maintain Halina's apparent interest if she wants to keep her. And Alexandra wants to keep her, and her inspirational presence.

"One of the architects?" Halina asks, a puzzled look in her eyes.

"Not quite," Alexandra replies, laughter in her voice, before she sips her cocktail. "I work on the reception wing."

Halina's eyes open wider with a glint of recognition. "Ah, so *you* are the Phantom of the Philharmonie. Do you know we can hear you sing sometimes?" she asks. She frowns playfully. "But since we never see you, I started to think the building had a ghost. But I thought your voice was much… deeper."

This time, Alexandra lets the laughter come out. "You heard my partner, Leo."

Halina takes a step back and raises one eyebrow. "Partner?"

The inquiry is not at all veiled, and Alexandra smirks as she places her fingers under her glass and holds it to her chest. It drives Halina's eyes to her cleavage. All Alexandra has to do is reel her in delicately.

"Business partner and my best friend. We've been working together for the last eight years."

Halina slides closer. "No partner or plus one either?" she asks, her voice dropped huskily to keep the conversation private.

Halina towers over her. The height difference pushes Alexandra's buttons and matches her pattern of partners. She looks up and slowly shakes her head. "I'm all by my lonesome," she replies, unashamed to purse her lips into a pout.

"What a pity," Halina says, before she chugs what's left in her glass and takes Alexandra's glass from her fingers. "What do you say we bail out of here, and you guide me through… Paris?" she offers, and her eyes follow the lines of Alexandra's body, conveying what parts of Paris she wants to pay her respects to.

Alexandra licks her lips when Halina returns her eyes to her face.

Halina's fingers trail along Alexandra's arm. "Meet you at the front. I have a chauffeur."

"Meet you there," Alexandra replies, hypnotized by the slight roll of Halina's hips as she walks away.

Jesus. Almighty.

Though it has the shape of a random hookup, Alexandra wills it to be more. It's simply an uncommon start to something with the potential to be great, an original, if naughty, story to tell years down the line when people ask how they met.

Getting ahead of myself, aren't I? Oh, well...

On her way to the cloakroom, she takes time to salute Loupan and some members of the board she doesn't know from Adam. It takes a lot of self-control to remind herself that running out will not help the respectful relationship burgeoning between her, Leo, and the powers that be, especially if she twists her ankle on these cursed heels. So, she walks briskly, as fast as she can without running.

On her way, she meets Leo. She gestures toward the ramp where Halina stands. He frowns at her, but a more detailed explanation will have to wait.

Halina looks toward the road, where a car approaches. She is talking to Ari. The memory of her encounter with the insufferable assistant from Hell makes Alexandra's hackles rise and she straightens as she approaches them.

"Ready to go?" Halina asks, holding her hand up for Alexandra to take. Alexandra walks between Halina and Ari; her hips nudge them out of the way.

"You bet," she replies, barely giving them a side glance.

"Are you sure, boss?" Ari asks, a twist to their mouth.

"I'll see you tomorrow," Halina says, accentuating the last word as she lightly puts her hand on the small of Alexandra's back. She keeps it there until they are in the black car that was waiting at the bottom of the ramp.

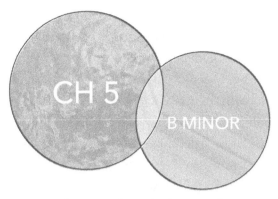

CH 5

B MINOR

White, Peach, and Olympic Blue

HALINA LETS HER INSTINCTS GUIDE her; she's out of her depth. She just met Alexandra, but she already wants to play with the many ways she can imagine taking her apart in her bed.

Oh God, she'll look so pretty on the dark silky cotton of my sheets.

The olive tone of her skin is lovely and will be lovelier once she's out of her dress and spread on the bed for Halina to take at her leisure. She wants her so much; she barely waits for the car door to close. She captures Alexandra's full lips in a kiss and keeps one hand on Alexandra's knee.

What Halina didn't expect, though, is how quickly she loses control of the kiss. Usually, her partners are overwhelmed by the sudden unleashing of her passion. They are too taken aback by the contrast between her professional chill and her seductive fire to even attempt to question her leadership. Halina's partners let her make them do what she wants or needs.

Now, she barely teases at Alexandra's lips before a hand cups her cheek and tilts her head. Alexandra's tongue licks languorously into her mouth. Halina kisses back, but Alexandra is the choreographer of this little dance.

When Alexandra sucks on her tongue while smiling into the kiss, Halina moans. When she licks the roof of her mouth, Halina's body tingles down to her crotch, just as surely as if Alexandra had reached between Halina's legs with her hand.

Halina opens her coat and paws at Alexandra's while pulling her as close as she can with their seatbelts on. Alexandra manages to open her own overcomplicated coat but never stops kissing her. Her fingers graze the line of Halina's jaw and neck. The touch is as light as a feather.

Halina doesn't waste any time. She caresses Alexandra's leg from knee to thigh. She expected Alexandra's legs to be soft. She does find softness, but also meets hard muscle as soon as she presses on the velvet of Alexandra's dark skin. The prospect of that strength around her face while she eats Alexandra out creates another wave of arousal, and Halina doesn't stop until she finds the junction of Alexandra's legs.

It's Alexandra's turn to moan into the kiss. Her legs are parted for Halina's touch. The car drives through the streets of Paris. She doesn't have time to explore it now, when a different type of geography awaits her exploring fingertips.

Yes, Paris can wait.

Halina bids her driver goodnight before they rush out of the car. Incapable of delaying any longer, she pulls Alexandra into a kiss on the hotel's threshold. She only drank one cocktail, but her brain is fuzzy: drunk on arousal, drunk on Alexandra's light, mysterious, delectable perfume; drunk on the prospect of a passionate night. After tonight, Halina will give her whole self to music. She'll take one last moment for herself and just herself.

Alexandra presses her against the elevator wall; her leg slides between Halina's as her hands hold her waist. Halina pants into the kiss when Alexandra's thumbs rub circles on her hips, slowly rolling her underwear under her jumpsuit. In the vibrant light of the elevator, Alexandra's gray eyes glow like pearls.

"Come on." Halina is short of breath as they make their way to her room.

Halima turns to face the door and almost gets the electronic key through the slot when Alexandra's breasts press against her back. Her hands delicately cup Halina's hips while her lips take advantage of Halina's jumpsuit's low neck to press against her bare skin.

Halina can't help but gasp under the onslaught of sensations.

Oh, but this is delicious. I should have tried different body types before.

The door finally opens, and they tumble into the room before slamming it shut. Alexandra forces Halina to stand against the door. She cups her face with both hands and kisses her. Halina puts her hands on Alexandra's waist, pulling her even closer, until their chests are pressed together as much as possible despite their height difference and she hums into the kiss to show her appreciation.

Alexandra pulls away and suddenly loses a couple of inches. A dull noise is repeated, and Alexandra's heeled shoes lie in the middle of the room. Now that Alexandra is without shoes and Halina still wears hers, they are face to breast.

The height difference doesn't throw Alexandra off balance. She uses her new vantage point to play with the neckline of Halina's jumpsuit and pushes aside the silky material to access her breasts. One hand on Halina's waist, her other finds the side of Halina's right breast. On tiptoe at first, she presses a trail of kisses from the hollow of Halina's throat to the skin under her breasts.

Halina expected her to go for her nipples, but she should stop expecting and forget what she was used to. Evidently, Alexandra plays by other rules.

Halina puts one hand in Alexandra's thick hair and guides her toward the spot where she is wetter and wetter. Alexandra lowers herself until she is blocked by the belt of the jumpsuit. She lets out a frustrated sigh, and the warm air on the trail of spit she left in her path raises goosebumps on Halina's skin. None of her previous partners managed to make her feel this way; only now that she's experiencing it does Halina realize what's been missing from her life.

"How do you get this off?" Alexandra mumbles, and Halina is only too happy to oblige, rolling her shoulders to remove the top of the jumpsuit. A shimmy of her hips drops it to the floor.

"Thank God," Alexandra comments, smiling. She takes a step back. "Look at you."

Her voice is laced with worship and awe and lust. Halina basks in it as she kicks the jumpsuit and her shoes to the side. She returns to Alexandra to cup her face and pulls her into a kiss as she walks them toward the bed.

Alexandra doesn't seem to mind relinquishing the lead; she keeps her hands on Halina's waist and walks backward until the backs of her knees hit the bed and she lets herself drop onto it with an expectant smirk.

Halina was right: Alexandra makes for a spectacular vision on her sheets.

"Shouldn't we get this off," Halina purrs, one knee on the bed for balance. She reaches for Alexandra's belt.

"I thought it was all about getting off," Alexandra replies with a laugh. She stretches her arms while she lets Halina open her dress. With the gesture, she becomes a silky, embroidered present.

I do love presents.

Alexandra's golden-brown skin and the breasts overflowing from her bra demand caresses, and they demand them sooner rather than later.

Halina lies on top of Alexandra, capturing her lips for a bruising kiss while putting a leg between Alexandra's. Her knee meets Alexandra's crotch, and, even through the material of her underwear, her arousal is obvious. Halina is in the same state of excitement. She rocks against Alexandra and the motion is enough to simultaneously stimulate Alexandra with her knee and herself against Alexandra's leg.

"Yes," Alexandra moans, voice turning rougher and rougher as she wiggles under Halina. Her hands are back on Halina's hips, guiding her downward and moving with her. "Come on, just—ah! Just like that, yesss…"

The moan spurs Halina forward. She moves her body faster, orgasm already within her grasp. Warmth spreads through her, and she barely manages to catch herself before she falls and crushes Alexandra. She lets out a short, breathless laugh as she rolls to the side.

Alexandra takes a deep breath before she sits up to toss down her crumpled dress and unhook her bra in one swift move. The lacy garment joins the dress on the floor. A handful of tiny petals, an explanation for the perfume Halina couldn't quite place, flutter in the air as the bra flies to the floor. She rolls to her side, closer to Halina, so she has one arm over Halina's waist to brush her side and one leg thrown over Halina's hip to get some friction for herself. She kisses Halina's shoulder.

"Off to a good start, then," Alexandra says gleefully, and Halina can only approve. "I knew you'd be spectacular."

"How did you—" Halina frowns, combing through her memories until everything adds up. *American, plump, kicked out by Ari—* "You sneaked into the concert hall to listen to me play. Did you enjoy the show?" she asks cockily.

Alexandra gives her a long, sweeping glance; Halina sees a sparkle of desire in her eyes. "All of it."

Halina wiggles as the compliment adds to the warmth in her body. She glances at Alexandra's relaxed form and smirks. "I really want to eat you out."

"Ditto."

Halina turns her head just in time for Alexandra to kiss her again, her lips tingling with the force of it while her hand blindly reaches for dental dams in the drawer of her nightstand.

"Come here," Alexandra says while she pulls Halina toward her. "I don't want us to be off balance."

"You want to eat me while I do you?" Halina asks for confirmation, raising to her knees on the mattress, the bedspread scratching her skin.

Alexandra laughs in response, and it makes her breasts bounce enticingly. "Sixty-nine seems to be the fairest deal," Alexandra replies with a come-hither gesture Halina is hopeless to resist.

"I'm all for fairness."

Halina gives a dam to Alexandra. Twisting her body, she positions her crotch over Alexandra's face. Alexandra grabs her ass, squeezing it as she guides Halina toward her. A small, appreciative sigh comes out of her mouth, which is already caressing Halina's sweat-slicked skin.

"You enjoy the view?" Halina asks, rotating her hips as she slowly lowers her body toward Alexandra.

"You have no idea how much appreciation I have for your everything," Alexandra replies with a light slap on the soft globes of Halina's ass, "but I propose to revisit this topic later."

"Another time" is quite the foreign concept as far as Halina and sex are concerned, but Alexandra did manage to make her come faster than ever. Maybe she'll break her rule of one-time-only.

Alexandra wraps her arms around Halina's thighs once she sits on her face, and Halina reaches for her hands to guide them closer to the junction of her thighs. Alexandra doesn't disappoint her; one hand reaches down to tease her while she licks at her folds.

Halina is already wet from her first orgasm, but her pleasure is only renewed; her body is responsive to Alexandra's eager tongue. Alexandra doesn't hesitate, doesn't tease, in her approach to Halina's body. Halina reaches for her own breasts, lost in her pleasure, then remembers to take care of Alexandra's. She'll be damned if Alexandra manages to make her come a second time before Halina even manages to reciprocate.

Halina bends over to press her pelvis harder against Alexandra's face. It dislodges her hand, but Alexandra returns it to Halina's hip, and Halina is closer to her goal. Alexandra's folds are shiny and wet, too attractive to resist, and Halina goes right for it, licking her way from Alexandra's clit to her entrance and back up.

Alexandra's gasp serves as an incentive; she finds a new position for her body against Alexandra's wicked and talented mouth so she can focus on her own task. A second wave of pleasure builds, and there is a competitive edge to the way Halina now sucks and licks her way around Alexandra's entrance. Halina may care more about her own pleasure than anyone else's, but Alexandra's orgasm is now a matter of principle.

She makes good use of her hands too, grabbing Alexandra's legs to caress them, the backs of her knees, the backs of her thighs, the insides of her legs. When Halina tickles a spot between Alexandra's thigh and ass cheek, her companion moans and bucks against Halina's face.

Now she's certain there will be a next time to explore all this chemistry and pleasure, to find new ways to make this infuriating, sexy-against-all odds woman moan so beautifully again and again.

She's not alone in her desire to give and get pleasure. Alexandra is relentless and alternates between kitten licks to Halina's folds and unprecise strokes to her clitoris. Try as she may, Halina can't hold back anymore and she comes, harder even than the first orgasm. To catch her breath and gather her wits, she stops using her mouth; one hand still teases Alexandra as she slips her fingers in deeper.

Halina still rides her second orgasm, so the competitor in her needs to make Alexandra find her peak of pleasure. As soon as she can breathe and focus properly, Halina dives back to her task. Her efforts pay off as more fluid gushes out. Despite how unsafe it would be, how unlike her it is to want such a thing, she wants to taste it. Alexandra's legs tremble under her touch. A glance upward shows a tension in her whole body, a wave of pleasure she needs to catch immediately while it is at its highest.

With a victorious smile, Halina runs her fingers along the edges of Alexandra's folds and then pushes them inside as she hollows her cheeks around Alexandra's clitoris. She is rewarded with a smothered shout, muted by her own body over Alexandra's mouth. Alexandra's whole body tightens and relaxes against Halina's with each jolt of pleasure. Teasingly, Halina trails her fingers through the fluid smeared on Alexandra's upper thighs. She shakes her ass to get rid of the tickling sensation born from Alexandra's panted breath.

"Oh, wow," Alexandra whispers, her voice a little bit rougher than when they started. She presses her forehead against Halina's thigh. "Come back here, you," she adds with a growl, forcefully pulling Halina back onto her mouth and pushing her tongue inside her.

Maybe it's the shock of the onslaught, maybe it's the satisfaction of getting her partner off, maybe it's just Alexandra who is so damn good, but a third orgasm, slower and warmer than the first two, surprises Halina. It makes her shout and straighten as she nearly blacks out.

Halina is barely conscious when Alexandra disentangles herself from her legs and gently rolls her on her back. She comes back to her senses when Alexandra presses a soft kiss to the side of her breast. Her whole body is sensitive, lit by an internal fire, and she groans, weakly batting Alexandra away.

So that's *overstimulation.*

Blinking, Halina searches for any sign of smugness, but Alexandra wears only a satisfied smile. Sweaty curls are stuck to her forehead in some places and sticking out in others. The mascara smudged at the corner of her eyes makes her look feline and wild.

"I owe you one." Halina rolls to her side and scoots to Alexandra until she has her on her back. "How can I make you come now?"

Alexandra pats her cheek; the gesture is lazy and tired. Halina finds herself enjoying the mark of affection and leans into the touch. "You don't owe me anything," Alexandra says, slurring a little. "It was my pleasure, believe me."

"Still," Halina insists as she slides her hand between Alexandra's legs. "Let me get us to deuce before you leave."

A frown draws lines on Alexandra's face, but it quickly passes. "I didn't intend to just leave, but—*oh, my God,*" she hisses as Halina crooks two fingers inside of her in a quest for her G-spot and, obviously, finds it.

Halina lies on her belly to get a better look, and Alexandra grasps the sheets in one hand while the other cups the back of Halina's head in a gentle touch, fingers tangled in her hair without pulling.

Halina quickly adds a third finger. Her hand comes back wetter and wetter with every pass inside of Alexandra's eager body, with every roll of Alexandra's hips against her touch.

"Come on, come on, *dzidzia,*" Halina mumbles. The endearment is out of her mouth before she realizes it while she moves faster, properly fucking Alexandra with her hand. Her fingers are crooked inside Alexandra while her thumb rubs at Alexandra's clit.

Alexandra lets go of Halina's head to cover her eyes with her forearm, the hand in the sheets tightens, and, as her legs open even wider, Halina cannot resist. She moves forward to suck at the nub while pressing her fingers against Alexandra's special spot again and again until Alexandra howls out her orgasm.

Alexandra's smaller, curvier body is frozen, lifted from the bed as she arches her back. Halina doesn't want the moment to end. She doesn't want Alexandra to ever leave her bed; she wants to find all the ways to make her look so carnal, so beautiful, such an epitome of lust.

But it ends, because all good things come to an end, and Alexandra's shouts turn into ecstatic, breathless giggles. "I believe—" she pants, running her fingers through Halina's hair, "I believe we've reached a more equal ground, if that concerned you."

"Good." Halina licks her fingers before she rolls on her back and clumsily reaches for the blanket.

Alexandra lies close to her, close enough to call it cuddling, but the pleasant warmth of her body lulls Halina to sleep before she can find the strength to tell her to leave, or the will to question why she doesn't want to.

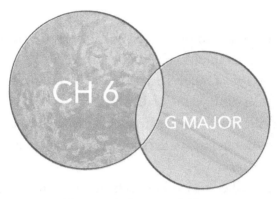

CH 6

G MAJOR

Shamrock Green and Ebony

DURING THE TWO WEEKS SINCE they started sleeping together, Alexandra has slowly but surely fallen head over heels and under Halina's spell. Halina keeps finding new ways to make sure Alexandra will want more: more of her, of her body, and of her presence.

When she came to Halina's hotel today, Alexandra had a very serious subject in mind, a question about the two of them that she's been holding back since the morning after their first night together. *Damn Halina for being so damn irresistible.*

Now Alexandra rolls onto her back, cheeks flushed and curls stuck to her forehead after yet another extremely pleasurable and, yes, a bit athletic, horizontal session with Halina. Halina's long fingers cup the curves of Alexandra's breasts, and that distracts her.

Alexandra does the only sensible thing and subtly moves away from Halina's grasp and sits back against the plush headboard. Halina pouts, but Alexandra won't be so easily seduced.

"Come on." She pats the pillow next to her until Halina huffs and comes to sit by her side. "There is something I'd like to talk about with you." Halina frowns; her look of confusion is adorable, but she gestures for Alexandra to go on. "I wanted to know why we… only fuck," Alexandra says bluntly, wincing internally at her language.

To Alexandra's surprise, Halina laughs. It's a full-on belly laugh that makes Alexandra see carmine red sprayed all over Halina's usual soft coloring. And it's better suited to a Marx Brothers movie than to Alexandra's question.

"Oh, you're serious," Halina says, voice still shaking with laughter, once she notices that Alexandra is waiting for her to stop. "What more would you have us do?"

Alexandra blinks at her as anger and embarrassment battle to dominate her emotions. "Go out? Movies, restaurants, walks around the city?" she lists, her voice louder with each suggestion while Helena gives her a blank look. "Talks? Dates, outside of this bedroom, as nice as it is."

Halina's hilarity ends abruptly. "Dates?" she repeats, her nose scrunched up as if the word tastes sour in her mouth. Her voice's color reflects it too, neon yellow on the backdrop of her natural peach. "Where did you get such an idea?"

Alexandra's lungs empty as if she had just been punched in the stomach. She gets out of the bed, nudity be damned, to look more properly at Halina. "I thought this," she replies, her hand waves between them, "was... something. A relationship."

Halina rolls her eyes, and red progressively seeps into the edges of Alexandra's vision. "It's something—a good fuck," Halina says slowly while she gets out of bed and puts her blouse on. "And nothing more. Trust me, if it wasn't good, it would have been the one-time performance and *cześć*."

The foreign word is strange, brutal in her ears and, on the backdrop of her eyelids, a swift splotch of khaki and brown. Alexandra frowns to shake it out of her mind.

She searches for her clothes, which are strewn around the room, a proof of their eagerness to get to bed, and gets dressed. She nearly tears off her sleeve in her haste. "I suppose I should be flattered?" she says in disbelief, and Halina, who looks the epitome of poise and afterglow calm, shrugs while she fiddles with a tumbler of gin.

"Yeah, you should," she replies before taking a sip with her eyes firmly on Alexandra.

Alexandra stands there, hands shaking, silenced by everything she wants to say, everything she won't say, lest she completely lose it.

"Is this your first casual thing?" Halina's beautiful face is marred by her scornful expression.

"Well, you're certainly the first woman to make me regret attaching stupid emotions to a physical thing!"

"The *first* woman?"

"Not the first one I fucked," Alexandra clarifies, the words out of her mouth as fast as bullets while she dresses. "I trusted you not to be defensive about feelings the way men are."

"You actually thought we were... dating?"

Disgust is no longer the predominant emotion in Halina's demeanor. Her eyes are wide and blinking as she turns sideways; her clenched jaw predominates in Alexandra's line of sight. "I was obviously mistaken," Alexandra says around the knot lodged in her throat. "Thank you for... clearing things up, but I should—I should go."

"You don't have to leave."

"Yeah, no. I definitely do."

Halina stands with a sigh and comes closer. She doesn't try to touch her, thank God, but she's close enough to invade Alexandra's every sense. "Come on, Alexandra." Alexandra's name is a purr, darkening Halina's usual peach into vermillion. "Why stop something so fun?"

Alexandra pauses while she puts her coat on. She focuses on buttoning it properly so she'll at least look decent on her way home. For a fleeting moment, she almost lets Halina's words convince her. She could carpe the fuck out of this diem. She could change her pattern and just take what Halina can offer.

No, she says firmly to the voice in her brain pleading for surrender. *Who would I be if I betray my own heart?*

"Because it's not enough," she replies as tears and embarrassment threaten to choke her. She blindly gets hold of the door handle. "Goodbye, Halina."

"Alex—" Halina starts, but Alexandra closes the door before Halina can make her lose her resolve.

THE COLD AIR SLAPS HER in the face. Alexandra buries her nose in her scarf. The best idea for her right now is to walk home, take advantage of the fresh air and let it distract from the negative whirlwind of thoughts developing in her mind.

There is a sale on the Boulevard Beaumarchais: antique dealers next to individuals selling toys children outgrew and presents they never appreciated. One man's trash is another's treasure, or so it seems. Usually, Alexandra would browse and enjoy. Today, as derogatory thoughts and self-blame swirl in her head, she doesn't bother to look. If anything, she quickens her pace when she passes stalls with instruments.

She bites her lower lip. *How stupid can you get*, Alexandra berates herself. Tears of anger roll onto her cheek before she wipes them brusquely away. How could she delude herself into believing Halina wanted more than to fuck her? She is all too aware of how different they are, how easy it would be—correction, will be—for Halina, with her classical beauty and model's body, to find another partner for her "good fuck."

It's not what she wants, though. Hell, if she did want it, Halina appears to be interested in keeping their arrangement… But how many times can she delude herself into reading a situation in ways that suit her, and not as it actually is?

At a red light, Alexandra taps her foot against the pavement and raises her eyes to the skies. It was obvious, if she takes the time to consider it, that they had widely different points of view on their affair. Alexandra was more invested in it—no, not just more invested. It's clear now that they didn't seek the same thing at all. She can't even blame Halina. The pianist never lied about what she sought in her acquaintance with Alexandra, did she? It's Alexandra who projected her own infatuation, who colored every interaction with Halina with her own feelings, who cast a veil over what didn't fit her "script."

"What an idiot, putain," she mutters under her breath, but not low enough to prevent the old man next to her at the light from catching her curse, if the shocked look on his face is any indication. "*Pardon*," she whispers, then increases her speed to cross the street. She doesn't need to scare passersby. She feels pathetic enough as it is.

Her phone vibrates in her pocket, but Alexandra ignores it. If it's Halina, she doesn't want to hear anything from her; if it's Leo, she is not in the proper mindset to deal with him. The rest of the world can wait too. She needs to get home, back to the nest she built with her clutter and knickknacks, back to Punshki and the comfort of his fur and his soft, compassionate grumbles. She also needs to bury, with something greasy and sweet, the misery gathered in her heart and threatening to choke her. She needs to be home, where she is safe from the world.

The moment she closes the door with a bag of cream puffs clutched to her chest, Alexandra rests her head against the door, lets herself slide to the floor, spreads her legs to let her dog snuggle up to her, and buries her nose in the thick fur of his neck to let the tears out.

My foolish, stupid heart, she tells herself before letting her bruised emotions roll down her cheeks.

HALINA STARES AT THE DOOR, her hands clenched into fists. Then she throws her glass against a wall, where it bounces before landing, unscathed, on the floor.

"*Kurde*! How dare she!"

She's certain she did nothing to lead Alexandra to believe their arrangement was more than a roll in the hay, a quest for pleasure. And now, Miss All High and Mighty While Being Naughty wants to claim they are, what? A couple? In a relationship? *Good Lord.*

No, Halina doesn't do relationships; sex is all she needs from other women who are not her equals on a stage, and even then...

Intimacy? Is she expected to just let someone in and take a chance on them? To allow them to see who she is behind her carefully crafted walls, to contemplate all her flaws and neuroses and defects? To give them a chance to hurt her when they reject her for the very qualities they claimed to love?

No, thank you.

Relationship? Letting the daily occurrences corrode what was admittedly a delightful lay?

No, thank you.

Alexandra was a fun fuck-buddy, a very talented one, sure, but nothing irreplaceable. As a matter of fact, Halina *will* replace her, and no later than today. Halina takes her phone and angrily types a message to Ari to inform them she plans to go to the club they went to on the day they arrived. Maybe the prospect of another shot at their dreamy barman will entice them to join her. In any case, if there is one place where she is bound to find someone else to fuck, at her pace and at her will, it's there.

ONCE AT THE CLUB, HALINA tries to get rid of the inexplicable disappointment over the whole debacle and enjoy herself. She dances, she flirts, she drinks the anger away.

To prove herself that Alexandra was not that good, Halina goes back to Camille the bartender. They end up in the stockroom for a quick encounter, but this only crushes her hope of leaving Alexandra in the past. As fun and gorgeous as Camille is, as close to her usual type as she may be, Halina can't quite focus. Something is amiss. Camille doesn't have what it takes to make Halina feel transformed, like the strings of an entire piano in the hands of a master. The way Alexandra made her feel.

Dammit.

* * *

THE NEXT DAY, THE ORCHESTRA has no rehearsals, and Halina and Ari visit the Louvre and spend some time on "touristy" stuff at the museum. But most of the time they spend in the aisles of the former royal palace finds Halina confiding in Ari about her misadventures.

"Forget about her," Ari says as they take a selfie with Albrecht Dürer's self-portrait and mimic his expression. "It's not as if she made such an impression, is it?" Halina remains silent, maybe a bit too long if Ari's widening eyes are any indication. "She did?"

Halina nods sadly. The museum's map is crumpled into oblivion between her nervous hands.

"Wow," Ari whispers with a pout. "Didn't see it coming."

"Is it such a surprise?" Halina frowns.

"Well, you can be quite difficult to please, and I didn't expect someone of her type to be... hardworking, so to speak."

"Her type?" Halina repeats, her voice betraying an anger on behalf of Alexandra she didn't expect.

"Oh, come on, Lina," Ari says with a small, uncertain laugh. "People like her, yeah. Didn't you say she is bi? And she's a fatty too. Neither have the best rep."

"No, I can't let you say that," Halina cuts them. "Sure, she is nothing like the size zeroes I banged around the world, but I wouldn't want her to be thinner. You said yourself that she's cute, but she's more than that. She's gorgeous, and *I* was an idiot for not giving bigger women a chance sooner. And she's the best sex I ever had," Halina adds with a wistful sigh.

Ari holds up their hands in surrender. "My apologies, Lina. I guess I have prejudices of my own, but you have to admit that your previous partners were pretty much cut from the same skinny cloth," they add with a pointed look.

Halina humphs. The whole museum visit has been slowly tainted by her sour mood.

"The best sex you ever had, uh?"

"No competition." She sighs as she slouches onto a bench.

Ari sits next to her with crossed legs, prim and proper as always, as they pretend to observe the painting in front of them. "Well," they say slowly, obviously attempting to protect her frayed nerves, "if she was so good, maybe you should—"

"What, join the monogamous club, get married, and decide who will carry the babies?" Halina snarls, and Ari visibly recoils.

"I was just going to suggest giving her a shot, but okay, if that's where you stand already, more power to you."

Halina remains silent, her eyes drawn to the painting for real this time. She takes in the curves of the woman inhabiting the canvas and she sighs. It's such a commonplace subject for a work of art, a nude portrait of a nameless woman, but Halina is lost in the body, the rich colors, the intimacy infused in the painter's strokes, and the painted woman's hidden gaze. Her mind drifts to the very woman she has tried to erase from it. She lets out another, sadder breath, and Ari frowns at her.

"I can't stop thinking about her," Halina admits softly as she shifts her eyes from the painting to her hands in her lap. She finally voices what has disturbed her. "About how good and simple it was to just be with her."

Ari utters a simple sound meant to make her say more.

"I didn't think I would ever say those words," Halina continues, keeping her eyes away from Ari, "but she is in my every thought. That infuriating woman stars in all my dreams—"

"TMI."

"As if. And every vaguely romantic piece of music speaks of her. I can't go on like this!"

"I hear this is what relationships are made of." Ari's voice is strangely neutral.

"I can't picture myself in a relationship," she replies, "and you and I share the same vision of romance in general."

They both shudder dramatically. Ari tilts their head to the side and leans back on their hands. "And yet?"

"And yet."

"What do you have to lose, when it comes to it?"

"I could get hurt. I could hurt her. I could lose my focus and my drive. I could lose the music. I could—"

"Nah, it's bolted to your body and your heart with unbreakable bolts."

Halina doesn't bother hiding her surprise. "You mean it?"

Ari scoffs. "Of course I do," they say. "Your passion and talent are why I slave away to make sure you're happy." It's a simple joke, but it stings a little. That must show on her face, because Ari wraps one arm over her shoulders. "The reason I used to slave away; now I just want to make you happy, my friend." They squeeze her arm and pull her closer. "And as for hurt, I won't say it's bound to happen with someone who hasn't figured themselves out yet, but *que sera, sera*, right?"

Halina smiles at them as she yields to the embrace and rests her head on their shoulder. "See, relationships really don't make any sense," she says. "Drama, drama, drama."

"Since you already have the drama, you might as well try out the relationship and its advantages."

"Advantages?"

"Cuddles, someone to confide in..."

Halina looks up, trying for her best puppy look. "Don't I have you for that?"

"Okay, cuddles with the potential to become dirtier."

"Oh."

"Yeah, you don't have me for that, doll."

Halina snorts, and some tourists give her a nasty look. "I have soaked in enough culture for now," she says, straightening her posture before she stands. "Let's go eat."

Ari pulls their phone from their pocket to check recommendations on different websites. "According to my BFF the World Wide Web, we should find a sushi bar nearby. And with a conveyor belt? Neat," they add with a new sparkle in their eyes.

"It could be fun," Halina replies. They link arms to walk away from the gallery. "Maybe I'll take Alexandra there for a—" she winces at the very idea.

"A date," Ari says, their expression slightly enigmatic.

"What," Halina says, with a squeeze of their elbow as an incentive to talk.

"Dare I say you are putting the cart before the horse here?"

Halina doesn't get what they mean. They both pause to let a group move into the room. "As in?"

"Well," Ari says, moving forward, "before a date, don't you need to, you know...?"

Halina raises her eyebrows to make them go on.

"Apologize and tell her you were wrong?"

Halina groans, drops her head, and lets herself be pulled along. She does need to grovel at Alexandra's feet, doesn't she?

*　　*　　*

GIVEN HER STATE OF MIND, perhaps she shouldn't have gone to a club only three days after the debacle. Then again, Alexandra is not in the mood to be sensible; she wants to drink, she wants to dance, she wants to feel desired again. She doesn't want to take someone home, not so soon after the—well, it was a break-up even if there was no relationship to break.

Merde.

All Alexandra wants tonight is to soothe her ego. To achieve that, she needs her armor. Leo used to call her little black dress her "fuck me" dress, usually before pulling it off her body. The dress doesn't match anything else in Alexandra's wardrobe, but it will certainly get her some much-needed attention.

The dress has not been exposed to the light of day in a couple of years, but it still fits. It hugs Alexandra's every curve, and, if she may say so herself, she looks so good in it, she's pretty sure it will live up to its name tonight.

Plus, it has pockets.

ALEXANDRA HAS BARELY STEPPED INTO the bar when a glass is pushed in front of her. "I didn't order anything," she tells the barmaid in French. She hopes her accent is covered by the loud bass, which pulses black and purple at the forefront of her mind.

"You don't need to, sweetheart," the barmaid replies with a wink; her chin is subtly angled to her right to point Alexandra in the direction of her generous patron.

Alexandra looks at the stranger, considers her, before taking the glass in hand to hold in a silent toast. As the tall woman crosses the crowd, Alexandra smirks around the rim of her glass and pats her dress.

Worked like a charm.

The woman, Lucie, doesn't have the most sparkling conversation, but neither does the man Alexandra dances with next. Conversation is not what Alexandra is after, though, and she lets them flirt and ogle her. She dances with them, and more drinks come her way, and, as the night progresses, Alexandra's anger and self-pity recede.

"Should we go back to my place?" Lucie whispers in Alexandra's ear, and she can only shake her head in response. "Seriously?"

Alexandra faces her with an apologetic smile. "It was really nice," she replies, only slightly slurring. "But I wasn't looking for anything else tonight."

Lucie frowns at her. Then she shrugs. "You little tease," she says without bite. "Maybe some other time?" she adds as she shakes her red hair.

Alexandra can't deny she's a beautiful woman, and it would be oh-so easy to just follow that attraction. But as Halina so generously pointed out, casual sex is not for Alexandra. And she's not ready to try a rebound; just as with her inspiration, she won't force it.

With a noncommittal smile, Alexandra returns to the bar. If she can't drown her sorrow in music and dancing and flirtation, alcohol will have to do the trick.

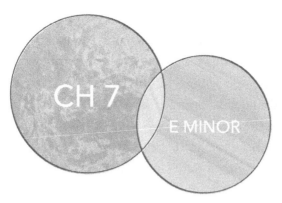

CH 7

E MINOR

Violine, Baby Blue, and Bordeaux

THE NEXT MORNING, ALEXANDRA CANNOT give her all to the task at hand, but the fact she's showing up at work at all is a cause for celebration. And if Leo notices anything amiss, either he is sensitive enough not to mention it, or he has grown a sense of self-preservation since their last big fight.

The panels come along nicely, and Alexandra spares a moment to curse Halina to the ninth circle of Hell for taking away some of the passion she'd had for the project. She'd started the gig with loads of enthusiasm, already reluctant to part with whatever pieces might emerge. Now, honestly, she can't wait to be finished with it, finished in particular with the main panel inspired by the colors Halina created in her mind, finished with this place where her music inhabits every curve and every room.

"Hey, boss, easy on the blue," Leo says, calling her back from her thoughts, "we don't have much to spare."

Alexandra frowns at him before dropping her gaze to the glass in her hands. She scraped the glass just on the wrong side of too rough; fractures have appeared at its edges and will need to be polished away, leaving this piece of glass the wrong size for its intended purpose. This will cost them precious material.

Damn it.

"Sorry," she mumbles as she hides her face by looking into her satchel to find some fine-grain sandpaper. "Got lost in thought."

Leo pauses in his welding, lifts his goggles to his forehead, and tilts his head. "Wanna talk about it?" he asks gently. He clenches his jaw. "It's the ivory-tickler, isn't it?"

He doesn't have to phrase it as a question; Alexandra might have gushed once or twice about Halina and her many fine qualities while they worked on the panels.

Alexandra nods sadly and sniffs. She returns her attention to the deep-blue panel.

Leo turns off the torch, goes to her, and puts his gloved hands around her shoulders. "If she let you go, she's an idiot."

"No, she isn't."

"I *know* she is," Leo insists, making her turn to face him. "I was in her idiotic shoes once, remember?"

Alexandra winces and pulls him into an embrace. "You are, were, not an idiot. We both decided to end it, remember?" She mumbles into his chest and circles his waist with one arm. "It was the best way to keep our friendship intact."

Leo hums and squeezes her shoulder. "It's still her loss," he says softly as he pulls away. "You'll be okay, *cara mia*?"

"I'll be okay when we're done with this and away from this place." She pauses to take a deep breath. "Let's weld the whole thing together, install it, get our check, and move on."

Leo smiles at her and ruffles her curls. "You do realize this will take us at least a couple of months to finish, right?"

"I'm sure we can make it a month and a half."

"All right!" Leo exclaims while he struts back to his station. "Let's do this!"

Alexandra returns to the blue glass. She appreciates his enthusiasm. Enthusiasm is precisely what she needs to put all the ugliness behind her.

LATER, SHE LEAVES THE FOYER to fetch a thinner piece of lead from the truck. She's resolved to finish the more intricate details of her pattern so it can be handed over to Leo, and there is a new spring in her step, a new sense of urgency. Her renewed speed is the only reason she catches any of the conversation when she returns to the foyer.

"...to put her back together, so just leave, okay? She'll be better off without you, and I'll take care of her. I know how—I have plenty of experience."

Leo's voice is filled with venom and anger, sparks of red sprayed over his usual copper. Alexandra can almost picture his posture: chest puffed and arms crossed over it to make him look bigger and more impressive.

"What happens between Alexandra and me doesn't concern you, Mister Neri, no matter what you want to convince yourself and her of. As much as you wish for me to disappear, no, I won't just leave, if it's all the same to you."

Alexandra did not expect Halina's peach color to appear; not so soon, and not in a confrontation with Leo. Halina had been clear about her lack of interest in any sort of relationship.

"Get out of here before she comes back. You hurt her enough as it is," Leo insists.

Alexandra is torn between the instinct to protect Halina and gratitude to Leo for defending her. A more deeply ingrained part of her rejects the need for a white knight.

"I'll leave if Alexandra tells me to leave," Halina replies, her petulance sprayed in purple dots over her usual peach. "You can just go back to... flexing your arms or something."

Leo lets out a familiar huff, usually a herald of one of his volcanic explosions when he can be cruel with his words alone. She should stop the confrontation before it can escalate.

The lead she brought back suddenly weighs a ton, and she deposits it on the worktable. She gathers inner strength and puts her hands in her pockets as she clears her throat to get Halina and Leo's attention. "What's going on here?"

Halina has her hands on her hips, and her cheeks are still flushed with the heat of the confrontation. She relaxes her stance. "Alexandra," she says softly, turning her back to Leo. Alexandra had tried to convince herself Halina wasn't as beautiful as she remembered. But to see her in the flesh confirms that she is even more stunning.

Have some self-respect, damn it.

Halina's leather pants, which showcase her legs, are not helping her focus on her anger.

"What do you want?" Alexandra says to Halina while she nods toward Leo.

Behind Halina's back, he clenches his jaw before nodding back, and tugs at the corner of his eye to show his mistrust.

Halina gets closer. Alexandra takes one deliberate step back and pushes her hands deeper into her pockets. "I wanted to ask you if we could…" Halina says, and her voice has a quiver of baby pink around the edges. That shade has never appeared before. "…If we could talk? Just for a minute." The apples of her cheeks redden. "In private."

Leo flips off Halina, and Alexandra does agree with the sentiment. As far as she is concerned, Halina can go fuck herself into the next millennium if she believes she deserves a minute of Alexandra's time. That's what Alexandra wants to believe, anyway. On the other hand, Alexandra's heart screams at her to give Halina a chance, to hear what she has to say, because some good might come of it.

"Leo, I think I left the keys in the car. Do you mind checking it for me?" Alexandra asks, her eyes on Halina.

Leo opens and closes his mouth with a snap; the muscle in his jaw jumps under his stubble. He drops his gloves and his blowtorch on his worktable with a stormy expression and leaves the room.

"What do you want?" she repeats once Leo turns the corner.

Super-confident Halina was hot as hell, of course, but unsure, almost shy Halina? Alexandra wants to date this woman, unwrap all her layers and revel in her complexity, but not yet.

"I want to apologize for the way things ended between us. I never meant to hurt you and I—" She bites her lower lip before looking straight into Alexandra's eyes. "I miss you."

Alexandra exhales slowly to control the crazy rhythm of her heart. "I missed you, too," she mumbles, breaking eye contact to look at her feet. She scuffs the floor with the toe of her shoe.

A tender sound comes from Halina, the soft yellow of leather against wool. When Alexandra looks up, Halina is smiling at her from much closer. "You did?"

"Of course I did," Alexandra replies begrudgingly. "I meant every word I said to you: This was more than sex for me."

Her hands in her pockets, Halina props herself against Leo's worktable. In her oversized knitted sweater, she looks ten years younger; another layer of vulnerability tugs at Alexandra's protective instincts. "I'm sure you meant it," she says softly. "And I wish I could have your faith in, in us. The thing you have to understand is..." She pauses to exhale slowly. "...I've never dated anybody and I'm scared shitless."

Alexandra's dismay must be etched on her face. "Never? Not even when you were a teenager?"

A sad smile appears on Halina's face. "When you were a teenager, going to high school and normal parties and going on dates, I trained and practiced and toured all around Europe, on my way to my first award."

"Oh." Alexandra tries to picture it: no childhood; no time to discover who she was, what she liked, whom she loved; a childhood and an adolescence spent honing a talent. No hobbies aside music? No friends? No love? A shiver goes down her back. "And later?"

"I didn't care for it," Halina says, crossing her arms over her chest. "There wasn't any point in any relationship I would leave behind a week or so later." Halina looks back at Alexandra and shrugs. "It made more sense to keep it purely physical, if you see what I mean? Besides, relationships, and the whole mess that goes with them, never seemed to be worth my time."

Alexandra has a deep-rooted certainty Halina is not telling her all the reasons she abstained from dating for most of her adult life. It's a subject for a later conversation, though.

"What about now?" she asks as she adopts a more relaxed stance.

A blush appears on Halina's ears and cheeks. "Now I'm going to stay in town for at least a whole season and I—" She pauses, a dejected expression on her face. "I missed you. I want to see what could be between us."

"You wanna date me?" Alexandra asks, more to make sure she's not imagining things than to make Halina spell it out.

"I care about you," Halina says in one breath, as if ashamed of it. "If dating is what it takes to, um, be with you, I want to give it a try."

"It?"

Halina rolls her eyes, but her lips are still drawn in a smile. "Us, okay? I want to give us a chance." She pauses, audibly gulping. "If you want to give me one, of course."

Alexandra considers it.

She does want to give them another try, a proper chance at properly dating. It could be fun to woo Halina even though they already know each other in the biblical sense, to show her Alexandra's Paris and take her on delightful dates. But she's not sure she will recover so easily from the blow if Halina hurts her again. Hell, it took her two months to be able to look at Leo and at her work without a tissue in hand, and that was an amicable breakup.

Hope and worry battle in Halina's blue eyes, as if she expects Alexandra to dismiss her entirely but still wishes for the best. That visible conflict, so similar to what she feels herself, is what Alexandra needs to make her decision.

"All right." Alexandra puts her hands in her back pockets as she walks toward Halina. "One rule, though."

"Whatever you say." A dimple appears in Halina's left cheek.

"No more sex until we really know each other."

A frown makes a brief appearance between Halina's brows. "What does sex have to do with us dating?" She quirks her lips into a crooked smirk. "I thought the benefit of a relationship would be guaranteed sex, not less of it."

Alexandra fights against an answering grin. "We rushed into sex and we forgot to talk, and look where it almost led us. I think we need to learn who we are, what we want, before we let sex, as fun as it was, take over our brains." She pauses. Halina makes a begrudgingly agreeing sound. Encouraged, Alexandra continues. "If we want to build something based on more than physicality, sex needs to be taken out of the equation until it is a component of our relationship, not the alpha and the omega of it."

Halina squints at her and then sighs loudly. "Fine, whatever you say."

Alexandra takes Halina's hand and lets herself be pulled in. "So," she says, her hands splayed on Halina's collarbone, above her breasts, "does this mean I can take you on a date?"

Under her fingertips, Halina's sharp intake of breath is all the answer Alexandra needs. "I suppose it does."

"Awesome." Alexandra takes a deliberate step back and lightly brushes the swell of Halina's breasts. "Tomorrow night, I'll pick you up at your hotel around seven."

"Tomorrow night," Halina repeats. "Can I get a kiss?"

Alexandra's cheeks turn feverish and she can't resist acting coy. "A k—yeah, sure, you can," she replies, wiggling her fingers at Halina in a come-hither gesture.

Halina wraps one arm around Alexandra's waist to pull her flush against her and she cups Alexandra's chin to lift it toward her. "Looking forward to *knowing* you better," she whispers with a devilish smile before pressing her lips against Alexandra's.

Alexandra may have had some remorse about not playing a hundred percent fair, but it dissipates in the light of Halina's own unfairness. The kiss is dirty, sexual, hot, and radically different from any kiss they shared in the past. As passionate as they were, those kisses did not convey the tenderness, the carefulness, with which Halina passes her lips over Alexandra's now. Alexandra's toes curl in her shoes, and she returns the kiss wholeheartedly. Her fingers find the few tendrils escaping Halina's braid.

"Till the morrow." Halina pulls away with a wink and walks out, looking over her shoulder one more time before she disappears into the hallway.

Alexandra cups her own chin and observes Halina rolling her hips on her way out.

Bring it on.

*   *   *

HALINA THOUGHT THAT GETTING OVER Alexandra was complicated and frustrating, but it's nothing compared to what she has to face now. Her nerves turn a dinner at a restaurant into an examination, with Alexandra's eyes on her to catch her when she fails. Whether she's imagining this or not, the result is the same: Halina fidgets under Alexandra's observant gaze as if sitting on a chair made of red-hot coals.

Halina reaches for the little tendrils of hair on her nape. Playing with them gives her something to focus on. The menu is a blur and when Halina does manage to read the names of the dishes, they make little sense.

She looks up, and flushes when her eyes once again meet Alexandra's gray ones. Whoever said gray is a cold color never saw this shade: so rich, so deep, so full of passion. Mesmerizing.

Halina clears her throat, as it won't do her any good to let her mind wander to how passionate Alexandra has proven to be.

"Until we get to know each other," ja pierdolę, *that could be a while.*

"You don't want to eat?" she asks.

Alexandra blinks and sits up straighter. "Beg your pardon?"

The button of Alexandra's shirt is about ready to pop, and Halina focuses on not staring at it. She shifts her gaze slightly, to the light reflected by Alexandra's choker necklace, and smiles. "You didn't read the menu. The logical conclusion for me is to assume you don't intend to order anything to eat, which would be a shame."

Alexandra puts her hands over the folded menu on the table. "Oh, I do want to eat."

Halina doesn't want to let her libido take over, but she cannot silence mental suggestions of exactly what, or who, Alexandra could be eating right this instant. She squirms in her chair.

Alexandra speaks up, cutting through the fog of lust. "I didn't pick this restaurant on a whim; it's one of my favorites. I know the menu like the back of my hand. Besides," she adds with a crooked smile, "the view is more interesting."

"Is it so?" Halina is unable to keep her appreciation for the compliment from her voice, as hard as she tries.

"Very much so."

"If you are so familiar with the menu, do you recommend a dish in particular?"

For Halina, this is the first step on a tightrope without any net.

Alexandra's smile turns into a full-on smirk. "Depends on how varied your diet is."

"Pretty varied, but I am a creature of habit." If Alexandra's phrasing was a challenge, she will learn how strong Halina's competitive side can be.

"Is that so?" Alexandra cocks one eyebrow.

"Omnivorous, but with a very selective palate."

"Mm hmm?"

"Not sure you're as picky as I am."

Alexandra raises her other eyebrow. "*Au contraire*, I am very picky. I simply have varied interests within the parameters of my likes and dislikes, if you will."

"Oh, I will."

A blush appears on Alexandra's cheeks, spreading like a drop of red ink in a glass of water. "Good—good to know."

A moment passes, just long enough to make Halina fiddle with a stray piece of thread escaping from the embroidery on her sleeve.

"Back to your question," Alexandra says, her voice sounding slightly strangled. "I recommend the brioche. It looks like a pastry served with jam, but it's actually filled with a filet of salmon cooked in Thai spices with a side of bell peppers and tomato chutney."

Halina searches for it on the menu and frowns at Alexandra. "The whole menu is like this. The Saint Honoré?"

"You'd think it's a cake, but it's actually a burger."

"And the dessert section, with the cold cuts?"

"An assortment of chocolates and miniature cakes, yes."

"This place is weird."

"I'm sure you'll like it, though."

"You seem so sure."

"Positive."

The weirdest thing is not the way Halina trusts Alexandra's judgment on this matter—or any matter. It's the warmth spreading through her whole body at the sight of Alexandra's smile.

"Aren't we doing things backward?"

Alexandra swallows her mouthful of gnocchi and tilts her head to look up at her. Halina's heart should not somersault at how lovely she looks across the table. "What do you mean?"

Halina puts down her cutlery and presses her napkin to her lips, which gives her the time to compose her thoughts.

"Fucking first, dating second. I mean…" She needs to understand where she's going with this experiment, and it's well worth the embarrassment of having her cheeks turn bright red.

Alexandra mirrors her moves, pushes away her plate and cutlery, folds her arms on the table, and relaxes. "Well, as previously stated, when we… fucked, as you put it, I was under the impression that it was the heated start of us as a couple, nothing less." With the thumb and forefinger of her left hand, she twists the thumb ring on her right.

Even though they haven't spent a lot of time with their clothes on, the comfort Alexandra gets from the gesture hadn't escaped Halina's notice. If she focuses hard enough, she can recall the way the ring felt against her heated body while they kissed, the way the light bounced off it when Alexandra ran her thumb over her nipple, and—

Well, aren't I fucked.

Alexandra clears her throat, and Halina returns her gaze to her face. "It was always about building something real, not just orgasms."

That is a loaded sentence if Halina has ever heard one. She takes a deep breath before diving in headfirst. "It's ... it's not just about sex. For me. At least, not anymore."

She's not proud of her stammer, but there, she said it, she admitted it, and she may even be a little proud of herself for managing to say it aloud, if only for the reward of Alexandra's responding smile.

"I'm glad to hear it."

They exchange a look before returning to their respective meals. The salmon is indeed delicious, just as Alexandra promised, and the smell of the herbs blends with the underlying tanginess of the caramelized vegetables and the sweetness of the sauce to complement the fatty taste of the fish. Alexandra's dish of gnocchi is odd, in its appearance at least. It reminds Halina of a *makowiec*, the pastry her father used to make when she came back from a concert away from home. It does look good, and this dish nails the restaurant's concept in Halina's mind. Entrées shaped like desserts, desserts disguised as savory dishes— it's disturbing. Alexandra didn't pick the place for their first date by accident; she picked a place she was familiar with in order to get the upper hand.

Halina spares a moment to ponder how it fits another aspect of Alexandra's life: It's good, sure, but Halina prefers to have things more clearly defined. In her admittedly limited experience of the world, choices need to be made, and one thing cannot fit in two boxes at once—a pasta dish cannot be a dessert, a dessert cannot be a pasta dish, and one cannot be attracted equally to different genders. She's certain she would be more comfortable in this relationship business if she could be sure of Alexandra's preference.

But for now, Alexandra seems to have chosen her, and Halina is a perfectionist.

"So…"

Alexandra raises an eyebrow and picks her glass. "So?"

"Enlighten me," Halina says, affecting confidence as she sits back in her chair, her fingers around the stem of her wine glass. "What does a date not meant to end in, um—"

"In bed?" Laughter rings in Alexandra's voice, reminiscent of the soft thrumming of the drums in the background of a piece, a vibration that spreads through Halina's belly.

"Precisely. What does such a date entail?"

Alexandra laughs openly, and the sound is as rich and warm and silky as the sweetest of *miód pitny*, just as intoxicating as the liquor, and just as addictive.

"Well, for starters, it entails getting to learn who we are, beyond our magical spots and the way we moan or sigh," Alexandra replies, her voice cracking with the remnants of her laughter. "What makes us, us."

Halina wrinkles her nose in unveiled contempt. "What, a variation of Twenty Questions?"

Alexandra's features turn predatory as she looks at Halina, as if she is getting ready to pounce on the mouse Halina has become in this game. It's not a role she's used to playing, but she can't find it in herself to mind.

"Exactly like Twenty Questions."

Halina can only focus on swallowing without choking on her mouthful of wine and on gathering what's left of her wits after the unexpected wave of arousal in her body. Why does learning things about Alexandra while revealing things about herself turn out to be so exciting?

"You start," she says, hands on her lap and legs crossed under the table. "This is way too much of an uncharted territory for me."

Alexandra smiles at the waiter when he takes their plates before returning her attention to Halina. Her eyes are like lasers. "Don't worry. I'll be gentle. First one: dream holidays?"

Halina is so surprised by the question she just snorts a laugh. Truth be told, she expected something a little bit more… traditional, or cliché, such as her zodiac sign or her favorite movie. Somehow, Alexandra manages to surprise her.

"Remind me of what a holiday is." She stalls to hear Alexandra's rich laugh once again. She could get used to this relationship business.

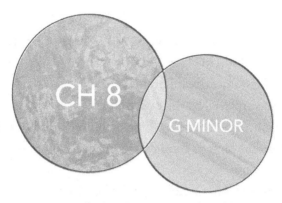

CH 8

G MINOR

Purple, Bottle Green, and Gold

THE MOMENT SHE CLOSES THE door behind Alexandra, Halina pulls her into a passionate kiss, all tongue and teeth and, yes, desperation.

During the day, on a search to catch a glimpse of Alexandra, Halina had an eyeful of Leonardo Neri, or *he-who-must-disappear* as she called him in the privacy of her mind. She saw the way he couldn't take his eyes off Alexandra. The sight accentuated every emotion Halina could feel brewing deep inside, from a lustful curiosity to something she could not yet name.

Most of their dates have had Halina walking on eggshells. Alexandra and her whirlwind of emotions, heartfelt words, and softness—both literal and figurative—pull her into a maelstrom of confusion and doubt. But this? Kisses that turn her partner's brain into mush? Using her body to find peace? This, Halina knows how to handle.

She pulls Alexandra closer, one hand on her cheek and the other on her waist, and doesn't give her any time to pause or talk. Halina doesn't give Alexandra a chance to throw her out of her groove; she just takes all she can while giving as little of herself as possible.

Her hand moves from Alexandra's soft waist to her even softer breast before traveling south to her generous buttocks. God, Halina had never been so interested in asses before, but there is something in Alexandra that effortlessly turns Halina's world upside down.

Alas, her partner is not so easily convinced, and though she kisses Halina back—and with as much passion, the little *diabełek*—Alexandra quickly pulls away from her embrace.

"Now, now," she says, voice soft yet strong in the two short words. "Didn't we say we would do this right?"

"Was I doing it wrong?" Halina asks as innocently as she can manage. At Alexandra's silence, she cocks one eyebrow and puckers her lips. "I must need to practice some more."

Alexandra lets out a throaty laugh as she twirls a long lock of Halina's hair around her fingers. "Nice try," she says, an echo of her laughter still in her voice like the ring of cymbals at the end of a movement, "but it's not what I meant."

Halina pouts and tries to get ahold of Alexandra's waist once again, but she takes a step back and puts a hand on Halina's shoulder. Her touch is feather-light, and yet it weighs on Halina like an anchor.

"Tut, tut. Let's go to that comfortable sofa over there and order all the most decadent items on the room service menu." She clasps Halina's hand in hers and pulls her toward the aforementioned piece of furniture. "And then we'll catch a movie and maybe kiss…"

"A regular date, with just kissing." Halina sums up, and Alexandra nods as she sits and pats the couch next to her. Such a short woman, but she has more power over her than Halina would ever care to admit.

Damned if she doesn't love it, too. Yes, women and their curves and their softness and their complications are everything one could desire. Why anyone would want a man when they could hold a woman is beyond Halina's comprehension, and she intends on convincing Alexandra of the same.

WHILE THEY WAIT FOR ROOM service to deliver the many delicious-sounding items Halina picked from the menu, she decides to woo Alexandra with her abilities as a mixologist. Camille was only one of the numerous bartenders Halina had seduced around the world and over the years, and she retained some ideas and recipes.

Her minibar and fruit bowl have just the ingredients she needs to make a Negroni. Sharp, tangy, delicious, it seems to be a perfect choice for Alexandra. She doesn't appear to be much of a drinker, but for one, of all the cocktails Halina enjoys and can prepare easily, the Negroni is the one with the most delicate taste. For two, Halina finds herself more comfortable with this whole seduction, this slow-paced relationship thing, than she'd thought. She enjoys the "make an effort to please your partner without any expectation" aspect—no expectation, but still an eventual reward.

Alexandra takes the offered glass, plucks the slice of orange from it, and sucks the peel. She smiles at Halina. "Trying to get me drunk?"

Halina quietly laughs and takes a sip of her drink. "I would never," she replies, one eyebrow dramatically raised. "Besides, do I really need to get you drunk to make you change your mind?"

Alexandra may want to be firm on her no-sex policy, but Halina doesn't have to make it easy for her. They share a look, and Alexandra seems unable to tear her eyes away. Halina can't either; the swirling gray of Alexandra's eyes pulls her in and gives her comfort.

Alexandra breaks the connection and takes another drink. "I suppose that's true," she finally says, before asking Halina how rehearsal went.

After a little chat about their respective work at the Philharmonie, they let a companionable silence fall over them as they enjoy their drinks. Halina feels nervous, out of her element; somehow, noticing her lack of nerves makes her nervous. And yet there is nowhere else she would rather be.

When a knock on the door disturbs their quiet, Halina jumps from the couch. Her hair frees itself from the loose tie she was using to tame it. Shaking the cascade of hair, Halina catches her reflection in the mirror near the entrance of her suite: Her appearance is wild, an incarnation of a filly introduced to human touch. The metaphor fits. She's slowly learning how to behave around someone who wants to domesticate her, how not to let her flight instincts take over, how to let herself trust Alexandra and get her to ride…

Oops. She just lost herself in the possibilities of the comparison. She opens the door.

"Mademoiselle Piotrowski," the young man says, "here is your order."

Halina signs the bill, gives him a tip, and takes the silver tray from his hands. "Thank you very much. Please make sure we're undisturbed?"

"Naturally, Mademoiselle Piotrowski."

Closing the door with her hip, Halina grins at the look of interest on her companion's face. "First, we have foie gras with toast and a fig and onion marmalade." She lifts the silver cover.

"Wow." Alexandra whistles under her breath. "You're not pulling your punches, are you."

"Followed by a chicken risotto."

"Yum."

"And for your sweet tooth," Halina adds with a smirk, "a *moelleux au chocolat.*"

The combination of Halina's accent, her choice of dessert, and all the work she put into setting up the date pays off. Alexandra pulls her into a dirty, dirty kiss, too brief for Halina's taste, then sinks back into the couch. She bites her lower lip, looking away to hide her crooked smile. With a deep intake of breath, she faces Halina. "Feed me."

Halina laughs. She delicately deposits a piece of foie gras on a piece of toast with some of the marmalade and offers it to Alexandra. "Hungry?"

"Starving," Alexandra replies as she kisses the back of Halina's hand before taking the toast. "Thanks."

Halina's cheeks probably turn an ugly shade of red, but she dismisses her bashfulness at Alexandra's gratitude with a wave of her hand and sticks the spoon in her mouth.

With a small moan of appreciation, Alexandra bites into the toast. She puts it back on the plate and tries the risotto.

Halina's eyes cross when she finds herself faced with a spoon. "What are—"

"You deserve the first bite."

They feed each other, alternating spoonfuls of risotto with foie gras toasts and trading light kisses every now and then. The food tastes incredible, if a little fatty, but Halina is not about to complain about that. She is a hedonist through and through, and generations of Polish heritage sing in her blood about how a little bit of fat never hurt anyone. Then too, the domesticity of feeding each other so playfully is more pleasant than she'd expected. Though she would never consider herself a romantic, Halina could be convinced this is not so bad after all. And they still have dessert, her secret weapon to get the mood of the evening slightly less romantic and more sexual.

Halina uncovers the dessert; the chocolate cake looks innocent enough on its porcelain plate. Alexandra gently presses a teaspoon to the top of the cake, which reminds Halina of a squeezed stuffed toy in all its fluffiness. She cuts into it; her hand is firm, and her gesture is assertive. They gasp as the molten center of the cake spreads out so the chocolate covers the plate. Then Alexandra holds her spoon up for Halina to take, which is just what Halina was waiting for.

Closing her lips around the spoon, Halina brushes her fingers against Alexandra's wrist. She flutters her eyelashes, closes her eyes to suck on the spoon, and lets out a long, throaty moan. Halina plays dirty, reminding Alexandra of how "thankful" she can be once she gets what she wanted, but she can't bring herself to feel remorse. Where there is a will, there is a way, and Halina is willing to do whatever it takes to get her way.

She savors the blush on Alexandra's cheeks, but Halina should have foreseen it wouldn't be so easy to get her back in her bed. She should have known it would take more to throw Alexandra off her game, more than a well-placed moan and Halina's flowing blonde hair. Halina had convinced herself she would have Alexandra between her legs once more before the end of the evening. She had even decided to reward Alexandra, an early prize for losing at Halina's game.

As if it could be so easy.

Alexandra doesn't open her mouth to accept the cake. No, the damned *psotnica* sticks her tongue out to lick at it with her eyes firmly on Halina. Mirroring Halina's earlier gesture, she wraps her fingers around Halina's wrist while she keeps licking it the same way she did when—*Oh.* Alternating between broad swipes of her tongue and kitten licks, Alexandra lets out little moans directed at Halina's libido and hums of delight that efficiently redirect Halina's blood flow. Halina can't be sure how much her face lets on, but her hands are certainly unsteady by the time Alexandra is finished.

Lesson learned: no more teasing you into bed before you say so, she thinks as she gulps.

"Delicious," Alexandra says with an innocent smile, and Halina can only nod and wait for her next bite.

The plates are covered in crumbs and half-eaten pieces of cake. Both women are content to just sit on the couch, close but not quite snuggling, hands on their stomachs, happily sighing. Alexandra turns toward Halina, who sits with one arm folded so she can rest her head in her palm. She smiles softly at Alexandra. An emotion she has tried to keep away for as long as she can remember blooms in her heart, making her feel warm and cared for, l—

Nah, it can't be that just yet. No, all she feels is caring and softness, and it is enough for now. Yet—for now—her mind still follows a road she thought abandoned, and her heart is drunk on a sea of words she understands now but never had much use for.

"What?" Alexandra asks.

"Nothing. You're beautiful."

Under her eyes, Alexandra's cheeks turn a charming, darker shade of pink. She brushes the comment off: "What about a movie now?"

"What about not a movie?" Halina waggles her fingers up to the side of Alexandra's thigh.

Alexandra glances at the fingers before crossing her legs primly so her thigh is out of reach. "Nuh-uh." She stretches the vowel. "I'm *pretty* sure a movie is on the program."

Halina ponders, for exactly two seconds, the benefits of challenging said program before she accepts it and gets the remote from under various magazines and music sheets. "Fine," she replies with a pout, a useful tool in her seductive arsenal. "What about porn?" she offers, half serious and half to check how Alexandra will react.

"I don't mind," Alexandra replies with a shrug. "Gay, lesbian, straight? Poly?" She cocks one eyebrow at Halina. "I really don't have a preference, though I'm not sure it fits the mood…"

Well, it may not fit the mood of this evening, but it is fodder for another evening. Halina doesn't need precognitive abilities to picture how much fun she could have experiencing a pornographic movie with Alexandra—but not tonight, not when Alexandra's rules about sex are enforced and Halina will be left alone to deal with her arousal.

"Might be better to pick another movie."

As she sits back on the couch browsing the movies, Halina feels Alexandra's hand on her shoulder, feels circles drawn on her skin. "Pick whatever movie you want," Alexandra tells her. "I just want to get my cuddle on."

It's so sweet, this demand for physical contact, as platonic as it may be. Halina can't resist smiling shyly at Alexandra before she returns her attention to finding the right movie and, as Alexandra said, getting her cuddle on.

Ha-ah! Perfect.

"*An American Tail*?" Alexandra asks with a look of surprise; the screen shows that the movie has been selected once before.

Halina sits back, legs folded, one arm thrown over the back of the couch in invitation for Alexandra to snuggle. "I love this movie." She fiddles with Alexandra's longest curls. "But I never got to see the end when I was a kid, or recently either."

"It's a good movie. I'm just surprised."

"Let's just say that I'm catching up on my childhood."

The couch moves with every inch Alexandra gets closer, but Halina keeps her eyes on the screen and the opening credits.

With one short sentence, Halina just opened more doors to herself than she has with anyone, and she doesn't even dread Alexandra's reaction.

Alexandra's short body fits perfectly under Halina's arm. She presses a small kiss to the corner of Halina's lips before they settle in to enjoy the adventures of Fievel Mousekewitz.

Halfway through the movie, more or less in the middle of Henri the pigeon's song, Halina glances at Alexandra, who has moved to settle her head on Halina's shoulder. Without a word, she bows her head to kiss her, simply because she wants to do it. It feels right on every level. Even if she agreed, albeit reluctantly, to let a "real" relationship unfold at its own pace, she doesn't want to deny herself any more of Alexandra's lips than she must.

So she kisses her, and cups her cheek, and deepens the kiss until Alexandra moves away. Alexandra sits up, mirrors Halina's posture with one leg folded under her body, and returns the kiss with a comforting languor. Somehow, this closed-mouth kiss is more loaded than a thousand dirty kisses Halina exchanged with some of her former, more temporary partners.

Halina doesn't mind that Alexandra is in charge of the pace and heat of their encounter. In some ways, Alexandra's subtle control makes her more comfortable, as it gives her a structure, borders to test and to be sheltered within. She smoothly slides one hand from Alexandra's cheek to her neck and to her breast. Alexandra picks up her hand and puts it back on her shoulder without breaking the soft kiss.

Merde.

Halina cups the back of Alexandra's head with her left hand while her right hand tightens around the knot of her shoulder, bringing her closer. But against her lips, Alexandra tuts, then moves away from her. The distance feels like an ocean and deprives Halina of her warmth and softness. Facing the screen with a pillow against her chest, Alexandra seems unaffected. The only sign she was not indifferent to the kiss is the blush spread over her cheeks and neck. Halina is not particularly proud of herself, but she can't help her disappointment. She drops herself against the back of the couch and sulks.

From the corner of her eye, she notices Alexandra give her a quick look before facing the screen again, but she is also laying her hand in the middle of the couch as an olive branch. It's a present Halina can't refuse.

Holding hands like stereotypical teenagers, they finish the movie. Alexandra stands, smooths her dress, and pecks Halina's lips with a perky "Don't go to sleep too late, babe." And out the door she goes.

Merde indeed.

*   *   *

"Stop, stop, stop!" The maestro slams his baton on the stand in front of him and turns toward Halina, and with him the whole string section. "Mademoiselle Piotrowski," he says, sickly sweet, with so much condescension it raises Halina's hackles, "would you mind keeping a firmer rein on your enthusiasm for Smetana?"

Halina frowns at him. "It is an allegro, maestro," she replies, not to be disrespectful but in resistance to a man who has a reputation in their little world for getting what he wants by pulling strings.

"*Ma non agitato*, Mademoiselle Piotrowski, *ma non agitato!*"

Halina clenches her hands on her lap and decides not to let this divergence of opinion get in the way of her enthusiasm for an entire evening dedicated to the Czech composer. She puts a pleasant smile on her face. "My affinity for Smetana got the best of me. My apologies, maestro, colleagues," she says with an apologetic nod to the assembled orchestra.

The maestro gives her an odd look before turning to the orchestra.

"One more time," the maestro says with a pointed look. "And no interpretation, just what's on the score, hm."

Halina nods, fingers at the ready over the keys as her mind goes back to the past evening and the not-so-small epiphany it brought. When she agreed to Alexandra's plan to build a relationship, Halina thought that her being so unromantic would complicate the process. But the major emotions from the past evening's date are neither reluctance nor the feeling of being pushed into a corner. The predominant ones are comfort and the feeling of freedom to be herself within a space carved for two.

Maybe, she thinks as the maestro stops the orchestra, *just maybe, I never wanted to settle in a relationship because it never felt right.*

"Good, good," the maestro says, tapping his baton against the stand. "Much better, isn't it, when we all stick to the sheet?"

Behind her, Halina catches Odile muttering about where he can stick his sheet, and subdued laughter flutters through the violin section. Troubled by this mutiny, the maestro clears his throat and gingerly puts his baton back on the stand. "Maybe a ten-minute break before we start working on the finale, yes?"

Halina looks at the orchestra filing out of the concert room. Some of the musicians are off to get a smoke; others stay to continue their jokes about the guest maestro and his rigor. Some busy themselves tending to their instruments. And finally, some leave in pairs to enjoy a quickie backstage; the twinkle in their eyes is one she's familiar with. Or at least, she used to be familiar with it.

Halina stays where she is, playing variations on Smetana's melody to get it out of her system before the conductor can snap at her again. The vivacious melody of the second movement slowly turns into something softer.

The modulations remind her of Alexandra: the soft heart and the iron will, combined to create a personality Halina wants to learn and decode. She rests her head against the fallboard of the piano at the memory of how powerless she felt last night after Alexandra's departure, how wanted she had felt, how willing she was to let Alexandra dictate the progression of their relationship. She is already wrapped around Alexandra's little finger, isn't she?

Shit, merde, o cholera.

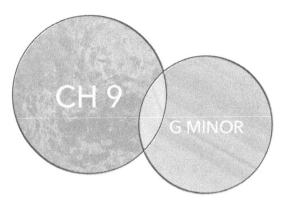

CH 9 / G MINOR

Red, Khaki, and Dusty Pink

THE DATE OFFERED MANY DISCOVERIES about Halina, and Alexandra wants to keep the momentum going. They have agreed on another date for three days later, and, while Alexandra has the perfect restaurant for it, she needs to up her game.

"Where could I take a musician on a Thursday night?" she muses, scrolling on her phone for different activities.

They could go to the Architecture Museum near Place du Trocadéro and look at the models. She is almost certain that she heard something about an exhibition of stained glass. But Alexandra wants to wow Halina, not just show her a different side of Paris. She bookmarks it anyway: at some time, the Palais de Chaillot may be a good date location, but not now.

"Leo, where would you—" she starts, but Leo lets a piece of lead clang onto the table.

"No."

"What? I just—"

"I just refuse to help you date her," Leo hotly retorts. "So my answer is no. Deal with it yourself."

"That behavior is just charming," Alexandra mutters to herself.

Leo humphs and grumbles. "Oh come on!"

"Count me out next time you're looking for advice on a good way to satisfy your partner."

"As if I need—never mind," he cuts himself short when Alexandra shoots him a pointed look. Alexandra has saved Leo's ass on more than one occasion, and sometimes quite literally, something she won't let him forget any time soon.

"I don't like her."

"You've made it abundantly clear," Alexandra says, returning her eyes to her screen. "I don't care what you think about her, though."

"You don't care?"

"I. Don't. Care," she repeats. "What matters is that *I* like her, and *she* likes me."

"And I have no say in this?"

"Why would you get one?"

Leo drops his goggles next to the lead. "Because it affects your work? You? Us?"

"Us?" she repeats. "If you're talking about work, maybe, and that's debatable. Otherwise, nothing about Halina affects us."

"I'm not allowed to be jealous?"

"Be whatever you want to be," Alexandra snaps, "except a pain in my *tuches.*"

"Oh, come on, Lexie, don't be that way," Leo says, dropping his voice to a velvety tone.

It could have worked, once upon a time. "I'll be that very way until you stop being a schmuck."

Another grumble, followed by a sigh of reluctant, mint-green-colored surrender. "Take her to a jazz club."

The idea gets her attention. "You think she'd enjoy it?"

Leo rests his arms on the table. "Whenever she tinkers, it's jazzier than classical. She might appreciate it, and more power to you."

Now there's an idea: there are several cool jazz clubs in Paris, one not too far from the restaurant she has in mind and it's one she is very familiar with. Winter has fallen over Paris like a blanket of cold. They could huddle close as they walk to the club, and once there, she will know whether Halina is a jazz aficionada or not. She pulls up the New Morning website to appraise their program for the coming week.

"Thanks, Leo," she says softly. "You don't have to dislike her on principle."

Leo gives her a long, soulful look. "I do," he says softly. "As long as you're with her, I won't get you back."

Alexandra rolls her eyes and throws a balled piece of paper in his direction. "Very funny."

Leo kicks the ball before it can hit him. He grins. "As always."

"Uh huh."

"You love me."

"Sometimes I wonder why."

"Still love me."

"Sure, sure."

Her phone beeps, a notification of new email, and she walks out of their workspace to open it. It's from her sister, saying she'll be coming to Paris with her son for Hanukkah and New Year's Eve "if it's not too much of an imposition, of course, and God willing. If you can make some time for us, it would be great. Can't wait to be with you in the City of Lights."

It's been years since the two sisters managed to spend their favorite holiday together. Of all she left behind when she moved to France, Alexandra misses her sister the most. It will be fun to have her and her nephew in Paris for Hanukkah and Christmas, and it also means she may get to introduce her family to Halina. Alexandra closes her eyes and lightly taps her cheek. *Stop daydreaming, silly,* she admonishes herself. *One step at a time.*

She'll consider an introduction to her family and its consequences when they reach that bridge. For now, good food and good music, and a little flirting.

* * *

ALEXANDRA HAS SURPRISED HALINA AGAIN, if the small sigh she lets out as they enter the restaurant is any indication. The unremarkable building is similar to hundreds of Parisian ones: Once standing tall and sturdy, it now looks closer to crumbling. The high step at the entrance is uneven, and the hallway leading to the stairs shows cracks and water stains while the lightbulbs flicker on and off.

"I agree to trust you, and you decide to take me to a serial killer, is that it?" she asks, then squeezes her hand when Alexandra huffs in mock outrage.

"Ha! Who's to say I am not the serial killer?"

"Ha!"

"And for your information, tonight will only eradicate any misconceptions you may have about Italian cuisine."

"Oh, joy."

They reach the first floor, and Alexandra turns to raise an eyebrow at Halina. She's one step higher on the stairway and uses the higher ground to tap her finger against the tip of Halina's nose. "What did I just say?"

"Killing preconceived ideas, got it," Halina replies, snapping playfully at Alexandra's finger. "What is this place, anyway? A speakeasy?"

Alexandra smiles at her and pushes the door open. "In a way."

They are welcomed by a large man with a friendly, booming voice who seats them at a quiet table next to the bar. Halina sits with her back to the room. Her eyes are drawn to the antique coffee machine taking pride of place on the counter. Alexandra takes in the décor. The restaurant is in a former apartment; the furniture is old, yet comfortable, while the walls bear large, colorful canvases. One thing is certain, this place doesn't look like the rest of the building.

"How did you even find this restaurant?"

"I saw it on TV," Alexandra replies, picking a piece of warm focaccia from a basket that has just been brought to them by the affable host. "The journalist wouldn't shut up about how authentic, yet modern, it was, and the plates looked drool-worthy."

Halina hums as she snatches a piece of the soft bread for herself.

The owner swiftly switches to English with a heavy accent to ask them if they want wine with their meal, and Halina asks for his recommendation. It's Alexandra's turn to be surprised: She didn't imagine Halina would take the lead, but she doesn't mind. She wants Halina to behave normally, not to be a subdued version of herself or a façade.

The man chuckles, purple and burgundy bouncing on deep yellow, and makes a couple of suggestions. Alexandra doesn't care much about wine and lets Halina decide on a glass of Savennières Roche aux Moines with her veal. He turns to her to joke that she should get some wine too, since "wine only adds beauty and glow to beautiful women." Alexandra smiles politely and declines the offer.

As he leaves them, Alexandra catches an unhappy frown on Halina's face. Alexandra is relieved when it disappears quickly.

Halina takes her hand as soon as they're left to their own devices. Alexandra absorbs the ambiance reigning over their table. The intimacy is almost tangible; their interaction is far easier than either of their previous dates. This third date together has the resonance of an anniversary, and Alexandra wants to bask in it.

"What else have you planned for us tonight?" Halina asks as she rubs her thumb back and forth across Alexandra's knuckles.

Alexandra angles her chest over the table, aware that her V-neck reveals her cleavage. "All of my plans should make you very happy," she replies with a crooked smile.

Halina's eyes follow the opening of her top, and she cocks an eyebrow. "I can only imagine," she says; her fingers subtly tighten around Alexandra's hand. Her voice takes on a deeper shade: coral and rosewood in dots around her usual peach. The colors are familiar, the mark of Halina's arousal. If she's honest with herself, Alexandra wants to follow this train of thought. Maybe tonight—?

Let's see how the evening goes.

In the meantime, Halina's hungry eyes do wonders for Alexandra's ego. Alexandra lets her own eyes wander over Halina's outfit and hairdo: her Blonde hair is in a ponytail of ringlets that falls over one shoulder and brushes the brass buttons on her chest. Her navy, military-style dress is severe, with a neckline that highlights her collarbones. Alexandra can't take her eyes from the hems of her navy cuffs. The contrast between the dark blue and Halina's fairness beckons Alexandra to brush the delicate skin of Halina's wrists with her fingers.

The first course arrives as Alexandra is about to do just that. She fiddles with her napkin to get over her urge. The plate is covered in grilled artichoke hearts, crushed mint leaves, and a generous amount of shaved Parmigiano, with a drizzle of olive oil and a sprinkle of sea salt: a delightful painting on a plate.

"Oh, wow," Halina says, eyes wide as she licks her lips. "I'm famished."

"Weren't you supposed to have a nice lunch with some members of the orchestra?" Alexandra asks, twirling her fork between her fingers before she picks a piece of cheese.

Halina groans and stabs an artichoke. "Don't get me started on this," she says, stuffing her face with the vegetable—not that it silences her. "Turns out, 'nice lunch' was code for a cardboard sandwich on the square in front of the Philharmonie."

Alexandra winces in sympathy as she delicately cuts the artichoke and a piece of dry cheese and takes a small bite. "Damn." The smoothness of the artichoke is highlighted by the sharpness of the cheese, and Alexandra savors it.

"With a bottle of cheap beer," Halina adds. Then she swallows, her eyes closed. "Now," she says, pointing her fork at the plate, "that's delicious."

With a smile, Alexandra sips from her glass of water. "Didn't I tell you it would win you over?"

"Full of surprises and delicious," Halina replies, with her glass paused between her mouth and the table. "Seems I have a type. In different aspects of my life."

"Are you comparing me to our delicious starter?"

Halina sets her glass down, leans one elbow on the table, and rests her head on her hand. "Metaphorically speaking, yeah."

Alexandra, enchanted by the layers of their discussion, is unable to look away from Halina's gaze. "I suppose I should be flattered."

"I may start calling you 'Artichoke,'" Halina teases. She spears another piece of the vegetable.

"Don't you dare."

"What, you don't like it, my little artichoke?"

'I really do not: *coeur d'artichaut* doesn't sound right."

"I shall find another—" Halina takes another bite, and Alexandra can't help but smile fondly at her. "What?"

"You're so cute," Alexandra says with a chuckle. "I love your enthusiasm for your food."

Halina glances away; a pink hue colors her cheeks. "I'm sorry." Her hand covers her mouth. "It's just so delicious. I didn't stop to think—"

Across the table, Alexandra pats Halina's hand to put an end to her unease. "I'm glad you can be yourself with me," she says softly. "I was just teasing, babe."

The flush intensifies, and a realization dawns on Alexandra: The endearment might be the source of it. That's something to study further at another time.

Clearing her throat, Alexandra takes the conversation in a safer direction. "Was it at least interesting?" Halina cocks one eyebrow at her, and she explains. "The lunch?"

"Oh," Halina says, using a piece of bread to soak up some olive oil. "Yeah, I guess. Moineau's knowledge of the inner workings of the orchestra and the politics of it all was very interesting. And she mentioned something about how you got the job, by the way," she adds, eyes crinkling.

"Odile Moineau, right?" Alexandra asks, going through her mental images of the orchestra and envisioning the stern older woman's face.

"Yeah. Have you met her?"

Alexandra shrugs. "I know *of* her; she performed for a couple of charity events I attended at the Hungarian Institute," she explains. "Colorful bow work."

"Colorful?" Halina asks, resting her chin on her joined hands.

Alexandra chuckles. "As in, in here," she replies and taps her temple with two fingers. "I... see music in colors. It's my main source of inspiration."

Halina's eyes widen considerably while the waiter takes their empty plates. "How so?"

Explaining the phenomenon is never easy. It puts her at the border between pride in its uniqueness and embarrassment over its strangeness. "It's called synesthesia," she says, her fingers wrapped around the stem of her glass. "I, uh, guess, technically, it's a brain defect, though I never considered it a flaw." Halina hums in interest, leans forward, enraptured, and encourages her to go on. "I have no control over it, but I use it as an inspiration for my art. It makes sense to turn it into something productive."

"How does it work, exactly?" Halina asks with a small frown. "As, right now, does my voice make colors appear?"

Alexandra chuckles and brushes a curl away from her eyes. "You sound peach or apricot; it varies with your mood," she replies honestly. "But most of the time, I tune out the colors from voices to focus on what is said. Music on the other hand, is harder to suppress."

"Fascinating," Halina whispers, her eyes sharp on Alexandra. "It's as if you constantly find new ways to pull me in."

"Not by design, I promise," Alexandra replies, her cheeks heating up at the praise.

"I still don't fully understand it," Halina says at a more conversational volume. She shakes her head, sending her ponytail into motion behind her. "Is it the same as what happens when you scrub your closed eyes?"

Alexandra laughs. "It's hard to explain; imagine having to describe music to someone who never heard a sound. I'm not talking about what it makes you experience, how music works, how notes can vary, but the physical process of it: how a stimulus enters your ear, hits your eardrums, how your nerves deliver it to your brain, which processes it and makes you understand you ... *heard.*" She shrugs. "I've come to consider it as an extra sense you have to experience to understand."

"Wow."

"My sister has a different experience with it, entirely: she sees letters in colors."

"Letters." The doubt in Halina's voice edges the peach with a light, springtime shade of green. "Letters have colors for her?"

"Yeah. When we were kids, she used to cry because my name was redder than hers."

"Huh?"

"Apparently, A's in Alexandra are red while E's in Elisabeth are yellow, and she hated, still hates, yellow."

Halina snorts and then covers her mouth. "The poor thing," she comments; her voice is now colored carmine.

"Oh, she even tried to convince me to trade names."

Halina joins her in laughter, and they both lower it to a contained snicker when the waiter arrives with their entrées.

"I hope you ladies keep on having a good time," he tells them with a wide grin. "Bon appétit."

They thank him in unison and start eating. Halina has a veal chop, perfectly grilled and tender, fragrant with rosemary and sage, served with vegetables. The plate could have come from a jeweler's window. Alexandra's dish is cep ravioli, covered in a rich tomato sauce, fresh leaves of basil, and delicate shavings of Parmigiano. The discussion is on hold. Clearly, Halina loves her meat, and Alexandra loves how she digs into it. Halina's hand hovers over the bone before she picks up her knife and fork.

"Remind me to cook you my lamb chops sometime," Alexandra says as she uses the last piece of ravioli to soak up as much of the sauce as possible. "Eating it with my hands is what I prefer about it."

A light appears in Halina's eyes. "A home-cooked meal? I could be interested."

"Would you?"

"I'm curious about your place." Halina dips the tip of her finger into Alexandra's sauce and then sucks on it. "How you decorated. How big is your nest? Let me guess… a bit of Goldilocks, not too small, not too big, and lots of clutter."

"Excuse you, it's called a perfectly organized mess," Alexandra corrects haughtily, before laughing into her glass of water. "What else do you have in mind?"

"Pictures on the walls, of places you've been to and loved ones." She pauses to sip the last of her wine. "Lots of pillows. Um… would you have a pet?" she muses, and Alexandra lifts one eyebrow. She thinks of Punshki, the corgi who is happily spending the night at a canine "spa" for his birthday. "Of course you have a pet, it would explain the long, light hairs on your clothes. I want to say cat, but…"

"Dog."

"Ah, of course. You're from California, aren't you?" Halina gives her an amused look. "Must be one of those annoyingly small ones, a Chihuahua or something equally ridiculous."

Alexandra snorts. Ridiculous he might be, from time to time, but Punshki is much bigger than a Chihuahua.

"That's for me to know," she replies to keep at least some mystery. Punshki is an experience, from the first encounter; she wouldn't dream of spoiling it. And he's hated Leo with a passion from the get-go; Alexandra should have considered that a sufficient warning.

"And for me to find out," Halina says, winking at Alexandra. The waiter comes with the dessert menu.

Alexandra checks her watch and shakes her head with an apologetic smile.

"Aw, leaving me so soon?" the man jokes as he brings the bill with two mints. "Have a good evening, ladies."

"Thank you," Halina tells him, following Alexandra out of the restaurant. "What's the rush?"

Alexandra grins at her as she hails a taxi. "That's a surprise!"

HALINA ENJOYS DATING MORE THAN she thought she would. Dinner was excellent, and she already plans to return to this restaurant often during her Parisian stay, with Ari and with Saral when he comes for the inaugural concert in January. Above all, Alexandra herself makes this whole dating business more fun than Halina expected. The easy way she navigates it makes Halina comfortable trying these unknown waters.

Right this moment, she shaves years from the mid-thirties age bracket Halina assigned her as she tries to cover Halina's eyes.

"If I promise to keep my eyes closed, will you stop trying to break both our necks?" she asks.

"Oooh," Alexandra says, stumbling and then straightening up. "Okay."

Her eyes closed, Halina's only option is to let Alexandra take her hand to guide her forward. She can hear a crowd around them and Alexandra's voice as she speaks in rapid French. They pass over a threshold and the sounds of the street disappear, replaced by those of tuning instruments.

"Ta-da," Alexandra whispers in her ear as they sit, and Halina opens her eyes.

They are in a bar with a stage, and there are two men on said stage. One tunes a battered, beautiful double bass while the other sits at the piano.

"Where are we?" she whispers, eyes drawn to the piano.

"Welcome to New Morning, one of the best places in Paris for jazz concerts," Alexandra replies with a small, hopeful smile on her face. "And these two gentlemen are Dave Holland and—"

"Kenny Barron," Halina, completely in awe at the legend not twenty feet away from her, cuts her off. "*O, mój Boże.*"

Alexandra laughs happily. A spark of pride lights her eyes when Halina, unable to completely close her mouth, turns to stare at her.

"How did you…" Halina's voice trails off as Barron starts playing.

"I had a hunch you'd be a jazz connoisseur, based on how you play when the rest of the ensemble leaves," Alexandra replies, "and this is my jazz place when I miss home too much."

Halina pockets the information and sits on the edge of her plush chair as the duet launches into one of her favorite songs. God knows she has recorded many jazz songs on her phone, standards of the genre that she adores and dreams of playing to her heart's content. And the interplay between the two musicians, in which the delicate yet strong piano notes perfectly respond to the smooth backdrop of the bass, perfectly illustrates what draws her to jazz. It's a conversation created between instruments to paint a different picture in each listener's mind.

From the corner of her eye, Halina peeks at Alexandra. Now, her explanation of synesthesia makes more sense. Halina doesn't pretend to have any artistic talent with colors, but Alexandra's parallel between her synesthesia and how Halina would explain music to someone who never heard it makes sense. If she were to try to explain how this music affects her, even to Alexandra, who seems so attuned to music, she's pretty sure she would fail.

Keeping her eyes on the musicians, Halina reaches for Alexandra's hand and squeezes her fingers. She trusts the touch to convey more than her words could ever express. Alexandra tightens her hold in return, and Halina lets herself be wrapped in the double warmth of the melody and the person sitting next to her to share it.

By the end of the concert, Halina buzzes with the energy of the music and she yearns to play something, anything. Any Chopin polonaise would do, or maybe some Sibelius to calm her excitement before sleep.

Alexandra walks next to her and lets her ramble about her favorite moments of the concert. She simply wraps her scarf around Halina's neck when the wind blows more harshly. The gesture brings Halina back to reality, and she lets Alexandra pull her closer with the ends of the scarf, which is permeated with Alexandra's discreet perfume, until they stand toe-to-toe.

"I guess I should go back to my hotel," Halina says softly, checking the crowd around them before she pulls Alexandra closer by the waist. "It's getting late."

"It is late." Alexandra fiddles with the hem of her scarf and then ties it in a soft knot around Halina's neck. "Or... we could go back home."

"Hm?"

Halina takes longer than she should to get Alexandra's meaning, but in her defense, she's had a pretty long day.

"My apartment is ten minutes away," Alexandra says, her head cocked.

Halina looks over Alexandra's head and takes a moment to weigh her options. She could stretch out her celibacy a little longer and learn how to enjoy the budding relationship. Or, she could get reacquainted with Alexandra's body, with her wicked ways.

It's a no-brainer. "Lead the way."

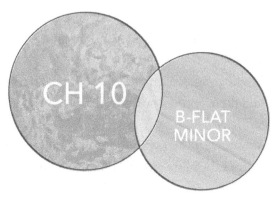

CH 10

B-FLAT MINOR

Violine, Blue, and Silver

ALEXANDRA CLOSES THE DOOR BEHIND them and lets Halina move past her and into the living room. She settles into the relief of being back in her nest before anything else can happen.

When she joins Halina in the living room, Halina's coat is off. The passion in her gaze is spellbinding. Without a word, with the lights still off, they find each other; hands caress and lips meet for a heated kiss.

They stumble into her bedroom, and Alexandra doesn't waste any time. She throws her beautiful sweater and her skirt in a corner, then pulls Halina to her. Alexandra wraps her arms around Halina's waist and grasps the zipper of her dress. She's not helped by the dress's inhabitant, because Halina cups Alexandra's face for one more kiss to her lips, one more to her nose, her cheeks, her jaw.

The zipper finally obeys. Alexandra's thumb trails down the line of Halina's back, and Halina's ponytail brushes against her hand as if returning the caress.

Halina shrugs to let the dress pool at her ankles and steps away from it. As she does so, the light from the streetlamp bathe her in a yellowish, almost sepia, glow. They both let out a shuddering breath, and Halina smothers a laugh when hers evolves into a snort. The sound dissipates the tension between them, and Alexandra kneels on her bed, wiggling her fingers at Halina. "Come here, babe," she says huskily, and Halina takes her hand.

Alexandra lies against her pillows, gently prodding Halina until she has her back to Alexandra's chest. Alexandra hugs her close, unashamed to rub her breasts against her back. It's teasing, but so comfortable, so inherently good, and, from the sound Halina's making, it's good for her too—win-win.

Alexandra presses kisses along the line of Halina's neck, mapping the ways she reacts to her mouth: not as much behind her ears, but so sensitive around the nape of her neck. She starts slowly, with her fingertips on Halina's thighs, and then slides up. Her touch stays feather-light, barely a caress, and she's rewarded with moans and pants.

"Oh, Xandra…"

Alexandra cups one breast and gently rolls Halina's nipple between her fingers. "Want me to tell you what I would do if you were to let me take my sweet time?" she asks, and Halina clutches her kneecaps.

"Y-yes?"

"I would use a toy," she whispers, pressing a wet kiss to Halina's shoulder followed by a soft blow of air on it to raise goosebumps, "all over you, from shoulders to toes."

"On—on my breasts too?" Halina manages, arching into Alexandra's touch when her fingers get to that zone.

"Yeah, on your breasts. Low vibration, around your perky breasts."

"On the nipples?"

"Nah." She laughs, and Halina relaxes even deeper into her embrace. "It would be too much. Or maybe I would," she continues, as if just considering it, "just graze them with the tip of the toy to make you squirm."

"What next?" Halina's voice has gone rough and throaty; it's almost orange. The change in colors is affecting Alexandra's arousal.

"Next, I would take it lower, around your ribs, your belly. Wherever you'd want, babe."

"Uh-huh."

Alexandra pinches the soft skin of Halina's stomach. "Are you doubting my ability to show you some new hot spots?"

Halina turns her head just a bit, so her profile is turned toward Alexandra. "Never."

Alexandra presses a soft kiss to the corner of Halina's mouth just as she slides her hand farther south, covering Halina's mound. "Thank you for your trust," she says against Halina's lips, her free hand on Halina's hip. "Now, where were we?"

Halina thrusts her hips in the air in a barely veiled attempt to make Alexandra's hand move. Alexandra chuckles at how easily Halina responds to her touch. It was the point of the whole evening, but she never envisioned such success.

"Right," she purrs. "Now, if I used one of my toys, I wouldn't go straight for your pussy, babe."

"No?"

"No."

"But why?" Halina's voice takes on a slightly desperate quality. Her skin reveals more than her voice as her blush spreads to her chest. Alexandra has yet to find out if it's a response to the term of endearment or to the suggestion.

"Because it's not fun to go straight for the grand finale."

"Hmph."

"Trust me, babe," Alexandra says; the words ring between them.

Halina freezes. And then her hand covers Alexandra's, which is still on her hip. "I do."

Alexandra lets out a breath she hadn't consciously held and caresses Halina's leg.

"As I was saying," she says, "I wouldn't go straight for the obvious. First, I would make sure your whole body is aroused."

"Oh, I am."

"More aroused, in that case."

Halina groans, and her head drops against Alexandra's shoulder, but she never lets go of Alexandra's hand.

"So, yes, I would caress your legs," she says, demonstrating with different touches, "and your knees, so…"

Halina holds up one leg, almost straight, and Alexandra giggles. "Sure, and your calf, like this."

Her hand cups the round muscle of Halina's calf. She savors the weight and strength of it in her palm before guiding Halina's leg back down to the bed. Tracing to the crease of Halina's thigh, Alexandra presses another kiss to her neck and arranges a strand of hair behind her ear. Her fingers trail over the shell of Halina's ear, if only to make her shudder delightfully. "And now I would push against your lips," she says, voice barely above a whisper.

Her fingers move around Halina's outer lips, more lightly as she gets closer to her clitoris before circling back. Halina whines every time Alexandra gets closer to where she wants her the most.

"I would turn the vibration higher," Alexandra says, increasing the pressure she applies and the speed of her strokes, "and I would also want to test how wet you're getting."

It's affecting her, too, this whole fantasy she paints for Halina, and she presses her legs together to get a little friction.

She dips her fingers between Halina's folds and she is delighted to feel how slick Halina is.

"Then I would lower the vibration and pay some attention to your clit. You want me to?"

Halina's answer is immediate. "Yes, yes, please, please, you're so good," she babbles, and Alexandra is only too happy to oblige.

Wetting her thumb, she massages the nub of nerves, making sure to go to the sides randomly. Halina's breath is labored now; her hips move in short, aborted thrusts. Her hands, blindly searching for Alexandra, grasp the sheets, and she closes her fingers around Alexandra's knees as she howls.

Alexandra tries to go on with her narration, but she can't deny how much this affects her. She clamps her mouth on Halina's neck in a bruising kiss as she slides her fingers inside Halina's body. Halina cries out and starts fucking Alexandra's fingers in earnest.

"So impatient," Alexandra murmurs, sucking hard on Halina's shoulder, letting her move the way she wants. "Come on, babe," she says, lifting her hand from Halina's hip to cup a breast and massage it, "come on, come, you've been so good, I want to see you come…"

Halina cries out Alexandra's name; her body arches against Alexandra's chest as she comes, and Alexandra's fingers are covered in fluid. Just as suddenly as she tensed, Halina relaxes against her, limp as a rag doll. Alexandra strokes her hair and brushes strands away from her sweaty forehead with her non-sticky hand, and presses a trail of small kisses against her cheeks. She particularly enjoys how hot they are, red as fire trucks against her lips.

Halina sighs and sits up, away from Alexandra, and fear takes hold of Alexandra's heart, its claws sharpened by the idea that Halina will leave as soon as she gets what she wanted, revert to her old self, and shatter everything Alexandra thought they'd achieved.

"Now, what would I do if I had a toy to use on you," Halina purrs, her body turned toward Alexandra.

She sits on her haunches, contemplating her with dark eyes. Alexandra has never been happier to be the object of such scrutiny.

Halina's body glints with sweat in the streetlamp's light. She becomes an incarnation of an ancient divinity of debauchery. "I have the perfect idea of what to use on you," she continues in the same infuriating, sexy tone.

"Oh, really?" Alexandra asks, her hands around Halina's thighs to bring her closer. "Pray tell?"

Halina scoots closer, until Alexandra could just take her nipple between her lips.

"I would love to use a strap-on on you." Halina's voice is dark pink with subtle purple accents as she rolls the R. "I would want to fuck you any way possible, make you come as many times as you have managed to make me come."

Alexandra is captivated by the vision Halina's words are painting. Halina in a strap-on making love to her for hours—that's a plan she would happily follow.

"And how would you want me?" Alexandra says, moving away from Halina. "On my back, legs spread for you to take me?" she asks as innocently as possible as she spreads her legs as wide as she can without hurting herself.

Halina's eyes drop, and she squeezes Alexandra's thighs with her fingers.

"Or on my stomach maybe, so I wouldn't be able to do a goddamn thing; it would be all yours," Alexandra continues while she rolls over and shakes her ass. She peers over her shoulder.

Halina's blush is back in full force, all over her torso, and her fingers slide around Alexandra's waist to pull her closer.

"Or," Alexandra says, delivering the pièce de résistance, "on my hands and knees?"

The moment she raises her ass in the air, Halina's fingers are in her. Her free hand squeezes Alexandra's ass. Alexandra clutches the sheets in one hand; her pillow is clutched between her teeth to smother her shouts of pleasure. Alexandra pushes back against Halina's touch and arches her body to get more friction. Halina slides her free hand higher, up to the small of Alexandra's back. She pushes, gently but firmly, until the angle is more to her satisfaction.

"Fuck," Alexandra groans between gritted teeth. "Oh, yeah, just like that, babe..."

Halina keeps her hand moving, adding a finger as she drapes herself over Alexandra's body. "I love how you call me babe," she whispers, tracing Alexandra's spinal column with her tongue. "It... works for me."

"It does?"

"Mm hmm."

"Oh, baby," Alexandra moans, stretching the word almost comically, and it makes Halina laugh.

Her next reaction couldn't be further from comedy as she pulls her fingers out and moves behind Alexandra to use her lips.

"Oh, wow," Alexandra moans, her whole body tensing as her orgasm builds. "Yeah, fuck me…"

Halina chuckles, the vibration of it seemingly attached to Alexandra's guts and the heat pooling there, before pressing the pad of her tongue against Alexandra's folds. Alexandra didn't notice Halina take the dental dam out of her bag, a proof of Alexandra's excitement or of Halina's discretion. Halina doesn't waste any time. She laps at and pushes her tongue inside of Alexandra with a hunger only matched by Alexandra's need.

When Halina's finger slides back inside of her, Alexandra is gone, shouting into the pillow and holding onto the sheet for dear life. When she starts to comes down, Halina uses both hands to roll her onto her back. Then she traces circles on Alexandra's soft stomach while Alexandra recovers from such an incredible orgasm.

"Okay," she says, respiration heavy, "You have a point."

"And you have one too," Halina replies, pressing a kiss to Alexandra's bicep. "Slow is good."

"Fast is pretty good."

"*We're* pretty good." Halina, with a satisfied smile, moves closer for a proper kiss.

"Indeed, we are," Alexandra confirms, her hand on Halina's cheek.

Just as they're about to settle in for the night with the blankets warm and soft around them, Alexandra can't resist the temptation to tease Halina. She giggles lazily. "It's such a shame, my toys are just right here."

"You bitch," Halina mumbles, scooting back into Alexandra's embrace, in the position of the smaller spoon. "Next…" She is interrupted by a yawn. "Next time."

"Next time," Alexandra repeats, her nose buried in Halina's hair.

*   *   *

A COUPLE OF DAYS LATER, Odile stops Halina after rehearsal. "You have a minute?"

"Sure."

They sit in the front row of the auditorium. Before long, the decorating crew will finish up with the paints, the wallpapers, lamps, and all, and the inaugural concert will be upon them. Before long, it will be showtime.

"How do you feel, Piotrowski?"

"Beg your pardon?"

Odile seems uncomfortable, almost awkward. "Are you happy here? Working with us?"

"I am. The Philharmonie is a good ensemble, very energetic."

"Thank you, I appreciate it." Odile pulls an electronic cigarette from her breast pocket. She twirls it around just long enough to choose her words.

Halina almost gets dizzy with the motion of the little glass and plastic device.

"And your girlfriend, you're happy with her?"

The question takes Halina by surprise, and she can only blink at Odile.

"Sorry if this is not my business," Odile adds, her French accent heavier with her discomfort. "It's just—oh, how can I put it…"

"Come on, Moineau, just spit it out."

"We all appreciate you, Piotrowski, and we want you to feel good here, good enough for you to stay past June."

"Oh."

"Yeah, oh."

"Th-thank you, Odile," Halina babbles, a watermelon-sized lump in her throat. "That means a lot to me, more than I can tell."

Odile pats her shoulder as she stands. Smoke curls around the temples of her glasses. "Trust me, Halina, I never say something I don't mean."

"Even as spokesperson for the orchestra?"

"When am I not speaking for them?"

They both laugh at the truth in her statement.

"Whatever you do," Odile says with a sigh, "keep the long-term in mind, will you?"

"Beyond the season, at least?"

"Precisely."

"I promise. Good evening, Odile."

"Good evening, Halina."

HALINA CAN TASTE THE COLD and the coming snow, and that puts a bounce to her step. In true Polish fashion, the cold doesn't affect her. Warmth runs through her body that has nothing to do with how many layers she has on or the cup of white mocha in her hands.

After spending most of her life on the road, going from country to country without paying attention to where she landed and where she took off, following her Sagittarian wanderlust, Halina's thirtieth birthday had been a wake-up call to her deeply repressed desire for some sense of balance. Halina's life needed stability, hence the decision to find a semipermanent contract, the choice of Paris Philharmonie to be with the orchestra for the season. But she hadn't expected Paris to bring this sense of rightness, the sensation of finally being woven into the fabric of the world.

Tonight, Alexandra is supposed to be in Halina's hotel room when she gets there. Asking for a second keycard to her room for Alexandra was a gigantic step, yet it created more excitement than anxiety. Halina knows she's changed since she landed in Paris, but this is the biggest proof of all.

Opening the door, Halina bites back the clichéd greeting on the tip of her tongue, the old-fashioned "Honey, I'm home" she wants to use when it comes to Alexandra.

"Why are you wrapped in so many layers?" she asks, unable to keep a smile from growing on her lips as she takes off her coat and scarf.

Alexandra is on the plush couch, enveloped in a silvery fleece blanket with the hotel's coat of arms embroidered in the corner. Her chin and mouth are obscured by the blanket, giving her a much younger and more fragile appearance. Her feet rest on the edge of the coffee table, and Halina fakes a cough to cover her laugh: As warm as they may be, her socks are mood-killers for sure; the cutesy faces of pink reindeer are not on Halina's sexy list. The ridiculousness of it all only doubles Halina's affection for Alexandra.

"I'm cold," Alexandra replies. Her voice is muffled by the blanket until she shakes her head so the blanket falls around her shoulders. "I'm from California. I can't help it! Winter doesn't agree with me."

Halina hums in sympathy, then sits with Alexandra and puts her arm on the back of the couch to invite her in. Alexandra scoots closer; the blanket follows her. The image is just too much, and Halina pulls her into a hug with a chuckle. "My poor, sunny girl," she coos, one arm wrapped around Alexandra's back, rubbing her upper arms to warm her.

Alexandra rests her head on Halina's shoulder and buries the bottom half of her face in the blanket again, but not quickly enough to prevent Halina from catching the fondness in her eyes.

She tilts Alexandra's chin up before she can bury herself even deeper in her layers. "Got something to say?"

The fondness grows in Alexandra's eyes, and she wiggles closer, so warm Halina wants her to stay close. Like her very own sun.

"What you just called me," Alexandra replies with a toothy smile.

Halina grins back, her embrace tighter around Alexandra. "My. Poor. Sunny. Girl," she repeats; small kisses on Alexandra's face mark each word.

Alexandra scrunches up her nose and sits back to face Halina. "And what should I call you, huh?" she asks, poking at Halina's chest with her hand still under the blanket. "My Ice Girl?" she continues with a kiss to Halina's left cheek. "My Snow Queen?" She kisses Halina's right cheek.

Halina stiffens and shakes her head. "Anything but that," she says harshly, softening her words and tone with a whispered "please."

Alexandra's face softens. "Fine," she says, not dwelling on Halina's reaction. "I've got it: my eastern babe?"

Halina snorts and bows her head. "God, shut up."

Alexandra somehow manages to cup Halina's cheeks; her hands, wrapped in the blanket, are two big fuzzy paws. "Make. Me."

Halina doesn't need a more official invitation. She pulls Alexandra into a deep kiss; her hand is near Alexandra's waist or hip. Alexandra tilts her head, licking at the seam of Halina's lips, and Halina parts them to let her in. Even though their tongues are now involved, the kiss remains soft and unhurried. Halina loses herself in it, smiling when Alexandra wiggles in her arms.

Alexandra's fingers appear from under the heavy blanket as she caresses Halina's face. The tender gesture creates a path through Alexandra's many layers: under the blanket, she wears a knitted cardigan in addition to a heavy plaid shirt and an undershirt. Halina blindly finds Alexandra's elbow to pull her closer.

Instead of turning their kisses into something more, Alexandra shrieks and shrinks down into her cocoon. "I can't believe you almost made me come out in this cold!" Her pout is visible, though her face is once again half-buried in the blanket. "Keep your icicles to yourself."

Halina chuckles, pulling her into a tight embrace and practically lifting Alexandra until she's in her lap. When she's satisfied with their position, she tucks Alexandra's head under her chin and rubs her back to convey more warmth to her sunny girl.

Alexandra nuzzles her neck, loving and affectionate as a cat, or as a dog, given the furry companion Halina has yet to meet; as a pet, in any case, and her warm breath sends tingles all over Halina's body.

"You're really hot," Alexandra mumbles, eyes closed from what Halina can glimpse of her face.

"Why, thank you."

"You're a big dork," Alexandra says with a kiss to a tendon in Halina's neck. "But I love... it."

Alexandra's pause and change of heart doesn't go unnoticed; Halina knows she stopped herself from saying those three words because of the way she freezes when they might come up.

A part of Halina wants nothing more than to embrace the relationship, to let her heart beat to the rhythm of Alexandra's. It would be easier if she could just, simply, love Alexandra back. But the bigger part of her is scared shitless to lower, even fractionally, the walls she has built around her heart, brick by brick, over the years. For now, she'll cuddle her *słoneczna* girl and share her warmth here in this room and keep the rest of the world at bay.

"Did I mention my sister and my nephew are coming to town next week?" Alexandra whispers, still nuzzling Halina's neck.

So much for keeping the world away.

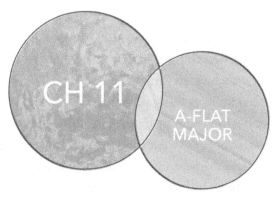

CH 11 — A-FLAT MAJOR

Malachite, Turquoise, and Orange

ALEXANDRA IS JITTERY AS A June bug as she waits for her sister and her nephew to walk through the doors at the airport. They couldn't leave California until her husband finally agreed to the religious divorce. Elisabeth booked her plane tickets, along with Zachary's, before the ink could dry on the official document. Now the plane has landed, and they'll spend Hanukkah and Christmas and New Year's together, the three of them—maybe four if things between Halina and Alexandra continue to progress in the right direction, beyond the tentative balance they've found.

"Sasha!"

Alexandra is pulled out of her Halina-shaped mental space by her sister's voice. She pulls Elisabeth into a tight embrace and buries her nose in her hair. The void left by her sister was even more vast than she'd thought, judging by the relief and warmth that spread through her body as the familiar scents of jasmine and mint fill her nose.

"Where is your luggage?" she asks when they finally dislodge themselves from each other.

Elisabeth smiles and carefully tucks a strand of hair behind her ear. "Zach wanted to handle it." They turn toward the door to search for the fourteen-year old.

In the middle of the crowd, Zachary's slim, teenaged frame is made more noticeable by his mop of auburn hair. He's with a cute blonde girl and nods while he pushes the luggage cart as she chatters.

"Does he have his aids on?" Alexandra asks with a frown.

Elisabeth nods. "Yes, he just turned them all the way down halfway through the flight."

"What the heck is he doing?"

"Trying to flirt with a girl who laughs louder than a pack of hyenas, God help him."

They stay silent, glancing at each other until a perfectly timed giggle cuts them short.

Hey, Lex, Zach says when he finally joins them, crooking his index in a mixture of the signs for "X" and "window," the way he has always signed her name. He pulls her into a hug, and she wraps one arm around his waist.

Hey, yourself, she signs. *God, you're so tall now,* she adds, glad she can make him blush.

"You're just s-small," he says out loud as he shakes his head at her, then steps away to bury his hands in the pockets of his hoodie. He scuffs the tip of his shoe against the floor.

Alexandra points at her own chin to make sure he faces her. *You sound very good,* she tells him. *I'm so proud of you.*

Zach shrugs through his blush, but his pleased expression is reminiscent of Alexandra and Elisabeth's father, his face as she remembers it from childhood. She exchanges a glance with Elisabeth, and the pride on her face reflects that in Alexandra's heart. Elisabeth yawns loudly in a very un-Elisabeth-like manner.

"Let's drive you home," Alexandra says, signing as she talks to make sure her nephew gets all of it.

Zach turns to her as he pushes the cart toward the elevator. "Is Punshki home?" he asks, and Alexandra smiles at him, enjoying his lively herb-green.

"Of course," she says, signing along. "Still asleep, the little bastard."

Once in the elevator, Zach reaches for his aids, pushes his hair out of the way, and turns them back on.

"Didn't take you for a Sharks fan," Alexandra signs as she speaks at the sight of the bright turquoise shining in his midst of red curls.

It's awesome, right, he replies with a wink. *I knew* you'd *appreciate it.*

"Don't encourage him," Elisabeth says with an eye-roll, her hands signing more harshly. "We told him to pick something a little more…"

"Dull?"

"Sensible. But he had to go and pick this blue one."

"Blue is pretty," Alexandra replies just as Zachary signs it, smugness written all over his face.

"Blue is pretty," Elisabeth mockingly repeats as the pair high-fives. Her voice is clipped, less purple and more blue. "I should have guessed you two would gang up on me."

"We're awesome; accept it. And you need to relax, Liz."

Under her hand, Elisabeth's shoulders sag. "You're right, of course; you're right."

"That's often the case."

"Should have remembered."

* * *

WHILE ZACH LIES ON THE floor and lets Punshki bury him in kisses and tail-wags and lick the crumbs of his brioche, Alexandra and Elisabeth sit on the couch and split an entire buttered baguette.

"So, you're back to being single?" Alexandra asks.

"Thirty-five, with a fourteen-year-old boy, and single, yeah," Elisabeth whispers, munching on her piece of bread. "And *'hag samea'h* to me."

"Honestly, granting you your divorce is the best present Matthew ever gave you," Alexandra says, putting her hand on Elisabeth's shoulder. "One that beats the miracle we're going to celebrate for eight nights."

Elisabeth glances at her son, who seems completely uninterested in their conversation. "At least Zach didn't take his side," she says softly. "I would have gone meshuga if I had lost him too."

"Zach is a smart boy." Alexandra comforts her. "And you didn't raise him to accept any kind of bullshit, even from his father or from you."

"True."

"Now," Alexandra says, tapping the floor to get Zach's attention, "you two need to stay awake at least for the next,"—she checks her watch—"ten hours to fight the jetlag. What do you wanna do today?"

Elisabeth and Zach make the same thoughtful face. The only sounds in the room are Punshki's panting and the ticking of the clock above the door.

"I want to shower, first," Elisabeth finally says, untying her hair from its tight bun. The curls, so like Alexandra's, if longer, show more white hair than Alexandra remembered. "We can walk to the Christmas market afterward?"

Both Zachary and Alexandra stare at her as if she has lost her mind. "What?"

"Christmas?" Alexandra asks, raising her eyebrows.

You want to go to a Christmas market? Zachary asks, his signs insistent in his disbelief.

"They talked about it in the in-flight magazine," Elisabeth replies, signing along, "I figured it could be fun to give it a chance. Besides, it's right on the Champs Elysées, isn't it?" Alexandra nods in response. "Well, it sounds perfect; something to keep us awake!"

Alexandra is glad to see her sister's enthusiasm, a sign she's already picking herself up. "Sure," she says, "let's get you two to your hotel."

"Do we need to take a car?"

"Nah, it's a ten-minute walk." Alexandra shrugs. "A proper introduction to my neighborhood."

"Awe-some," Elisabeth deadpans with a twist of her mouth.

Snob, Zachary comments. His chuckles turn into a full-on belly laugh when his mother reaches to cuff the back of his head and fails to make contact.

"I'm glad you two are here for the holidays," Alexandra says when they step out of her building. Punshki is on his leash and in his little bright pink coat, the pompoms bouncing with each step, in time with the wagging of his tail.

"Not as much as we are," Elisabeth replies with a light peck before walking ahead. "Um, where to?"

Alexandra laughs loudly as she takes the lead. "That's so you," she says, clipping Punshki's leash to her coat to free her hands so she can sign while she speaks. "You always act as if you're running this show when you don't have a clue."

Zachary laughs, but he doesn't comment. He's too busy taking pictures of the buildings and restaurants on their way.

* * *

THE NEXT EVENING, WHEN ALEXANDRA and Elisabeth are alone and Zachary takes Punshki out for a walk, Elisabeth suggests they cook together.

"Let's make a *krupnik.*" It seems so innocent, the proposition to prepare a soup they ate through their childhood, whenever their father got nostalgic for his own youth. Kitchens and recipes have a magic of their own to create a bubble of comfort so words can be freed, at least in their family's tradition. Cooking is a prelude to a discussion. Elisabeth waits until the meat is seared and the vegetables and barley are in the pot. The aroma of it all, and the memories attached to it, fills the apartment when Elisabeth says softly, "We need to talk about Mom."

Alexandra sighs. She sits on the bench by the window and pulls her knees up to her chest. "We do," she says, her voice smothered by her cardigan. "How is she?"

Elisabeth sighs even more deeply. Her whole body moves with it, and she sits next to her sister, crosses one leg over the other, and brushes Alexandra's ankle with her toe. Her hands twist a towel. "Not good."

"Last time we talked, she didn't want to go to the doctor." Alexandra's voice lilts into a question.

"No, she doesn't," Elisabeth says tiredly. "And Dad keeps saying she is the best placed to decide what is good for her, so he just lets her—"

"—do whatever she wants, as in exactly the opposite of what she needs," Alexandra finishes for her. Irritation rises at the mention of her father. Her anger turns inward seamlessly, for letting Henry Graff affect her so deeply still.

"Is there anything we can do?" she asks, though the answer is obvious.

"I could take her to the doctor myself," Elisabeth replies with a shrug and a sad smile. "Use the pretext of a shopping trip or a girls' lunch. Though I'm not sure Dad will be very happy to have me around."

"What turned you into a pariah?" Alexandra asks with a frown.

Elisabeth's mouth tightens, and she wiggles her ring-free hand. Her gesture includes Alexandra and the city outside the window. "This."

Alexandra's shoulders tense, and she has to tear her eyes away as a familiar coldness trickles down her back. "He still regards me as contagious?"

"Sasha, it's not—"

"It is, Liz. How can someone so smart be so stupid?" The question is rhetorical, and Elisabeth lets the distant, soft lavender of the bubbling pot answer it. "I'm his daughter, and, since I'm not what he planned me to be, Mister Henry Graff gets to keep me away from my family, to treat me like my private life tarnishes his reputation?"

Elisabeth's jaw clenches. "His pride has always been his downfall. Don't let it be yours too. Take the higher road, Sash."

"I'm the one who has to forgive everything?" Alexandra tightens her fist in her cardigan. "That's not fair, Liz."

"I didn't—" Elisabeth sighs. "He will never give you an apology, Sasha, and if you want to see Mamuschka again…"

"Forget about him." Alexandra shakes her head, unwilling to waste any more time, energy, or heartache on their father and his small-mindedness. "What do you say about visiting my latest creation at the Philharmonie?"

Elisabeth squints knowingly, a gaze Alexandra carefully avoids. Her sister may let the subject drop to save Alexandra more pain. She clicks her tongue before smiling at her. "Sure, I'd love to."

*　*　*

THREE DAYS INTO THEIR STAY, Alexandra decides it's time to make good on her suggestion, and, if they cross paths with Halina, well, it will only be a pleasant bonus. She invites Elisabeth and Zach to come at the end of the day, once the orchestra has rehearsed.

When they arrive, Alexandra notices Zachary's frown.

What's going on in that brain of yours? she asks as they walk around the corridors.

I'm curious about the music. Don't mind me.

How curious? Elisabeth asks.

I want to find out what I can hear of the music with aids, Zachary replies slowly. *Whether the vibration is enough to make me feel something, something as vibrant as what you hear,* he adds, his head tilted toward Alexandra.

Oh, munchkin, Alexandra replies. *I'm just weird that way. And don't forget. In this family, we all see sounds.*

Still, he insists, "I want to hear it for myself."

More than anything, his vocalization of his wish instead of signing inspires Alexandra to let him try his experiment. She even has an idea to make it happen. All she needs is for Halina to still be in the concert hall.

The months spent with Halina have taught Alexandra that she must be reminded to leave her piano. Sure enough, when they step into the massive room, Halina is bending over the piano with the tuner-in-residence. The two of them are immersed in an animated discussion; it's unclear if they are agreeing or not, and since they don't seem to be speaking either English or French, Alexandra can't be sure.

"Lina?" she calls, stepping away from her guests and walking toward the stage.

Elisabeth and Zachary are frozen, staring at the ceiling and the many "bubbles" of seats for the future guests floating up there.

"Alexandra!" Halina calls enthusiastically. "Who is with you?"

Alexandra accepts a small kiss before answering; she's missed her far too much, though she's appreciated the last two evenings spent with her sister and Zachary. "Halina, this is my sister, Elisabeth, and her son, Zachary. Liz, Zach, this is Halina, the Philharmonie's pianist and my... girlfriend."

She signs it all while Elisabeth and Zach walk up to them, and Halina observes their hands curiously.

"Why are you signing?"

"Zach has a hearing loss because he was born prematurely," Alexandra explains, still signing.

"I won't mind if you say I'm Deaf, Lex," Zachary says, and Halina's eyes widen.

"You talk!"

"I do."

"Like normal people!"

Elisabeth and Alexandra wince together. Zachary straightens and graces Halina with a look of ironic amusement only teenagers seem to be able to pull off. "I can vocalize instead of signing," he replies, "because my mother didn't raise me to be rude with people I just met and who mean something to someone I love."

The judgment is clearly stated, and Halina has the decency to blush. "I'm sorry," she says, her hands in front of her chest. "I didn't mean to be rude, it's just—" she hesitates before straightening and facing Zachary.

"I've never met a Deaf person before, but it's not an excuse. It won't happen again, I promise."

Whatever, Zachary replies. He moves to the piano and holds his hands above it but doesn't actually touch it.

"What did he say?" Halina asks, and Alexandra puts a hand on the small of Halina's back.

"It's fine," she replies. "Zach is not one to hold a grudge, but please, don't say he's not normal because he's Deaf ever again."

"I won't."

"Now," Alexandra says loudly while clapping her hands to get everybody's attention. "I have an idea, if you don't mind playing some more." She looks at Halina.

Halina sits at the keys immediately. "As if you ever have to ask."

Zach, she tells her nephew, *go to the back of the piano and put your hands and ear to it, please.*

Zachary raises one eyebrow at her in a perfect imitation of his mother's doubtful face, but follows her instructions.

Elisabeth takes a seat in the now-empty orchestra, behind Halina. "He used to love Liszt's nocturnes when he was younger," she says, her eyes on Halina as if gauging her. "I'd put the speaker against the crib, and the vibrations would soothe him to sleep."

Halina cracks her neck and rolls her shoulder. "I love Liszt. What about 'Dream of Love No.3'?" she asks, and Elisabeth nods, reclining in the chair with her arms over her chest.

Sitting next to her sister, Alexandra sees the tension in Halina's shoulders, her posture more controlled. She lifts her hands above the keys as if gathering energy, building momentum.

Alexandra can't decide what to focus on: the subdued energy of the music and the colors it creates in her mind; Halina playing; Zachary's amazed face as the music travels through his skin; Elisabeth's face, a mask of relief and grief.

She lets her synesthesia take over and closes her eyes to appreciate the photism to the fullest. The main melody is deep, chartreuse green.

Little explosions of orange and yellow cross the background; the melody dictates their appearance. As the music takes a darker turn, the chartreuse slowly morphs into a greenish gray, reminiscent of some types of marble or of the stones their father brought them from Eilat every time he went to Israel when they were kids.

Following a pattern of dark greens and grays, rivers or lightning bolts of light turquoise contrast with the darker parts. Some of the melody from the beginning returns, and with it the sparkles of orange and yellow. It expresses itself in a lovely and delicate manner, as fleeting as ephemeral rays of sunlight through foliage during a walk in the woods. It doesn't speak to Alexandra of dreams or of love at all. She can understand why Zachary used to love this piece: It's very peaceful and soothing.

Alexandra cocks her head to get a proper look at him. His face is somewhat obscured in shadow, but she can see that his eyes are wide open and tears gather at their corners. His hands—and against the dark wood, they seem so big, she can't believe her nephew's hands are so big—are flat against the body of the piano, with his fingers spread wide as if to absorb as much of the vibration as possible.

She turns to watch her sister, and Elisabeth's eyes are closed. She takes deep breaths, arms crossed, with one hand covering her heart while the other clutches her side. Tears roll down her cheeks, but there is a tentative smile on her lips.

The catharsis the experiment must provide for Elisabeth suddenly comes to light in Alexandra's mind. If the piece was one of Zachary's favorites in childhood, she must remember listening to it with Matthew in the periphery, if not directly involved.

Alexandra never particularly liked her ex-brother-in-law, but he did make Elisabeth happy for a while. Alexandra cannot deny his contribution to Zachary either, and that counts for something. As bitter as the memories may be now, Alexandra doesn't believe Elisabeth will ever regret having them.

When Halina stops playing, Zachary stands up. Alexandra would laugh at the way both Abernathys wipe their tears away in exactly the same way, if her instincts didn't scream at her to pull them into a hug and never let go.

Halina seeks Alexandra's eyes and raises inquisitive eyebrows. Alexandra replies with a soft smile before standing and walking to Zachary.

Your conclusion? she asks, and Zachary's eyes sparkle with unshed tears she won't mention.

It's very different listening to music with my aids, he replies, *But it's just as interesting. It may be worth studying back home.*

"Awesome," Alexandra says, clapping his back. *Didn't you forget something?* she adds, discreetly nodding toward Halina, who still seems uncomfortable.

"Thank you," Zachary tells her while simultaneously signing it, "it was very pretty."

"You're welcome," Halina says with a bow of her head. "Thank you for letting me be a part of it."

They look at each other awkwardly until Halina's stomach grumbles.

"What about we continue this conversation over dinner?" Alexandra offers, her arm linked with Zachary's.

"In or out?" he asks her, and they turn to Elisabeth and Halina, who exchange a silent question.

"Out," Elisabeth finally decides.

"Out it is."

IN THE EVENING, BACK AT the hotel, Alexandra snuggles with Halina, whose head is pillowed on Alexandra's chest.

"Sooo," Halina starts, her fingers drawing random patterns on Alexandra's skin.

"Hmm?"

"Twins, huh?"

Alexandra laughs. Her fingers are buried in Halina's hair. "Please tell me you don't have some kind of fantasy about getting twins into your bed."

"I don't," Halina says, too quickly, and Alexandra chuckles silently until Halina looks away. "Okay, so maybe I thought about it when you both came back from the restrooms tonight."

"Oh my God."

"Can you blame me, though? You two *are* twins." She presses a kiss to the side of Alexandra's right breast, the number one spot in Halina's list of places to rest her head. "And yet so different. It's... intriguing." She punctuates the end of her sentence with a light suck on Alexandra's nipple, making her groan and arch her body toward Halina's mouth, just as intended.

The little devil.

"Good—*oh, dear God, your mouth is made of sin*—good luck with making such a vision come to life," Alexandra replies. "My sister is straighter than a dance pole."

"Nice comparison."

"The straightness of arrows seems a bit exaggerated."

Halina scoots up in the bed to face Alexandra and rolls her eyes in the semidarkness before she bends for a kiss. "You're such a dork."

"Yep."

"You're lucky it's cute."

"I'm lucky *I'm* cute," Alexandra echoes before pulling Halina to her. "Now come back here, and let's get some sleep."

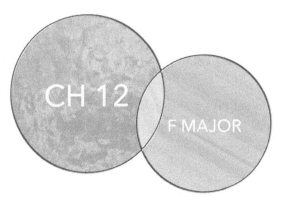

CH 12
F MAJOR

Gold, Imperial Purple, and Celeste Blue

WHEN ALEXANDRA TOLD HER TO come to her apartment for a "celebration," Halina anticipated various outcomes. It could be a night spent in bed with Alexandra's curves and her soft skin. It could be her chance to visit the apartment in detail, to snoop around and learn more than what her night there taught her. It could be another dinner, a pre-Christmas thing. It could even be a celebration for her thirty-first birthday; even if that subject has never come up, Halina wouldn't be surprised if Alexandra knows the date. In all those scenarios, the one constant was that it would be one evening shared between the two of them. Maybe it would be a chance to finally meet Alexandra's mystery pet. No matter how much Halina asked, Alexandra insisted that her dog, from breed to name, had to be introduced in the flesh.

"Punshki, sit."

Alexandra's voice is soft yet firm, and the dog slouches on its haunches at the command.

Halina is suddenly interested in a scenario in which Alexandra uses this tone on her, full of authority and care, oozing confidence.

"Punshki?" she repeats. She frowns at the dog, who seems solemn and serious in his evaluation of her. "As in...?"

Alexandra picks him up, all fluff and fur and short limbs flailing in the air. "As in my big, fat doughnut," she coos while she kisses the top of the dog's head.

Halina revels in the picture of companionship the pair makes and tentatively holds her hand out toward the dog. Punshki observes her progress with the utmost dignity in spite of his posture. When her fingers are within reach, Punshki bends over Alexandra's arms to sniff, pausing at her rings before he moves to the rest of her hand.

Taking her eyes away from him, Halina finds a secret, private expression on Alexandra's face, one directly connected to Halina's heartstrings.

Captivated by a gaze so full of fondness, Halina squeaks in surprise when Punshki gives her fingers a tentative lick. She giggles, delighted by the rasping, warm doggy kiss bestowed upon her, and scratches the fluff under his jaw.

In a perfect imitation of his owner, Punshki half-closes his eyes and tilts his big head to give her more access. His fluffy tail bats Alexandra's arms with even more vigor.

"Okay, mister, off you go," Alexandra groans, practically dropping her dog to the floor. Punshki makes a steady landing and walks a couple of circles around his owner's feet before he gives the same treatment to Halina's. Seemingly satisfied, the dog sniffs and struts back to the living room.

"Say," Halina says thoughtfully as she takes off her coat, "why didn't you tell me you can speak Polish?"

Alexandra pecks Halina's lips before taking her coat from her hands without replying. Halina follows her to the living room, where Elisabeth and her son shower the dog with caresses and praises.

In the daylight, Halina notices more details of Alexandra's apartment. The whole place gives off a very peculiar vibe, an "Alexandra" vibe, to be precise: small and compact and so warm, Halina is at home even though it's only her second time in the place. Her eyes linger on the high-paneled bow window. It's not much of a stretch to picture Alexandra here, in the morning light, all sleepy-eyed and disheveled.

Halina moves on to the comfortable sofa and armchairs, her eyes following Alexandra as she pushes away the curtain creating a boundary between her living room and her bedroom. The bed, with its dark wood and plush, burgundy quilt, looks just as comfortable as she remembers it being from their night spent in its cradle. Halina would love to get reacquainted with it.

She almost regrets not paying attention when she was here the first time. From the comfortable materials, reminiscent of her demeanor, to the artworks, posters, and decorations, Alexandra's apartment is an interior-designed self-portrait.

Alexandra lays Halina's coat on the quilt and brushes invisible lint from the lapel. "What do you mean? I don't speak Polish."

"*Pączki*," Halina says. "It means 'doughnut' in Polish."

Alexandra's expression turns to one of amusement. "Really? 'Cause it's *ponshkes* in Yiddish, and it became ponshki when I was a kid, and then... well, it made sense for him when we met."

"We have more in common than we thought," Halina says, her voice suddenly husky.

"So it seems."

Halina lets the words hang, heavy with meaning and decisions yet to be made.

"Come on, we have candles to light!" Elisabeth's voice is teasing. It's so like Alexandra's, and yet Halina has never heard her companion speak in such a breathy tone.

They both startle from whatever trance they were in at this reminder of reality.

"Coming," Alexandra replies, her eyes still on Halina's face.

"Candles?" Halina asks, gathering her thoughts and herself by smoothing over the pleats in her dress. Did she mention her birthday and forget she had?

"First night of Hanukkah," Alexandra tells her, as if her words are a sufficient explanation.

Halina knows Hanukkah is a Jewish holiday with candles and doughnuts and spinning tops—the combo never made much sense to her—but what she doesn't understand is what she is doing here. She is not Jewish, she is not a part of the family, she…

You don't belong here.

Halina shakes her head to silence her mother's voice. "You do know I'm not Jewish, though, right?"

"I invited you to celebrate it with us because it's the only Jewish holiday worth celebrating, in my opinion," Alexandra replies. The amusement on her face goes up a notch when Elisabeth protests behind them. "And since I wasn't sure where you stand on the whole concept of Christmas, and I wanted to give you a present no matter what…"

Halina's heart does a flip at the prospect of getting a present. She can count the number of Christmas presents she's gotten over the years on one hand. Halina wraps her fingers around the curve of Alexandra's hip and leans closer to whisper in her ear, "I have some ideas about what I want for Christmas, Santa."

Alexandra turns her head to peek at her over her shoulder. "Good thing Hanukkah is bountiful in presents, babe," she whispers, a kiss to Halina's cheek. "But first, candles and food."

On the coffee table in the living room, two candles are set in a beautiful wood and silver candelabra. A little silver top sits next to it. Only one candle is lit.

"I thought you said this was the first night," Halina points out.

"It is," she replies, signing along, "but we use this one," pointing at the lit candle, "to light the others. And every night, we add more candles until all nine are lit."

Next to his mother, Zachary snorts, but he looks away, fiddling with a lighter, when he sees Halina looking at him.

"Liz, go ahead," Alexandra says next to Halina.

"You sure?"

Alexandra and her sister exchange a look loaded with history. "I figure the prayers should come from someone closer to the Big Guy," Alexandra replies, and Elisabeth gapes.

"All right." She elbows her son's arm to move him forward. He lights one candle that he hands to her. Raising it in the air, she recites a prayer while Alexandra signs it.

The foreignness of the Hebrew reminds Halina of John Cage's work. It sounds experimental, yet melodious.

"Amen," Alexandra says while Zachary holds one hand up, palm up, with his other hand held in a thumbs-up gesture. He draws a small circle in the air with his thumbs-up before hitting his palm.

Halina catches his eyes, replicates the sign, and is rewarded with the hint of a smile.

Elisabeth continues the prayer, and Halina loses herself in the flicker of the flames.

"Amen," Alexandra repeats, and Halina signs along with Zachary.

Elisabeth puts the candle back in its higher spot and reaches for Alexandra's and Zachary's hands. She says one more prayer before the sisters say "amen" in unison.

Halina assumes this is it, but Elisabeth tightens her hold on Alexandra's hand. "Can I do just one verse of 'Ma'oz T'zur'?"

"Knock yourself out," Alexandra replies.

"Come on, Sasha, sing with me," Elisabeth insists, and Alexandra rolls her eyes playfully and nods in agreement. Halina is familiar with this tone, pleading and playful, almost whiny, and she smiles to herself when Alexandra herself can't resist it. Alexandra pulls Elisabeth into a one-armed hug. As they start singing, Halina's eyes widen.

Ma-oz Tzur Y'shu-a-ti
Le-cha Na-eh L'sha-bei-ach
Ti-kon Beit T'fi-la-ti
V'sham To-da le—

There's no denying Halina has quite a lot of layers to unwrap to get to the mystery named Alexandra Graff. Alexandra's musical ear is an established fact, and so is her unique connection with music, but Halina didn't expect her to chant so beautifully. *We make quite the pair,* Halina muses in amusement and delight, *the musician who can't sing to save her life, and the synesthete who sings perfectly, an* aniół *in the flesh.*

Their voices rise into a bridge until Alexandra squints at Elisabeth. Her sister snaps her mouth shut and holds up her hands in surrender.

"And now," Alexandra says, tapping her foot nearer where Zachary stands to get his attention and signing, "presents!"

"And latkes; I'm starving," Elisabeth groans on her way to the kitchen.

"What are latkes?" Halina asks.

"Potato pancakes served as a dessert."

"Pot—what holiday is it exactly?"

"Told you, the only kind worth celebrating," Alexandra says while she pulls presents from the bow-window seat.

Zachary goes into Alexandra's room and returns with four wrapped presents, one considerably smaller than the others, and winces toward Halina. "Sorry," he says, hesitantly. "We didn't know what to get you."

The fact that a member of Alexandra's family thinks he has to apologize for not bringing her a gift warms Halina as surely as a bowl of *rosół.*

"It's okay," she replies. "I didn't get the memo about presents to begin with."

Elisabeth returns with a plate laden with golden, crunchy-looking potato pancakes, very similar to *placki.* She also holds, expertly, a jar of cream and a sugar bowl.

"You deal with the presents," she says and signs to her son. "I'll deal with the food."

Zachary grins at her and hands Alexandra a large box. He gives a smaller package to Punshki.

The dog jumps at it, vicious against his mortal enemy, and tears the paper to shreds, revealing a squeaky toy in the shape of a bottle of wine, complete with a label and a cork made of felt. Halina hides her laugh behind her hand.

"Oh, you guys," Alexandra says softly. Her unwrapping is much more delicate than her pet's and reveals a set of old books, bound in leather, with golden lettering on their spines. "They're beautiful."

Halina scoots closer, reading the titles. "They are beautiful books," she comments, slowly moving her hand to brush her fingers along a spine. "Fairy tales?"

"Yeah," Alexandra replies, eyes soft, as she scans the pages of a book. "Liz and I used to read them together and turn them into plays."

"Oh, so these are your childhood books?"

"In a way," Alexandra says, her eyes on Halina as she keeps on caressing the spines. "Ours were never as richly bound. I suppose Liz smuggled them out of the house for rebinding."

"Exactly," Elisabeth says. Or Halina assumes that is what she said, since she talked with her mouth full.

Halina takes a plate too, and spoons some of the cream and sprinkles a little sugar on top of the latke. The potato pancake is crunchy on the outside and yet meltingly soft on the inside. If this is a Jewish tradition, Halina will gladly add Hanukkah to her own assortment of celebrations.

Alexandra sets the books aside, away from the food and out of Punshki's reach. She waits for Zachary to distribute the two other gifts before wiggling in her seat. "My turn!"

Pulling her pile of presents toward her, Alexandra practically vibrates.

"Youngest first," Alexandra says while signing and passes an envelope to her nephew. "Some Hanukkah *gelt* for you, but in a way you should appreciate," she explains.

Halina's confusion must show on her face, for Elisabeth shuffles to get closer to her. "It's tradition to give money, or gelt, to kids for Hanukkah," she explains softly.

"Thanks," Halina says.

Zachary has opened the envelope and pulls out a plastic card. His eyes go wide immediately, along with his smile.

He makes a universally recognizable gesture to signify just how crazy his aunt is and almost leaps over the table to pull her into a brief hug.

"What did you get him?" Elisabeth asks, elegantly dabbing her lips with a napkin, in perfect contrast to the way she ate.

"An Amazon card for bonuses on his role-playing video games," Alexandra replies, patting Zachary on the back. "Here you go, Liz." She passes a gift to her sister. "Though I wouldn't necessarily open it in front of the kiddo."

Elisabeth's eyes widen. "You didn't get me a… a *toy*, did you?"

"I didn't," Alexandra says, pausing with a short chuckle, "but now that you gave me the idea…"

"Alexandra. Drorit. Graff."

"Kidding, kidding!"

Halina observes the whole exchange; a bitter thought unfurls. It would have been better, easier perhaps, if she'd had someone by her side when she was younger, someone who knew her better than anybody else, someone irrevocably in her corner against the rest of the world.

Instead of letting the gloom take over, Halina chooses to focus on the tidbit of information she just received on a silver platter. "Drorit?" she repeats, her head tilted to grin at Alexandra.

Alexandra winces and rolls her eyes. "Our parents wanted us to have Hebrew middle names. It means 'sparrow,' or 'freedom.'"

"Suits you."

Alexandra's cheeks turn a pinkish hue, and her expression turns more playful when she points her thumb at her sister. "Want to hear hers?"

"What about I just open my gift, and you just shut your mouth?" Elisabeth cuts her off with a glare, before returning her attention to the package, which she opens gingerly. A blush spreads on her cheeks and neck. "Lingerie," she whispers. The contents of the package are shielded from Zachary's gaze by the wrapping paper. "Lexie…"

"Don't mention it," Alexandra says, waving her hand. "You deserve pretty things."

"Who will I wear it for?" Elisabeth says softly, more than a little sad.

"Yourself, for starters," Alexandra tells her, squeezing her hand.

"Right."

"Of course. Give yourself some credit, you deserve it!"

"Right!"

"Better," Alexandra comments, and Elisabeth quickly folds the paper back around the gift. "Your turn," Alexandra continues, pushing a medium-sized box toward Halina.

Halina blinks a couple of times, tentatively putting her hands on the present. "You were serious about getting me a present," she says, her eyes trained on the shiny bow.

"Of course I was," Alexandra says. "Go on, open it, I want to see your face."

Halina smiles, delicately opens the present, and sets the bow aside. The box revealed is mysterious, shiny black with no indication of its contents, and Halina's curiosity only increases when Alexandra leans closer to watch her open it.

Halina flicks her fingers on the latch of the box and opens it and her breath catches in her throat.

"A baby grand," she whispers, her mouth covered with one hand.

"A toy piano," Alexandra points out, shuffling forward on her knees. "I thought you'd like to have an instrument in your hotel room and—hmph!"

The rest of Alexandra's sentence is lost, as Halina thanks Alexandra with kiss after kiss.

She has no idea what she did, in this life or the previous ones, to deserve to have Alexandra in her life, but she will find a way to repay her kindness.

ALEXANDRA LEAVES HALINA WITH ELISABETH to fix tea and coffee in the kitchen, and Zachary follows her with a purely adolescent smirk on his face. She puts the water on to boil and gets to work with the mugs to make sure everybody gets the drink they want: a pinch of white tea leaves with dried cranberries in a tea ball for Elisabeth; two spoonfuls of coffee with a teaspoon of cocoa and two cubes of sugar for Halina's closet sweet-tooth; green tea with as many mint leaves as humanly possible and three cubes of sugar for Zach; and, finally, a couple of honeyed slices of ginger in her cup of Saenggang cha, a flavor she became addicted to while working with Sue Ji.

While she waits for the water to heat, Alexandra props an elbow on the counter and observes him.

What's on your mind? she asks Zachary. There is no way he followed her into the kitchen out of the goodness of his heart, just to help her with the drinks.

He smirks at her and fidgets with one of the magnets on her fridge. *So, you and her…* he starts, and Alexandra raises one eyebrow.

You can say it, she replies, and Zachary barks out a short laugh. The conversation in the living room halts before picking up again.

She is your— Zach says, but Alexandra has never seen the last sign he uses, a scratch on his chin.

Again? she asks, and Zach rolls his eyes in true adolescent fashion, with a sense of superiority Alexandra didn't look for in her teenage nephew.

B-A-E, he says, spelling the word for her, and Alexandra opens her mouth in an "Oh" before she replicates the "scratching" sign.

Bae? Is that a pet name or something?

Zach nods; his smirk turns into a softer grin. *You two are cute,* he says; a hint of pink tips his ears. Alexandra would bet good money on her face reflecting that awkwardness.

She focuses on taking care of the water; at least she'll have the steam to blame for her flushed appearance. *Thanks,* she replies quickly. *Not sure how long it will last, though.*

Why?

Alexandra opens a cupboard to take a tray and sighs. *Oh, come on,* she starts, and Zach lifts one eyebrow. *She is so pretty and delicate, and I'm…*

Zach puts one hand on her shoulder and then keeps signing. *You're pretty, too, Aunt Lex,* he says, as serious as he's ever been. *You two are different kinds of pretty. Don't be hard on yourself.*

Alexandra pats Zach's hand and beams up at him. *When did you get so wise?*

I've always been wise, he replies with a wink before gently pushing her aside.

Wanna talk about your love life? She teases, satisfied with the blotchy spots of pink and red all over her nephew's face.

Um, no thank you, he signs emphatically. He grabs the tray and, as dignified as possible with bright red cheeks, he goes back to the living room.

Alexandra gives herself an extra minute of quiet before following him. She tries not to read too much meaning into the smile Halina gives her when she sits down next to her—baby steps.

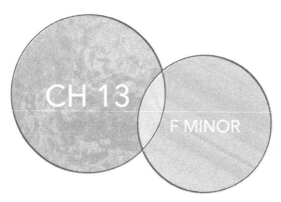

CH 13

F MINOR

Gold, Burnt Sienna, and Alizarin Crimson

THE MORE TIME SHE SPENDS making small talk with Ari while she waits for Halina to be through with rehearsals, the more Alexandra understands, piece by piece, why they are so important for Halina, professionally and personally. Alexandra and Ari are not the best friends in the world now, not by any stretch of the imagination, but they manage to be at least amicable.

Many conversations are focused on Halina's plans for Christmas Eve, on her desire to entertain the Graff family with the best Paris has to offer, or so Ari says.

"Where does she expect me to find a Polish restaurant open on Christmas?" Ari laments, their eyes glued to their phone as their voice grows progressively greener and greener. "And on top of all the craziness around the inaugural concert, too." They sigh. "I'm too young for this shit." Ari pauses before they cock their head at Alexandra, properly acknowledging her for the first time since their conversation started. "What about you? How is your installation going?"

Alexandra looks up at them. "We'll install the last panel right before the holidays," she replies. "We'll just need to come back the first week of January to check on the lighting system, make sure it's crowd-ready, so to speak."

"Awesome," Ari says, their phone once again the center of their attention. "Which means you can help me with Halina's weird idea!"

"Huh?"

"A Polish Christmas, seriously…" Ari mutters, the phone exiled to their pocket as they bite their pinkie fingernail and tap a foot in a rare show of exasperation.

"What about a regular Christmas dinner, somewhere nice," Alexandra muses as she leans against the wall next to them, "followed by midnight Mass at the Polish church?"

"Are you sure Paris has a Polish church?" Ari asks, one eyebrow cocked.

Alexandra shrugs. "I never searched for it, but I'm pretty sure there are all kinds of churches in Paris; why not a Polish one?"

"Makes sense."

"We should make sure it exists, but it could be a good compromise," Alexandra says. "Not a lot of Polish restaurants in Paris, if any, and I'm pretty sure they wouldn't open for Christmas."

"While plenty of regular restaurants do open on Christmas Eve," Ari muses, pulling back their phone and frenetically typing away. "*Yesss*, Polish church. Ooh, rue Saint Honoré, *fan-say*…"

Alexandra covers her mouth to smother her giggle at the sudden playful accent and is rewarded by a smile, one actually reaching their eyes, gracing Ari's face.

"Doesn't answer the restaurant part of the evening, though."

"I'm sure we'll figure something out," Alexandra replies, her hand already raised to pat their arm before she reminds herself that their relationship is not quite there yet.

"We?"

"Oui."

This time around, Ari does laugh. They snicker into the crook of their elbow to conceal it. "God, I understand now."

"What?"

"What Halina sees in you."

"Thanks, I guess?"

Ari examines her silently, their eyes reminiscent of Halina's searching gaze. "Yeah, you'll probably be good for her in the long run."

Alexandra wasn't aware her merit was questioned, but she'll take whatever compliment Halina's assistant sends her way. She has a sneaking suspicion she cannot bypass befriending Ari, as opposed as they may be, if she wants her relationship with Halina to survive.

*   *   *

HALINA PRACTICALLY VIBRATES WITH EXCITEMENT as they all wait for the elevator to take them to the restaurant on the rooftop.

"It's supposed to be the best view over Paris," she tells Alexandra, who fondly pecks her cheek.

"So you said."

"And their chef is amongst the culinary stars right now."

"You already told me, babe."

"And I made sure we could walk through the Duchamp exhibition after dinner."

"I—you didn't?!"

Ha, I finally managed to surprise you. "I did," she replies, hooking her arm with Alexandra's. "The curator is a big fan of my work, so I called in a little favor in exchange for a signed picture."

Alexandra looks down, and Halina is surprised and secretly delighted to catch her blushing. "I do love Marcel's work. Thank you for pulling strings to get us in."

"Oh, it's Marcel now."

"Yeah, he's my homeboy."

It's Halina's turn to laugh, but Ari clears their throat, pointedly nodding toward their two other guests. *Right, I should be a better hostess to the rest of the party.*

"I made sure to tell them we needed kosher options," she says, facing Elisabeth and Zachary and enunciating clearly without exaggerating.

"It's very kind of you," Zachary replies with a little bow of his head. Elisabeth brushes her fingers on the back of his neck and tweaks his bowtie just so, with such pride on her face Halina has to hide a wince at the pinch of her heart.

The little voice in the back of her head, her mother's irritating presence, makes a sudden appearance.

You never made me *so proud.*

You never deserved my love; what makes you expect you deserve hers?

What is love to you *anyway?*

Halina tries to shrug it off, as though her shoulders could be a shield, and Alexandra peers at her with a question in her gray eyes.

"Got a chill," she says softly, and Alexandra rubs her arm.

Maybe this love will be enough for now.

The elevator doors open, and a charming hostess welcomes them. "*Bienvenue chez Georges.* Do you have a reservation?"

"Piotrowski," Ari, the epitome of professionalism and class, replies, stepping forward on their high heels. "Booking for five, special kosher requests?"

"Of course," the hostess says courteously. "May I get your coats? My colleague will take you to your table."

Halina takes off her heavy coat and rearranges her hair. She spots Alexandra's outfit, and her breath catches in her throat. She has been lucky enough to admire her in various sexy outfits—the sexiest being nothing at all, in Halina's book—but this one hits all of Halina's buttons. It's not just the folds of the jumpsuit's neck, reminiscent of Alexandra's outfit on their first night together, or the subtle makeup Alexandra has put on her eyes to make them appear larger than life. It's all of it combined, with the little hint of lace Halina spots between the folds, proof that Alexandra took an extra step to make Halina's Christmas special.

See, she retorts to the voice, *she does care about me, in ways you never could.*

"You're gorgeous," she says reverently. Her hand follows the seam of Alexandra's sleeve to her smooth skin until she can cup her elbow.

"So are you," Alexandra replies, her head cocked. "Your dress is… magical. As if you just stepped out of one of my books."

Halina glances down at the dress she bought as a gift for herself, at the elegant neckline and the wrapped fabric of the bustier. The silky fabric of the skirt brushes against her legs, revealing them with every step. "That was its point," she says softly, "thank you." She pecks Alexandra's cheek, and they walk through the rows of tables to a large table right by the window.

On their way, Halina doesn't miss the way some patrons gawk at them. She stomps on an irrational need to put her hand, her mark almost, on Alexandra. Alexandra is hers, and these men don't deserve to be competition. No one should be competing for Alexandra's affection, but the idea of men as potential rivals is a sore spot.

Leonardo Neri, in particular, is a sore spot—the way he hovers over Alexandra whenever Halina enters their workspace, the way Alexandra is oblivious to his obvious endgame and how negatively it affects Halina, the very presence he has in Alexandra's life. The man has many maddening characteristics, but his attitude toward Alexandra takes the cake. But he will not disrupt this lovely evening, physically or in her thoughts, and she pushes him out of her mind.

Ari and Alexandra sit next to each other, while Elisabeth takes the head of the table. Alexandra's sister is very elegant, too, if in a more conventional way. The turtleneck dress highlights her curves perfectly; it's sexy without revealing anything. Halina tries not to focus too much on the way both sisters inhabit their curves.

"Wow!" Zachary's voice pulls Halina from her thoughts, as he fidgets with his tie and takes in the view over the roofs of Paris. "Spectacular."

"It is, isn't it," she replies as she sits next to him. Zachary looks at her with a little hesitation, but also with a warmth Halina isn't sure she deserves.

They order bottles of sparkling apple juice with their first course, and toast to the holidays.

Halina makes sure to clink her glass with Alexandra's, maintaining the eye contact for a touch too long, if Ari's visible amusement is any indication.

As it turns out, Ari was right to book their dinner reservation for so early in the evening. After dinner and their special preview of the exhibit at the Centre Pompidou, they barely have enough time to catch a taxi to the church. Halina never goes to church, except for *Wigilia*, the Polish Mass for Christmas Eve.

Despite the distance she's put between herself and her home country, the ritual brings her peace and comfort. Her entrée was no *barszcz*, by any stretch of the imagination, but the whole meal did have the comfort Halina associates with her memories of her early childhood in Wrocław, memories she had thought buried under years of resentment. All it took to remember the sweetness of that time was having the right people to share it with.

The choir starts singing, and though it has been years, decades even, since Halina's sung these hymns, they all come rushing back. She lets them come out, keeping her voice low to protect the ears of the people around her.

Next to her, Ari taps their foot with the beat of the carol. Zachary seems focused on the decor of the church; his eyes are trained on the arches of the dome. Elisabeth and Alexandra are enraptured by the choir, and Halina hears them humming in harmony with the singers.

Alexandra's musical ear must run in the family. Halina momentarily loses track of the song itself and listens as they follow the melody and even build a third interval around it. Then they stop suddenly and laugh in silence with their dark heads bowed together. They remind Halina of the illustrations in her childhood books depicting naughty little girls caught in the act. It only increases Halina's affection for Alexandra.

The service ends with the choir performing a moving rendition of
"*Lulajże Jezuniu.*" Halina stifles a laugh when her four companions look
up at her in unison for guidance.

"Come on, Scooby-gang, let's go."

Ari mutters under their breath, asking who is who in this metaphor.

"You don't want to hear the answer." She pokes out her tongue at
them.

Zachary signs something that makes his mother dissolve into peals
of laughter. She seems free in a way Halina has not seen before.

"What was the joke?" Ari asks. "Did you say I was Scooby-Doo?"

"Actually," Elisabeth replies, still laughing, "he said he was fine being
Scooby-Doo himself if you were Fred."

Ari seems to consider Zach carefully before nodding. "I suppose I
could deal with this arrangement."

"We should go back to our hotel," Elisabeth says, once she manages
to compose herself.

"I'm off to a party," Ari says with a self-satisfied smile. "Guess who
will get to play with Santa's candy cane to get off the naughty list!"

Halina turns to Alexandra. "May I get you all a taxi back to your
side of Paris?"

"Actually, I—"

"Don't worry about us," Elisabeth cuts in, pulling Alexandra closer
to kiss her cheek. "We can manage on our own. We'll take a taxi back
to your place, take care of Punshki, and then back to our room. Tonight
was delightful. Thank you and Merry Christmas, Halina," she adds,
stepping closer to pull Halina into her hug. "Take care of her, will you?"
she whispers in Halina's ear. "Good night!"

"G-good night," Halina says, a little dazed by the soft-spoken
demand. "What about you then?"

Alexandra shakes her head, making her curls bounce. "I want to go
back to your place."

"Oh?"

"Got a surprise for you there."

ONCE THEY'RE IN HALINA'S HOTEL room, the scent of Alexandra's surprise hits Halina before she can turn on the light.

"You got me a Christmas tree," Halina says, covering her mouth with one hand while the other brushes the needles of the potted miniature fir tree. "And ornaments too."

She marvels at the little baubles hooked on the tiny branches: There's a wooden piano, vividly red against the green of the tree, but mostly small glass pieces, miniatures of traditional Polish *bombki*. "It's so pretty," she whispers, brushing the ornaments with the tip of her finger. "Did you make them?"

Alexandra nods and comes to stand next to her. "I wanted to make sure you had the best Christmas possible," she says softly, wrapping her arms around Halina and resting her head on Halina's chest. "Oh, and if the website I used was not mistaken, you need to break one, don't you? To chase the bad spirits away?"

"It is tradition, yeah," Halina replies, but no way in hell will she smash one of these delicate pieces of art that Alexandra blew herself. She doesn't contain her surprised squeal when Alexandra pulls an actual *polska bombka* from her pocket.

"We don't want any bad luck."

Halina takes the bauble and observes the pattern of holly and snowflakes drawing hearts and clefs around the sphere before putting it on the table next to the tree. "No, we don't," she replies. She covers the sphere with a towel before she smashes it with her clenched fist.

Alexandra claps her hands. "All right, Mrs. Claus, let's fill you with cheer," she purrs, as she walks backward to Halina's bed while untying her jumpsuit and letting it fall open.

Halina follows her, taking care of the bodice of her own dress in a hurry.

Merry Christmas to me indeed.

* * *

THE RIDE BACK TO THE airport on January second is not as much fun as Elisabeth and Zachary's arrival was. Alexandra clutches Elisabeth's arm all the way to the security doors and pulls her nephew into a fierce hug. The airport is gloomy so early in the day, and the pain of separation only adds to the heavy atmosphere.

You take care of her, okay? she tells him.

You take care of yourself, he replies cheekily. *My mom is strong enough without needing any white knight to defend her.*

Of course she is. But sometimes, she needs a reminder.

That I can do.

"I don't ask for more," she says, pulling him back for another hug. *Come back any time you want.*

I'll hold you to that.

"Does the invitation extend to me?" Elisabeth asks, practically crushing Alexandra into a bear hug.

"Of course, Liz."

"I miss you, Lexie."

Alexandra buries her nose in her twin's long hair and takes in her perfume. "I miss you too. Be safe. Have fun." She signs the last two sentences to pull Zachary back into their conversation.

"I will, I will," Elisabeth replies with a tearful smile. "I have some ideas to put my degree to good use."

"Oh?"

"We'll talk about it when my plans are fleshed out," she says, winking before she squeezes Alexandra's hands in hers. "Be safe, bubbeleh."

"I will, *motek. Nesiah tovah.*"

Thank you, Elisabeth and Zachary sign in unison; they wave back at her until they are completely out of sight.

Alexandra wipes off her tears, takes her phone out of her pocket, and taps her most frequent contact. "Wanna go for a walk around the Marais?" she asks without preamble, and her smile comes back when Halina sleepily tells her to just come over.

*   *   *

THE END OF JANUARY COMES faster—and gloomier—than Alexandra anticipated, and with it, the completion of her installation at the Philharmonie. The installation is state-of-the-art and deserves a white paper describing the whole process in a technical publication.

The Philharmonie's board agrees with her assessment. Leo's talent in the creation of these self-lighting panels doesn't go unnoticed; she makes sure of it. With a handshake and a final deposit in the studio's bank account, she says her goodbyes to the job. But it's not goodbye to the orchestra; her presence in Halina's sphere has been noticed, and she's invited, more than once, to get a drink with them after rehearsal.

The closer they get to the inaugural concert, the more relaxed they all seem to become. It's odd, to her, but Halina explains how, by now, "rehearsals are more for the maestro than for us. We could play those pieces in our sleep."

They launch into a new streak of dinner dates. Alexandra makes sure Halina has a taste of the best Paris has to offer, while Halina, with some help from Ari, takes her to the trendiest restaurants popping up, as frequently as daisies, around Paris . Sometimes their ideas coincide, as with the American diner near the Moulin Rouge.

There, they busy themselves tearing into a massive plate of barbecued ribs while Halina gushes about the arrival of another famous musician for the inaugural concert.

"He's more than a remarkable musician," Halina says, waving a bone, "he's also the sweetest musician in the business. I wish I were more like him, though we have a lot in common, with the whole child artist thing, yada, yada, yada…"

"Yada, yada, yada," Alexandra repeats, her beer hiding her face.

"Ha ha, yeah, laugh at me, you caught what I meant. Anyway, it's such a pleasure to play with him, it's as if we…" Halina pauses, a hand to her chest. "We are in resonance, if it makes any sense?"

"It does," Alexandra says with a nod. "The same goes for Leo and me. We get each other's art without needing to voice it."

Halina twists her mouth for a split second, long enough for Alexandra to notice. "It's not as though I want to fuck the guy, though," Halina comments.

"Neither do I," Alexandra replies coldly. The last piece of spicy corn on the cob is rightfully hers now.

"Uh huh."

Alexandra is pretty sure Halina couldn't drip more condescension and doubt.

"You can't deny there is still something between you two," Halina points out. "Friends don't fuck each other. But maybe *you* do," she adds with a condescending pat. Alexandra wants to throw what's left of her beer in Halina's perfect face and storm out, but… no. She's not capable of such a dramatic exit without making a fool of herself and she doesn't want to support the melodrama Halina would try to make out of it. The calmer her reaction, the more ridiculous Halina's paranoia will be.

"We're just friends," she replies sweetly. She hopes she achieved sweet and not constipated. "I have no intention of rekindling that flame, trust me."

Halina's attitude turns apologetic, but she still mumbles under her breath about the trust issue not lying solely with Alexandra, but also with Leo.

"Anyway, you were saying?" Alexandra asks, seeking safer conversational territory.

"What was—oh, yeah, Lang Jian!" Halina exclaims, her good mood mercurially returning. "So, naturally, he'll play Ravel's concerto in G major for the first concert, but apparently, he also wants us to duet!"

"That's great," Alexandra replies earnestly, shoving her belligerent side to the back of her mind. "As in, a *pièce à quatre mains*?"

"You got it," Halina says with a wink, soaking up the last bit of barbecue sauce with a garlicky fry. "We have a grand plan."

"You're not going to tell me what it is, are you?"

"Nope."

"You're just mean. I won't even be there."

"'Course you will."

Alexandra snorts a derisive laugh and stabs a couple of fries. "Wish I could, but the season is completely sold out—I looked. And free tickets weren't part of my deal with the board."

Halina shrugs. "You'll be my guest."

"I thought your manager was your guest?"

"I'm the soloist for the orchestra. I'm pretty sure I can have more than one guest."

Alexandra covers Halina's hand and gives it a quick squeeze. "You're very sweet," she says, "but I don't want you to get in trouble. I'll just catch it on TV or something."

"Why settle for a small screen when you could see it live?"

"Halina, promise you won't play the diva card?"

"I want my girlfriend at the inaugural concert and I will have it."

"You're hella pushy when you get an idea in that thick head of yours, aren't you?"

Halina covers Alexandra's hand with her own. "I promise I won't play the diva," she replies, "but I will try to get you a seat. I can give you a good show," she adds with a wink.

"Oh, I don't doubt it."

*　*　*

HALINA SITS IN THE SECTION behind the orchestra on one of the breaks the maestro granted them, soaking up Lang's absolute mastery on the keys as the man plays with a Metallica song for his new colleagues. Ari comes rushing in, eyes wide and manic.

"What's wrong?" Halina frowns, offering a one-armed hug as soon as Ari is close enough. From the stage, she now hears the sound of angry, frightened discussion among the other members of the ensemble.

"Terrorist attack in the middle of Paris," Ari replies in one breath. Halina tightens her arm around them. "A magazine's headquarters, close to the Bastille. Apparently, the police think the shooters are—they are driving toward Porte de Pantin."

Halina's blood freezes in her veins. "Isn't that where we are?"

Ari nods frenetically. "We're on lockdown until the Prefecture of Police allows us to go out. They don't want to create a panic."

Halina nods, trying to focus on what is known instead of picturing the worst. "Okay. Okay. We're safe here."

Ari wraps their arms around their own torso. "Yes. We are. Safe?" Their voice lilts into a question, and Halina pulls them closer.

"Ari. We're good, they won't attack musicians," she says comfortingly.

"They attacked cartoonists, Lina," Ari replies between their teeth. "Why not a concert hall next?"

Halina rubs their arm. "We're going to be okay. Give me my phone; I need to tell Alexandra I'm safe."

Halina taps a quick text to Alexandra and tries to convince herself Alexandra is safe too. Her studio is not in central Paris; it's far away from the Bastille anyway, right? But isn't Alexandra's latest project right in the midst of it, close to Halina's hotel? Nah, she's fine, she has to be fine, the commission on Place des Vosges is not scheduled to start for a month or two, *She's safe, she's safe, she's*—

The depth of Halina's worry and just how hard she tried to convince herself all was well become obvious as relief sweeps through her when Alexandra confirms that she is safe. She asks Halina to "keep on breathing, babe, and come back to me."

Halina joins the group. She finds some solace in the companionship that's built over the past months between her and the orchestra.

Odile hugs her. "You're okay?"

"As okay as can be," Halina replies truthfully. "You?"

"We're discussing the impact of this on the plan for the opening," the concertmaster replies with a grimace. "I mean, it's next week. Surely the board should consider canceling, but there is so much money riding on the whole thing…"

Halina is shocked by the musicians' preoccupation in such a dire time, but she also understands: Focus on the mundane to avoid the unthinkable.

A couple of minutes or hours later, she can't be sure, the director enters the hall. It's hard to notice anything amiss in Loupan's attitude, but for those acquainted with the "Silver Lady," it's obvious how rattled she is: She's not wearing any makeup and her shirt is untucked.

"The Prefecture wants us to stay in the Philharmonie one more hour, while they sweep the neighborhood," she announces. "And given the years of planning it has required, it has been decided, in agreement with the President's team, to maintain the opening."

Some musicians protest, but Loupan raises one hand. "Please," she says, her voice raised above the murmurs, "we need to show to these… beasts, that they may have guns, but they can't silence art. They can't silence us. Thank you."

Halina exchanges glances with Lang Jian, with Odile, with other musicians she's become closer to. She squares her shoulders and straightens up to her full height. Their weapon is music. It doesn't seem much in the face of bullets, but they will wield it.

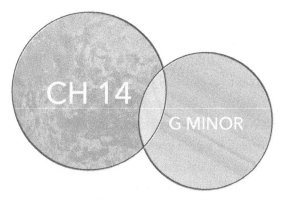

Midnight Blue, Rosewood, and Verdigris

ALEXANDRA STILL DOESN'T UNDERSTAND HOW Halina managed to prepare for the concert without losing her mind, or how she got Alexandra such a coveted ticket. It is a big night for them both, and she wants it to be the closure they need after the hardship of the past week.

As strong as Halina has tried to appear for the rest of the world, Alexandra has learned to read her, and she's done all she can to allay the fear clutching Halina in its claws. She's made sure they stayed in, and at Alexandra's place, to keep Halina away from the vicinity of the attack and the flock of journalists it attracted.

Alexandra is still reeling from the nonsensicality of the violent act, and from the overwhelming wave of loving messages from her sister and her friends, all of whom have needed assurance of her safety. Never did she imagine witnessing such an attack in Paris, and the French people's reactions to it have only increased her love for her adopted city. Some of the journalists covering tonight's event have messages of support on their cameras and in some cases, on their jackets: "Je Suis Charlie" armbands and badges fill the room.

Alexandra doesn't mingle; she walks around with a nice Bramble in her hand and observes the rooms she never visited while she worked here.

"Miss Graff?"

Alexandra nearly smacks herself in the face with her long hoops when she turns toward the accented voice calling to her in English; the hubbub around them is suddenly covered by its dark red hue.

The man is about Halina's size, with a build Alexandra usually associates with swimmers—large shoulders, tiny waist—accentuated by the cut of his suit. It's dark green, with a mandarin collar following the lines of his jaw. On his chest, over his heart, a truly impressive piece of jewelry sits: a large brooch of gold and green gems, shaped to resemble a teardrop. Alexandra can appreciate a good accessory, especially when it so definitely sets the man apart from the crowd of black suits around them. The twinkle in his eyes and the dimple in his cheek put Alexandra at ease.

"You found me," she replies, her head tilted as she considers him. "Have we met before?"

"Not in person," he replies, charming to the tip of his manicured fingers as he takes Alexandra's hand. "I'm Miss Piotrowski's manager—"

"You're Saral," Alexandra exclaims, shaking his hand enthusiastically. "I've heard all about you."

"If Ari is the one who talked about me, don't trust one word of it," he says with a smile, giving new depth to his dimple.

"I should tell you the same," Alexandra replies, taking a sip of her drink. "Ari may not be the most reliable source when it comes to me."

"Only good things, I assure you," Saral replies with a bow of his head. He stops a waiter to pluck a flute of champagne from a tray. "To a beautiful building where beautiful music should come to life," he toasts, and Alexandra raises her glass.

"To art, our rampart against barbarity."

"Here, here."

They sip their drinks. The lights dim, announcing the impending start of the concert.

"So, you're not backstage, giving our girl words of encouragement?" Alexandra asks while they walk. Her eyes are on the stairs. Her heels are going to make the journey quite adventurous. Alexandra isn't quite sure what made her choose them. Oh, right: the glint in Halina's eyes when she showed them to her.

Saral laughs, a full-belly guffaw; his dark red morphs into a kaleidoscope of ruby shades. It makes his double-pin brooch clink melodiously against his champagne flute, drops of pastel blue on a silver sea. "I would never spend time with Halina before a performance." He leans closer to speak more discreetly. "For one, she's a ball of nerves and tension before going onstage. And second, she usually blows off some steam with a, ah, partner, and I have no voyeuristic tendencies."

Alexandra freezes; her jaw is painfully clenched at the image he's painted in her mind of Halina doing whatever it takes to relax with some nameless woman, with no regard for what they have, what they've built in the past month. What she feels is close to jealousy, but worse; it's a mash-up of all her fears, striking at the first sign of weakness.

Her thoughts must show on her face or in her eyes, as Saral backtracks. "I mean, it's what she used to do. I just learned not to disturb her before a concert!"

Alexandra licks her lips and attempts to compose herself. "She can be quite dreadful when she's tense, can't she," she replies. "Besides, I'm sure she has other ways to relax now," she adds, willing her head to trust her heart. "Let's find our seats."

Saral offers her his arm. "Let's."

IN, AND OUT. IN. AND out.

"Meditation is crap," Halina mumbles with her hands on her stomach, trying to get just on the right side of pre-performance jitters.

A French horn chuckles from his corner. "Let it go, princess," he says, and the piccolo answers with a fast-paced version of the Disney hit. "We'll be fine. Besides, Lang Jian is the one carrying the heavy load tonight."

"You're the heavy load," Odile shouts. "All right, let's show these fine people how much we deserve the splurge of their money on our new home."

The orchestra files out of the room, some of them following strange rituals. It's establishing old rituals in a new place, Halina figures, a way to turn the new concert hall into a real home. Soon, it's just Odile, Lang Jian, Ari, and Halina in the musician's room.

"Showtime," Odile says with a wink. She picks up her violin and follows the group.

Ari hands Halina a bottle of water, snaps candids of the two musicians, then takes their favorite spot at the stage entrance.

It's just the two of them then, at least for the next hour or so. Lang Jian will take the stage for the concerto; Halina is more than happy to hand it over to him, since she abhors Ravel and his overcomplicated tendencies. Give her a good Stravinsky any day: melodramatic, sure, but not an injury risk.

The Chinese pianist, still in an armchair, seems relaxed; his fingers tap a mute melody on its arm. "How do you find Paris so far?" he asks, his tone friendly. "All to your satisfaction?"

Halina's thoughts jump to Alexandra and the many facets of Paris she has shown her. "Quite the discovery," she replies with a secretive expression.

"And what are the plans afterward?"

Ah, precisely the point she has avoided so far, to Saral's annoyance. She has delayed any consideration of what will happen beyond the end of concert season, beyond the end of her engagement with the orchestra.

Alas, this is not her first contract; she discovered, long ago, the various behind-the-scenes processes of her field beyond the simple joy of music. Halina is acutely aware of how deals are made by concert halls around the world as they secure soloists and guest musicians for their programs and to attract donors. She cannot bring herself to consider her next engagement and not involve Alexandra, whether it's to leave her or stay. She has just gotten used to the idea of being in a relationship; it's too soon to consider its end.

"My manager is in Paris for a couple of days," she replies, her attention seemingly on the hem of her dress. "We'll have some time after the opening to talk about it."

Echoes of the first piece played for an official audience in the concert hall surround them, and then thunderous applause. They both exhale deeply.

"It never gets old, does it," she says, eyes turned toward the ceiling.

"Let's hope it doesn't," Lang Jian replies with a boyish grin. "Otherwise, what's the point of all our hard work?"

"Good point."

LANG LEAVES THE STAGE AFTER the performance of his first piece, then brings Halina back onstage with him, and the crowd, already on its feet, cheers with new energy as she takes the stage. God, if she thought the room was impressive during rehearsals, it pales in comparison to how daunting it is when filled with an audience and alive with their cheers and applause.

Halina lets those vibrations resonate through her body and chase the nerves away. They're replaced by an energy just begging to come out through her fingers. Hand in hand, she and Lang bow to the orchestra, the audience, and the maestro before they sit side by side on the piano bench.

Lang Jian starts, one note repeated over and over again, while Halina plays the two higher-pitched arpeggios. Saint-Saëns's melodic poem unfolds as they play, and their four hands run along the keys in a perfect choreography of fingers and notes.

As if through a heavy curtain, Halina hears the orchestra around them marking the measure on their stands, following the tempo of the "Danse macabre" with them. She notes the reaction of the audience to this off-program surprise, but all that matters are her fellow pianist, the Steinway, and herself. She lets the melody sweep her from her thoughts and use her as a medium to share this magic with the rest of the world. This is why she sacrificed everything: to become one with the keys, with the strings, with the music. She lets herself smile when they get to the end of the piece, the end of death's waltz.

They both play the final notes, the tremolo, and then sit back, detaching themselves from the piano to return to the mundane world. They exchange a look in the second when the music is still present as an echo through the room, and the audience is still enraptured before exploding into applause and cheers.

They stand, arm in arm, and Halina is saved by Lang Jian's hand from making a fool of herself when she starts to bow too low. Scanning the audience, Halina quickly finds Alexandra on her feet next to Saral, cheering, awe written all over her face.

Oh, right, Halina reminds herself, *it's the first time she's seen me in performance mode.*

From the look of it, Alexandra enjoyed what she heard, what she saw. Halina wonders how it manifested for Alexandra: this beautiful, if a little bit frightening, piece of romantic music. She has the intermission to ask her all about it, but she must also focus on the next part of the program. Lang Jian will take over the celesta, because the instrument is one of his "hobbies," but the Escaich piece is no walk in the park for either of them.

ALEXANDRA STILL CLAPS SLOWLY AS people file out to stretch their legs, or get some drinks, or mingle with the celebrities in the audience. Her mouth is stretched in a stunned smile. The flash of colors is still vivid at the forefront of her mind, along with the sight of Halina's back, offered to Alexandra's eyes through the lace of her red dress.

Her beauty really is magnified in this outfit. And to watch her perform with such an audience is completely different from the numerous rehearsals Alexandra has attended. Trust Halina to hold back some of her energy for the actual performance.

Halina feeds on her public's energy, the spotlight; she connects all of it to the keys to give back to her audience, in a virtuous cycle. If Alexandra had any doubts about whether Halina belonged to the stage or not, they have completely vanished now. This creature who walks toward her? Electric, untouchable, passionate? It's the woman Alexandra has come to love, transformed, amplified to a whole other level.

"Did you enjoy our surprise?" Halina is aglow as she rests one hand on Alexandra's arm and the other on Saral's shoulder.

"It was splendid," Saral replies with an air-kiss. "And you are sensational, my dear."

Halina smiles coquettishly at him as she thanks him. It's a good thing Halina has repeatedly mentioned the pride she feels in her status as a gold-star lesbian, or Alexandra would be very jealous of the whole exchange.

Halina only has eyes for Alexandra when her smile turns soft as she says, "Paris must suit me."

"Hmm, must be it," Saral says, glancing over Halina's shoulder to wave at someone. "All right, Goldfinger. I must schmooze on your behalf. And, um, *na szczęście!*"

Halina shakes her head; one small ringlet escapes her complicated braid. "He always butchers it," she mutters, the fondness in her voice contradicting her judgment. "Did you like it?" she repeats, now completely focused on Alexandra.

"Oh, babe," she gushes, "it was... wow. Inspiring. Awesome. Brilliant."

Halina blushes light pink on her cheeks and the hollow of her throat. "I hoped you would. Was it... pretty?" she asks, tapping her temple in a mirror of Alexandra's usual gesture to signal a photism.

Alexandra laughs at her gesture and grasps Halina's hands. "It was. I'll show you, if you can find time to come by the studio."

Halina cocks an eyebrow at her. "Is this an invitation into your kingdom?"

"Consider this an open invitation whenever you want to drop by."

"I will." Halina pecks Alexandra's lips. "I need to get back. But I'll catch up with you later?"

"Of course. Blow them all away."

Halina beams at her. "I always do," she says with a wink, before she whispers in Alexandra's ear, "and it always gives me quite the rush."

"The r—oh," Alexandra says when Halina suggestively trails her fingers up her arm. "Let me think about that."

"Counting on it."

For the life of her, Alexandra can't take her eyes from the smoothness of Halina's skin undulating in front of her as she walks away.

Is this payback for my early teasing? Fine, I'll play.

AFTER THE CONCERTO, A SHORT break to move the pianos lets the audience return to schmoozing and Champaigning. Saral wishes Alexandra a pleasant evening and leaves, whispering with an important-looking lady. Ari takes advantage of the free seat and leans toward Alexandra. "She's changing, but she'll be here in a minute," they say conspiratorially. "Told me to tell you, so you wouldn't worry."

Alexandra keeps her eyes on the stage, where the piano and the smaller piano-thingy are being moved. "Thank you," she whispers back. "You are very handsome, by the way."

She means it. Ari's outfit brings out all their assets. The sober three-piece suit is perfectly tailored to their body. Their blond hair is swept into a gravity-defying pompadour. With the glitter on their chest, the winged eyeliner, and black lipstick, Ari makes a truly spectacular picture.

They pat their hair in a coy gesture. "Why, thank you m'lady."

"You're very welcome. Thank you for such a visual delight."

Ari gives her a sideways glance, playfully offended. "Are you hitting on me, ma'am?"

"Nope. Already taken."

"No need to tell me. Never thought I'd live to see the day Boss Lady would settle down." They pause as the orchestra tunes for the last part of the concert. "But I must say, you're a breath of fresh air compared to her usual type."

"How so?"

"Ya know," Ari replies, East Coast accent thick and turquoise in their whispers, "girls with the same slim physique, but without her brains and talent."

"And what am I?"

Ari snickers. "The opposite. Same level of brains and talent, but diametrically opposite body types."

"I suppose."

"It's a good thing that opposites attract and all," they add, patting her hand patronizingly.

Alexandra is about to ask them about it when they nod toward the free seat. "Hi."

Halina changed indeed. The red dress has been replaced by an outfit not so different from Ari's: a black tuxedo and a ruffled, crisp, white shirt. Her shoes and hairdo are the same, though, and Alexandra brushes her fingers against the braid, which is wound around a side ponytail. The style is playful, yet elegant.

"Hi."

Halina leans over the armrest to put her fingers on their preferred spot: high on Alexandra's thigh at the hem of her dress. "I hope you enjoy this as much as I do."

"Oh, yeah," Alexandra replies in the same tone and puts her hand on Halina's fingers before they can slip under the fabric. "The orchestra is very good."

Halina tangles her fingers with Alexandra's. "Can't wait to go home with you."

"Oh?"

Halina whispers in Alexandra's ear; her fingers draw abstract patterns to the beat of the music. "I want to take you home and undress you," she says softly, her face a mask of interest as she keeps her eyes on the musicians. "Make you keep your shoes on while you show me how you pleasure yourself." Alexandra gulps; her legs cross and uncross in an effort to put up a bold front. "And I'll make sure not to waste any of the lesson."

Halina's fingers move until they are brushing back and forth in the crease between Alexandra's hip and thigh, an unsubtle suggestion of what she intends to do.

"Oh."

"And afterward, maybe we can… play."

"Play?"

"I perused the stores around the hotel." She leans closer. "Are you familiar with 'Passage du Désir'?"

"Y-yes."

Of course, the adult pleasure store is one Alexandra has visited often. It's easy to picture Halina in it, perusing the different objects they have to offer, asking for guidance—*oh my.*

Halina's smiles, predatory yet playful, the best representation of the cat about to get the cream Alexandra has ever faced. "I have faith you'll approve of my choices."

"I'm pretty sure I already do."

"Good. Shhh, this is the best part, I don't want you to miss it."

It may be, as Halina says, the best part, but Alexandra cannot focus on the music; her mind is entirely occupied in controlling the wave of arousal breaking over her.

The little vixen.

BACK IN HALINA'S HOTEL ROOM, much later—so late, in fact, it's practically morning—Halina kicks off her shoes and sits in an armchair, obviously firmly on board with her own voyeuristic plan to watch Alexandra as she pleasures herself before joining in the fun. Usually, Alexandra would have no problem at all with such a plan. She'd be at ease with the spotlight on her as she put on a show for her partner. But Ari's words ring in her head.

How different Alexandra and Halina are! How different she must be in comparison to Halina's previous partners, the partners she would blow off some steam with before performing, and God knows how many there have been. All the confidence and love for her own body

Alexandra has built over the years crumble away, leaving her self-conscious and clumsy.

"Something wrong?" Halina asks when Alexandra keeps her hands on the zipper of her skirt for maybe a bit too long.

"N-nothing, just got caught in my own head," she replies hastily, pushing the skirt off to kick it aside. Of course, because it's her luck, the skirt catches her heel and nearly sends her toppling to the floor. Now embarrassed by her own lack of grace in addition to her self-consciousness, Alexandra tries to get her balance back. She takes her top off and stands for Halina with her hands on her hips.

This is not about me, she reasons, *this is for her, to celebrate* her.

Halina has her head cocked; her eyes slowly follow the curve of Alexandra's legs up to the lace of her bodysuit.

"That dress definitely suits you, słoneczna," she says, her face filled with fondness. "Remember, keep the shoes on."

"You have a fetish," Alexandra comments, slowly relaxing as she shakes her head to get rid of the static. Her earrings ring a bell-like chime, droplets of purple and turquoise. "Want me to keep these on, too?"

"Sure."

"Fetishist."

"Of you in very sexy attire you wear only for me? Sure, let's call it that."

Alexandra laughs at her and throws her bra in Halina's face. Some jasmine petals flutter to the plush floor. Halina chuckles too, with her nose buried in the cups to take in Alexandra's perfume.

As she scoots back on the bed with her back to the headboard so she faces Halina, Alexandra tries not to let her mind derail to the parts of her body bouncing and jiggling or to the way Halina's whole body is firm and toned.

"Okay, what's wrong," Halina growls as she sits at the other end of the bed. "Something's bothering you, and I'd rather have you comfortable when you're pleasuring yourself on my behalf."

Alexandra tries to deny it, but Halina's care gives her no escape route. She folds her legs closer to her chest. "It's just… something Ari said."

"They're full of shit. It doesn't matter."

"They told me I'm not your usual type?"

Halina acquiesces. "Okay, it's true."

"I just—it made me self-conscious, or something."

Halina sits closer and puts her hand on Alexandra's knee, soothing her by caressing circles on her skin. "Alexandra, listen to me," she says softly. "No, you're not my usual type. But, I never slept twice with girls who were my 'type.'" She makes air quotes, then puts her hands back on Alexandra's legs. "Maybe that's what matters? That I find you interesting and beautiful enough to want more of you than an easy physical thing?"

"I guess," Alexandra mutters, letting Halina's words and caresses appease her. "It's just a tough standard to match."

Halina chuckles softly and runs her hands down Alexandra's calves and to her ankles and back. "No bigger challenge than what we are building together."

"How so?"

"I never in my life had what we have, whatever it is. It's… honestly? I'm terrified."

Alexandra moves up on her haunches to get closer to Halina. "You don't think I'm terrified by it?" she asks, lifting Halina's chin to gaze into her eyes. "Every day, I wake up with the thought that today may be the day you decide this is not worth it."

In for a penny…

"The day you finally run away." *From me.*

Halina keeps her eyes on her, slowly blinking as she absorbs her words. "See," she says, voice dropped to a husky whisper, "I told you, we're not so different."

Alexandra smiles at her, leans back on the pillows and pulls Halina against her body. It's a weird position they end in, legs and arms tangled in fabric, but comfortable enough that she doesn't try to alter it. Halina, however, rolls to the side, pulls off her pants, and opens her shirt before nestling her head on Alexandra's chest.

"I am not a mind reader, though."

"Hmm?"

Alexandra settles into the embrace, marveling at how quickly they went from a moment that was supposed to be hot, sexy, and fun to one so intimate, nearly platonic, and serious.

Halina doesn't move, but Alexandra tilts her head to see her face. "You need to tell me when you are insecure about me, about us," Halina says softly. "I can't read your mind."

"I know."

"And I need to feel like you trust me, so I can trust you."

The hesitation is palpable in Halina's voice; it's colored rosewood around the edges.

"I do trust you, babe," Alexandra murmurs. "You're right. I'll try?"

"Ditto."

Silence stretches between them, interrupted only by the sounds from the street below. Alexandra tightens her hold around Halina, and Halina returns the gesture with a nuzzle to her cheek.

"Tell me about these."

Alexandra is very comfortable in this mood, just enough to drift into sleep. "Mmm—'bout what?"

Halina covers Alexandra's elbow with her hand and lightly taps her diamond-shaped tattoo—the inked rainbow is visible even in the semidarkness—and then slides her hand to the top of her spine, where there is another, cardiogram-like rainbow tattoo. "About *these*?"

"Right now?"

"Please?"

Alexandra focuses on her. Maybe their communication is improving. "All right," she says, twisting her arm so Halina can trace it with her fingers. "It's not much of a story, though."

"Ple-ease?"

Alexandra snorts and lightly rests her palm on Halina's face to push it away. "Put those puppy eyes away; you're going to hurt someone," she says, still laughing. "I got this one as a reward for myself, for getting my diploma. Right after college, before my internships, before I left California," she says, fingers on her elbow. "And I celebrated my first commission here with this one," she adds, her hands finding the nape of her neck.

"Why did you leave California?"

"I didn't belong there anymore, not after my father told me I disgraced the family name because of my relationship with Sue-Ji."

"He cut you from his life for being a lesbian?"

Alexandra winces. "Can we—can we not talk about it? For now?"

"Of course." Halina kisses Alexandra's forehead. She rolls on her back and settles for the night; her fingers remain around Alexandra's wrist.

"Lina?"

"Hmm?"

God, she's falling asleep already.

"I'm glad you decided to fuck me."

Halina lifts their joined hands to press a kiss to Alexandra's knuckles. "I'm glad you made sure it wouldn't end up there."

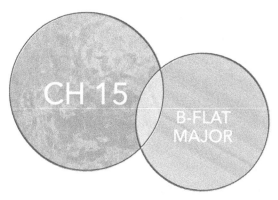

CH 15

B-FLAT
MAJOR

Violine, Green, Crimson, and Silver

ALEXANDRA EXTENDED AN OPEN INVITATION to come to her workshop since she doesn't work at the Philharmonie anymore, and Halina takes advantage of it a couple of weeks later. She is more than a little curious to witness the process of making stained glass and she can use the time away from the Philharmonie—away from Ari.

The whole idea of relationships is mind-boggling on its own without Ari pointing out, passive-aggressively, differences between Halina and Alexandra, mostly that it's beneath her to date someone as plebeian as Alexandra, even if she's "very nice, naturally." At some point, the phrase "slum it up with the bi" came up, and she doesn't need them to point out something she already feels tender about.

The more time they spend together, the more Halina wonders why Alexandra doesn't accept the lesbian label to the fullest. As far as Halina is concerned, no woman could be so good in bed, so intuitive about her partner's needs, and not be a lesbian.

Ari also asked, quite petulantly, what she was doing tying herself down when Saral has several options lined up for her beyond June, prestigious options that would secure Halina's fame and lifestyle. The jabs at Alexandra were one too many and Halina, having had enough, sent Ari on an impossible errand.

They both need the time out, Halina decides as she rides one of the city's thousands of public bikes to the address Alexandra gave her.

The building, a plain house with a white façade, isn't as artistic-looking as she imagined it would be. Two things separate the place from the rest of the neighborhood: how small it is, sandwiched between two taller buildings; and the third floor, which appears from the street as a single triangular window set in the blue gable of the roof. The only proof she is at the right place is a small metal label on the door.

"Graff & Neri."

She tries not to let it affect her, but Halina can't help but grit her teeth at the sight of that man's name. Her gut tells her he's not to be trusted at all and that he's not completely honest about his goal with Alexandra. Halina is not comfortable with jealousy, a novel feeling for her. Besides, since he has such a prominent role in Alexandra's life, Halina doesn't fool herself into believing she would be Alexandra's choice over Leo, should the situation devolve to that point.

That doesn't mean she has to like it, either.

The Fates must be laughing at her, for none other than Leo himself opens the door. The easy, fake smile on his face melts into an expression of disdain when he recognizes her. "Alexandra is busy," he says in lieu of greeting. His body fills the doorframe.

"Alexandra told me to come by anytime," Halina retorts, straightening to face him on a more even level. He's still taller and bigger, but he doesn't dwarf her.

The neutral line of Leo's lips turns into a sneer. "Be that as it may, she. Is. Busy. You know, working? With *glass*? I'm sure even *you* can understand how complicated and stressful it is." He pauses to cock his head as if to convey how little faith he puts in Halina's intelligence.

"It's not as if I want to barge into the studio while she's wielding fire." Halina takes a deep breath and puts on a more agreeable mask. "Why don't I just come in, and you can tell her I'm here to s—"

"Absolutely not." The aggression and venom in Leo's voice are unmistakable.

"Excuse me?"

Leo checks behind him, steps forward, and closes the door behind him. They're on the same level, now, and Halina does her best not to let his bulk intimidate her.

Talk down to me one more time, idiota, *and I'll John Cage your face with a hammer.*

"No," Leo repeats. He crosses his arms one more time; the gesture makes her roll her eyes before she mirrors it. He continues. "What we're going to do is have a little chat, you and me."

"I'm not interested in what you have to sell."

"Not interested in selling you anything either, with all due respect to our girl's taste," Leo says with a sniff of contempt. "No, I just want to give you a... let's call it a friendly warning."

Halina's eyebrows climb to her hairline at both the oxymoron and the word "friendly."

"Enjoy it while you can."

"Ex-cuse me?"

Leo rests his back against the door; to any onlooker, he's the epitome of relaxed and handsome, as loath as she is to admit it. "To have Alexandra as your... plaything. Enjoy it while you can, 'cause it won't last."

"She's my *girlfriend,*" Halina spits back. "And you can't understand what we have."

A small part of her is proud she didn't fall into a panic attack at the words, while a not-so-small part of her, the one she tries her hardest to silence, points at the ugly truth in Leo's words.

"Oh, I understand plenty," Leo says, in a voice so sickly sweet it's venomous. "I can remember having Alexandra in my bed, being in her, her body against mine, the way she laughed at my jokes, made me believe I was the only one able to keep the world on its axis."

Shit.

Leo gets closer. "I also remember that she only forgives once."

Merde.

"And you've already had your one strike, haven't you?"

Gówno.

He almost sounds sincere. If Halina didn't know as much as she already did about him, she would believe Leo's intentions to be compassionate. The sneaky... repulsive... *drań.*

"Yeah, you have," Leo continues, needing no confirmation from her as his expression turns vicious again. "And sooner or later, whether you want it or not, you'll blow it. Again. For good, this time."

"You may have your experience with Alexandra," Halina cuts him off before he can poison her mind any further, "but you don't know *me.*"

Something akin to compassion glints in Leo's brown eyes, but they're soon back to dark and sullen. "Oh, I know you plenty, lady." His voice drops to a growl. "We're cut from the same cloth."

"You wish." Not her best repartee, but it will have to do.

"Let's see." Leo slouches as he counts on his fingers. "You never doubted your power of attraction, did you? Getting what you want demanded work, yes, but again, you never thought you wouldn't get it in the end. You've never tied yourself to people, because people always end up leaving anyway, so fuck them, right; you're better than all of them anyway. The soonest you can walk away from something vaguely akin to actual commitment to someone else is not soon enough."

Halina clenches her fists. Punching him would only get her injured and out of commission for the orchestra; it's not worth it. She glares at him. "If we're so much alike, why do you want her back?"

Leo's stance immediately changes. He leans away from her as if she's poisonous.

"I'm right, aren't I," Halina continues, her voice dropped too, in case Alexandra, in an extraordinarily unlucky coincidence, decides to investigate right this moment what's keeping Leo for so long. "You want her back."

"What if I do," Leo hisses back. "We belong together. It's the natural way of things."

Halina laughs sharply, derisively. "You just said you weren't able to stay in a committed relationship," she says with an exasperated shake of her head. "And we're both aware that Alexandra needs this level of commitment to be happy. So what is it? If you can't have her, she can't be with anybody else?"

Leo clenches his jaw and avoids her eyes while huffing and puffing, an answer in and of itself.

"As long as she doesn't tell me to fuck off, you better get used to having me around, pal," Halina adds in conclusion. "Now," she says, a bit louder and with perhaps too much enthusiasm, "would you mind letting me in to see her?"

Leo shakes his head, but he goes inside, leaving the door open behind him.

"Caveman," Halina mutters before following him inside.

The unpleasantness of her encounter with Leo fades before the scene that welcomes her to the studio. If anything, the surroundings shed a new light on all the good things that come with Alexandra D. Graff.

The light from the spots on the ceiling is soft and nearly dwarfed by the fire visible through the small furnace door. It's enough to bathe Alexandra in a glow; she seems lost in her own world, hips moving to the beat of the music from a hidden system while her upper body is completely focused on the task at hand. Sunglasses protect her eyes.

On a marble table are two translucent, heavy-looking blocks, . They must be perfectly polished glass. Alexandra rolls molten glass over one of them with her pipe. Halina can almost believe Alexandra handles lava. Her face glows, and the sweat and light from the molten glass turn her into a magical creature from Halina's childhood tales.

Here stands the woman Halina has discovered over the months and, yes, has come to love. To the outside world, to anyone not paying close attention, Alexandra Graff may seem curve and softness incarnate, but that appearance hides so much more. By now, Halina has learned of the strength under it all, the unstoppable force animating every soft curve. More than Alexandra's prowess in bed, beyond the curiosity she's created in Halina's heart, Alexandra has attracted Halina with her contradictions and made her fall in love with her.

When did that happen?

Why am I not only not *scared by it, but drawn to it?*

Leo walks faster, bringing a string of mini-lights from another table as he approaches Alexandra. As much as it pains Halina to admit it, they work beautifully together. The perfect choreography of their movements reminds her of Halina's duet with Lang Jian.

Alexandra rolls the heated glass on top of one cube and follows each roll by carving into the surface with a small knife.

Halina steps closer. Alexandra has drawn a curved line in the softening surface of the glass.

Even in thick gloves, Leo's fingers move delicately to place the string of tiny lights in the crevice Alexandra carved.

Alexandra returns to the glory hole and puts the stick and the glob of glass back into the fire.

Halina can't take her eyes off Alexandra. Her face shines ethereally as she turns the pipe around; her arms and chest are covered by a layer of sweat, and her sunglasses surreally reflect the fire. Alexandra could be made of gold at this moment; Halina would love to start a cult devoted to her.

Leo moves to the other side of the table and crouches as he pulls on the two ends of the string. Alexandra returns; the glob of melted glass glows brighter, hotter too. Halina observes the way Alexandra rubs the cube in a methodical, back and forth motion, and how its surface takes on a softer appearance, briefly turning orange too.

The next instant, the pair springs into action at a pace Halina can't follow. Leo keeps the structure steady while Alexandra rubs her glob of light on the sides, leaving a trail of liquid glass on the line separating the two parts. It stays rough until she returns with a pair of tweezers and gently presses, smoothing it with one hand while she rubs a wet rag on it with the other. The process seems endless, and Halina must admire Leo's perfect stillness as Alexandra works on the massive, translucent monolith they've created.

Alexandra steps away to put her tools on another stone table. She pushes the sunglasses on top of her sweaty curls. Leo relaxes, once again crouching slightly as he slowly turns the piece around.

"It's not perfect," Alexandra muses with a disappointed twist to her mouth. "But it's a good start. Hi, there," she adds, turning to Halina with a radiant smile.

"Hi," Halina replies, slightly breathless, even though she did nothing but stare and try to make sense of the mastery in front of her eyes. She gathers her wits while Alexandra takes a Polaroid of the piece, then leaves Leo with the camera. "It—you were... wow."

Alexandra exudes pride as she wipes her face with a clean cloth. "I'd kiss you," she tells Halina, "but I'm all sweaty and smelly. Give me a minute to freshen up?"

"Of course," Halina says, still gobsmacked, her eyes fixed on Alexandra as she leaves the room.

"She's a goddess," Leo says softly as he takes several other Polaroid pictures of the final product.

"She is. A modern Perun."

"And you don't deserve her."

"You don't deserve her either."

"Oh, I'm aware." Leo stays silent, eyeing the new piece of art before using a switch to turn it on. The small lamps glow from within. "Are you?"

* * *

ALEXANDRA HAS BEEN TENSE FOR a couple of days, and Halina might know why, if her calculations are correct: pre-period jitters, the limbo of hormones whipping a frenzy through the body, that time when it's difficult to decide whether one is hungry or horny, tired or excited, emotional or hormonal, or all of these at once.

But to be the partner of someone who goes through such a turmoil? It's all so new, being in a relationship, and Halina wants to make it last.

It would be so stupid to throw away what is burgeoning between them just because of some frayed nerves.

When she gets to the apartment and rings the doorbell, the sounds of Punshki's claws on the wood floor and Alexandra's soft footsteps come to greet her.

"Good evening, słoneczna," she says as Alexandra opens the door. Alexandra's face shows exhaustion; she keeps one hand on the side of the door and the other cups one of her breasts.

Lucky her.

"Ow."

"So bad?" She detours to the kitchen to leave the bottle of wine she brought, then joins Alexandra in the living room.

Halina spares a moment to pat the excitable corgi's head. But her attention quickly reverts to Punshki's owner, the woman who single-handedly changed her opinion on romance. "Want me to make it better?"

She gently, innocently even, puts her hand on Alexandra's knee, then waits for her reaction. Alexandra's gray eyes turn stormy, and the smile she gives Halina shows such hunger that Halina's body warms in response. Pavlov's bell has nothing on Alexandra Graff's ability to cause arousal.

"Punshki, basket," Alexandra orders in reply. Without missing a beat, the pudgy dog is in his cradle, his furry butt turned to them, his tail wrapped around the edge of the basket in protest.

Halina doesn't waste time putting her hands around Alexandra's breasts and massaging them to relieve some of the pressure, but the moan from Alexandra is not one of pleasure.

"Owww," she whines, and Halina quickly adjusts the pressure she exerts on the soft flesh to small soothing circles.

Note to self: handle Alexandra's body as if it's a Chopin piece, not a Bartók: all smooth strokes and no intense pressures.

Alexandra's face relaxes, her eyes flutter shut, and that is more rewarding than any prize or trophy Halina ever received.

"Yeah, mmm, like that, it's just perfect," Alexandra murmurs as she twists her body to lean more completely into Halina's touch. She bends one leg at the knee, then moves in for a kiss.

Halina is only too happy to follow Alexandra's lead. "What do you need from me, słoneczna?" she asks, trailing her lips down Alexandra's chin to the junction of jaw and neck. The spot never fails to make Alexandra utter a high-pitched moan Halina wants to translate into a piano piece someday.

"Yesss," Alexandra hisses, straddling Halina's legs and pushing her to a reclining position against the couch.

Halina doesn't think she could ever be bored with Alexandra snuggled against her; her smaller, fuller body is just so damn fuckable. She is addicted to the way Alexandra's darker skin looks against Halina's own paleness. Halina can't have enough, either, of Alexandra's softness, of how her body follows Halina's silent commands the way keys obey her fingers.

It's time to make some silent music.

Keeping one hand on the small of Alexandra's back, Halina slides her hand from Alexandra's breast down to her stomach and the waistband of her yoga pants, then trails her fingers over the inseam.

"So warm," she marvels quietly, her voice dropped to a purr. She tilts her head to access Alexandra's neck and sucks on the soft skin of her throat. "So wet, I can tell; all for me?"

"Ngh," is Alexandra's very articulate reply as she rocks her hips against Halina's touch. "Y-yeah, for you. Shit, babe, you got it, hmm…"

The use of the endearment awakens something warm and possessive in Halina's gut. She starts playing a tune against Alexandra's covered crotch and laughs internally at herself when she recognizes what her fingers are doing: Bach, how appropriate, "Jesu, Joy of Man's Desiring." She alternates between kissing and sucking on Alexandra's throat. "My słoneczna," she whispers in Alexandra's ear, sucking on the lobe, "so needy, so insatiable. I'm sure you'd love someone else to join us, wouldn't you, hmm…"

Halina only means to tease Alexandra as foreplay before going down on her and maybe having Alexandra reciprocate, maybe, afterward, drinking some wine and settling down to bask in the afterglow with a good dinner and a movie…

She doesn't expect Alexandra to freeze and lean back to glare at Halina, a very different storm in her eyes: a hurricane with the strength to destroy everything in its path.

"What is that supposed to mean?" Alexandra snarls as she stands and adjusts her shirt. She brushes her dark curls away from her face, but they bounce back.

Halina sits up stiffly. "I only meant that you are—you were—horny." Her voice lifts into a question as her defensive walls rise.

"Uh huh." Alexandra frowns. "So this had nothing to do with what you think of me?"

"What I think of you?"

"Your perpetual condemnation, how I can't be trusted? How you had to lower your standards to put up with our relationship? Pick one."

"I do trust you, Xandra! I don't judge you for dating men in the past; you probably didn't know better. But do you expect me for one second to go through so much hormonal shit for someone I don't trust, someone I don't care about?" Halina jumps to her feet, wincing as the words replay in her mind. She regrets the sentence even before she finishes it, but there is nothing she can do to take it back now.

Hands on her hips, Alexandra suddenly seems much taller than her five-and-a-bit feet. She's formidable in her anger, and Halina is both frightened and aroused.

"Well, excuse me, Miss Perfect Golden Lesbian." Alexandra is seething. "Excuse me for being a fat, temperamental, greedy bitch!"

"Xandra…"

"And while we're at it, excuse me for being too enthusiastic about too many things and excuse me for having my own priorities, for not worshipping the very ground you deign to float upon!"

"Alexandra, I never—" Halina tries to cut into Alexandra's rant, but there is no way to stop her now.

They have a good thing going, but now it is clear Alexandra has more insecurities and grievances than she let on. As Alexandra catches her breath, Halina tries to reason with her. "I never said I wanted you to worship me."

"But you *would* be more comfortable if I were a perfect lesbian," Alexandra retorts, eyes piercing, unforgivingly so. Halina has never found her more beautiful.

"Do I wish I didn't have to compete for your attention?" she replies, letting her own worries out of the bag. "Do I feel like I will never be able to trust you not to cheat on me? Do I wish fucking Leo wasn't still in your life, in more ways than you let on? Of course I do!"

Alexandra rolls her eyes, dismissive and condescending, and Halina's own temper rises to match hers. "But it would be the same with any of your exes, with anyone who mattered for you before me," she insists. Deep down, she knows she's lying. After all, they met because of one of Alexandra's exes, and Halina never spared a thought for her or any other woman.

She quickly pushes the little voice to a more remote part of her mind, because now is not the time to admit that Alexandra might be right.

"Would you, though? Be more comfortable?"

Damn her for seeing right through me. Halina twists her hair into a messy bun on top of her head. "Listen, I have had some… difficulties, okay, accepting your orientation and what it could do to us, but you're impugning my motive here, and—"

"I don't want you to accept me, Halina," Alexandra replies, her shoulders sagging as her eyes leave Halina's. "I just need you to love me as I am, not as you want me to be."

"I meant…"

"It's time for you to go."

"You can't be serious right now!"

"I may be impaired by my hormones," Alexandra squares her shoulders, voice filled with irritation, "but I am fully capable of making a decision to ensure my well-being, and right now…" She pauses to take a deep breath. "…I need you to fuck off."

"Xandra," Halina begs as she picks up her bag from the corner where she left it, "we need to talk this through, please?"

Alexandra takes another deep breath and then hugs herself. "I think we both need some time to get a hold on ourselves and figure out what we want."

"There's no n—" Halina starts, but she chokes on the end of her sentence.

Alexandra cocks her head. "See?" She opens the door. "We can definitely use some time apart to clear things up." She stops, biting on her lower lip. "Once and for all."

"Once and for a—are you breaking up with me?" Halina asks, shocked by the fragility she hears in her voice and even more shocked at how much the idea of Alexandra finding their coda in this fight troubles her.

"No, Halina," Alexandra replies, some of her usual softness returning to her voice, "I'm saying we need a break to find out if we're what the other needs."

It's hard to breathe, and tears build in her eyes. Halina doesn't want to cry on Alexandra's doorstep, not when she hasn't let herself cry in so many years. She clearly fucked up long before Alexandra lashed out; what happened tonight brought it all to light. Tears won't help them, not in their respective states of mind. So she swallows the tears and the sob and squeezes Alexandra's wrist on her way out. She is relieved that Alexandra doesn't recoil from her touch.

Small mercies.

"I—um, I brought a bottle of wine, it's in the kitchen," she says softly, voice barely above a whisper. "And… um, call me?"

Alexandra's eyes shine in the soft light of the lamp above the elevator door as she gives her a curt nod. "I will," she replies, glancing up only once before she closes the door.

Halina, alone with her thoughts and her questions, has only one certainty. Alexandra will call her, because her girlfriend has never lied to her, not once since they met. Why did Halina doubt her in the first place?

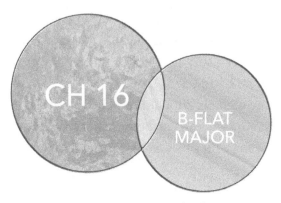

Brown, Orange, and Lilac

THE MIRRORED WALLS OF THE hotel elevator show a woman who is tired. Alexandra needed three days apart to stop aching, to mend her cracked heart while her mind replayed the whole evening.

She sees now that her temper had taken over, and she'd let all the uncertainties she had about her and Halina boil into a maelstrom of emotions that made almost no sense when it came out. But her anger was genuine, as was the pain Halina's words had elicited—words Alexandra has had to deal with since she came out.

The prejudice against bisexuals, especially women, is strong, in both the straight and the gay communities; but until now, it had never been used against her by someone she was dating. Not even Leo had mentioned it while they were together.

Other times she and Halina spent together replay in her mind, and Alexandra closes her eyes to focus on the moment they are in now. It's more important than their willingness to build a relationship, more important even than discovering each other. This moment, the now, will determine if there is still a chance for a "them" at all.

Stepping into the room is harder than she thought it would be, but Alexandra puts her fears aside to enter the ring ready for battle.

"I'm glad you came." Halina offers a glass of something glowing amber, but she refuses it. She'd rather keep a clear head.

"I said I would, didn't I?"

"You did." Halina exhales shakily. "I want to tell you I'm sorry." Halina's words trip over each other in her hurry to get them out. "And I won't let it happen again."

"How can I be sure you won't..." Alexandra's words die on her lips; anger and disappointment are still fresh and bitter. She swallows them and glares at Halina.

Alexandra was prepared for a confrontation, for Halina to be defensive and harsh, for an opportunity to unleash her resentment. She is unprepared for Halina to be contrite and apologetic as a misbehaving child who is aware she has done something wrong but can't, in her self-centered ignorance, figure out what.

If Halina truly understood what was wrong in what she did, what she said, if her apology was sincere and complete, Alexandra would be in her arms in a heartbeat for a hot, sweaty, debauched reconciliation on the fluffy pillows sitting on Halina's bed. But as it is, Halina's confused frown is all Alexandra needs to clarify the mess they're in. While her girlfriend is obviously aware she made a mistake, she doesn't understand the gravity of the situation.

Time to enlighten her, then.

God, if she could borrow just some of Liz's diplomatic talent.

"What you said," she starts all over again, slowly, taking deep breaths to calm herself, "was hurtful, Halina."

"I didn't mean to hurt you," Halina replies, wringing her hands in front of her.

"Whether you meant to hurt me or not, your intent has little to no importance when it did wound me," Alexandra insists, "and it was insulting. I may have overreacted, sure, but the basis of it all stands."

"I'm sorry," Halina replies, hands flailing in a definitely uncharacteristic fashion, "I'm sorry if I hurt you. I'm sorry I don't even—" She pauses to take a deep, shaky breath, and Alexandra is shocked to see tears in her eyes. "I'm sorry I can't even find what I said that set you off, what I did when all I want is for us to work for what we could be if you gave me a chance..."

Alexandra's first instinct screams at her to take Halina in her arms. After all, this is what she wanted to hear, desperately so, no matter what she claimed and wanted others to believe. Halina's confession that they share more than a superficial attraction, more than a very beneficial friendship, is all Alexandra could ask for, even though she hadn't put it into words for herself.

But for once in her life, Alexandra listens not to her heart, but to her brain. Her brain is telling her to go through with this not-fight, this discussion, to secure a more balanced basis for them to get back together.

"What you did, babe," she explains, her voice soft, "is use my past, my sex life, as a weapon against me."

"Not a weapon," Halina protests, but her voice is soft too.

The quiet turn the discussion has taken lets the sounds from outside vibrate within Halina's room. The ding of the hotel elevator, the roar of a couple of cars, the babble of an indistinguishable conversation: all these noises are yellow, wiggly lines, stark against the dark gray of heavy silence stretched between them.

"You used my sex life against me," Alexandra repeats, willing to amend her choice of words if it allows her to convey her thoughts to Halina. "You still consider my past relationships, with men at least, as some temporary lapse of judgment, a flaw you would generously gloss over, forgive, and move on."

"I'm sure there are some things in me you don't find attractive and yet accept," Halina replies, "such as my temper or my selfishness."

Alexandra groans; a wordless scream is on the tip of her tongue. "No! Right there!" she exclaims, walking in circles on her side of the room. The impression of entering a battle is back, more present than it ever was. "That's what I meant! Me being bi is not a flaw of character I could work on if I applied myself and made a little effort!"

Halina remains silent; her whole demeanor is the epitome of hostility. Nevertheless, her silence is proof she's still listening.

Thank God for small mercies.

"The only thing I could use against you the way you have used my bisexuality…" Alexandra's voice is back to its normal volume as she tries to find the proper argument to make Halina understand. "…would be to remind you how much of a slut you have been."

Halina's reaction is immediate. Her hands close into fists as the apples of her cheeks turn bright red: exactly the reaction Alexandra was expecting, as if Alexandra just slapped her.

"What does it have to do with you dating men? I'm not that person anymore; you can't doubt it."

"You see my point, then."

"What point?"

Alexandra's shoulders sag as she feels the will to fight drain out of her. She must continue, though not against Halina—quite the contrary, for both of them.

"The past," Alexandra says softly, with her chin dropped to her chest and her emotions back under control. "What both arguments have in common: the past. I used to have sex with men before you, you used to have casual sex with many women before me, yeah, but it's… in the past," she adds with a gesture as if to brush all of it away. Tilting her head to find Halina's eyes, Alexandra takes a deep breath, hoping her voice won't shake. "And as for who I may date if we go our separate ways… it shouldn't matter."

"It doesn't."

"As long as it comes back in a discussion, fight or otherwise," Alexandra exclaims, all of her emotions boiling over, as quick as milk from a forgotten pan on the stove, "it clearly matters and my bisexuality should. Not. Matter."

She punctuates every word with a clap of her hands, and the last one rings between them, highlighting the silence that once again suddenly stretches over the room, deep as molasses and just as dark.

"The only fact that matters, Lina," she says softly, "is that we love each other and we stay faithful to that."

It's the first time she has used the "L" word. What a moment to cross that threshold!

Halina nods; she keeps her eyes glued to her feet until Alexandra's phone beeps a familiar melody. She takes it out of her pocket to make it stop. Halina queasily considers the device.

"Do you—do you have to go?" she asks, her voice small and more fragile than Alexandra expected.

"Punshki," she replies. "I have to take care of him, walk him, and give him his pills."

"Of course," Halina says sincerely.

From anybody else, the two words might have been laced with malicious intent, but Halina's concern for her furry companion is genuine. Good God, she loves her, flaws and incomprehension and all.

Oy vey.

"Can we—" Halina starts, wringing her hands around the hem of her top. "Can we talk? Tomorrow? After you're done with your work, after my rehearsals are complete. Can we talk some more? Please?"

"Sure."

"See you tomorrow, Xandra. Go home safely."

"Good night, Lina."

*   *   *

THE FOLLOWING DAY IS FILLED with jitters and nerves, and Halina is completely unable to focus. She loses her temper at Ari, who remains mysteriously out of her sight for the rest of the morning. They don't speak more than three words to her when they return. If this is what Love, actual Love, capital L, does to a person, she's glad she didn't have to deal with it before. It's messy and complicated and it's interfering with her true purpose in life; it keeps her from connecting with the music.

Her brain disputes that statement. If anything, Alexandra's presence in her life has brought a new dimension to her music, to her way of feeling the notes: a new depth and more emotion. Sure, it is difficult to focus on the sheet music when the only things Halina wants to read are Alexandra's laugh lines and the variations in the gray of her eyes. But when her mind focuses on meeting with Alexandra later, Halina feels a weird sensation, a mixture of excitement and peace that is more difficult to understand than any thought.

In a way, they're worth it, all the difficulties they face, when she weighs them against all that Alexandra has brought to her life. How ridiculous: It's worth it, worth fighting for, and Halina was stupid to let Leonardo Neri slither his way into her head and between the two of them.

"All right," the maestro calls, tapping his baton against the rostrum. "One last time for today, if you will. Miss Piotrowski, whenever you're ready."

The tone is both judgmental and condescending, but Halina is not surprised. It's common knowledge that the guest conductor has a special place in his heart for Prokofiev. He must resent Halina for not giving her all to a work by the Russian composer.

Halina bows her head with her hands paused above the keyboard. The whole orchestra is here, though the concerto doesn't require it; the conductor obviously wants to go with a symphonic interpretation. Now she has pulled herself together and shelved all the things she wants to say to Alexandra in the storeroom of her mind. Now she's ready.

Halina listens to the vivacious beginning of the first movement and closes her eyes to let it carry her through the quick pace of the composition. That's where she's been wrong all day, wasting their time with her personal block: She thought too hard about it and forgot that the music plays her as much as she plays it.

The flutes, oboes, and violins take over, and Halina sits up, getting ready to get back into the melody. From the corner of her eye, she catches the collective breath of relief exhaled by the orchestra when the maestro keeps them going, finally satisfied with Halina's performance.

DURING HER BREAK, HALINA PONDERS the epiphany she just had and how it can translate to the mess with Alexandra. Maybe it's the same problem, because she has the same issues with her professional and personal lives. Maybe it's the same solution too: She needs to learn to let go and stop blowing everything out of proportion. She stopped assuming the maestro worked against her; she trusted him to be there with her and the whole group with him. Now, if she were to apply that to her current situation with one glass artist...

Her hands return to the keys and she touches them lightly, playfully, to match the circular melody Prokofiev wrote all those years ago. Halina closes her eyes once again.

How will it look through Alexandra's synesthesia?

The thought lingers; it's been present ever since she discovered Alexandra's peculiar relationship with music, and Halina is glad when the bassoons play. Their astounding sound is what she needs to silence her brain.

Whatever the outcome, there is a piece of music she wants to play for Alexandra; whether it will be an apology or a farewell is yet to be decided.

*　　*　　*

"YOU TOLD HER WHAT?"

The music on the radio fits Alexandra's mood quite well, as the electropop at the top of the charts translates perfectly what brews in the studio: swirls of reds and light-green sparks build her increasing belligerence. Something Halina said about Alexandra and Leo's relationship didn't sit well with her and, if she's not mistaken, Mr. Neri must have tried to play a dirty trick.

"Not only did I tell her to fuck off, but I'm glad I did it, too."

"What do you mean, you're glad you did it?" she shouts as Leo turns the LEDs on and off.

Their innovation at the Philharmonie has been the talk of the art world, in Paris and beyond. Since then, they've received many commissions asking for similar installations. Their latest contract takes them to the Place des Vosges, across the square from Halina's hotel, and their client is none other than one of the last Ashkenazi synagogues in Paris, which brings back a lot of unnecessary memories for Alexandra.

As if I needed more layers of emotion and complication.

Right now, the empty frame that will hold the *mekhitsa*, a folding screen that will separate men and women during prayers, stands in the middle of the studio, a welcome physical boundary between her and Leo. Alexandra needs to remember it's a blowtorch she's holding before she throws it at Leo's stubborn head.

He raises his eyebrows, all casual nonchalance and not a regret in sight. She could smack that expression off his face if she didn't want to get some answers first.

"I repeat and I'll repeat it as many times as needed." He moves on to test another display, and the flickers of light make Alexandra lose her grip. "I'm glad I told your precious ivory tickler that she didn't deserve you and that you were destined to come back to me."

"Have you lost your mind?" she says, crossing the studio to pull on his shirt and force him to face her. "One, I, and I alone, decide who deserves to be with me. Get that into your pea brain."

Leo twists his mouth, his jaw tight.

"Two, and I think this needs to be the most important thing: you and I? It's over. We're friends now." She pauses, letting him go as she takes a shaky breath. "Or so I thought."

This seems to rattle some sense into him. Leo stops playing with the LED's commands. "Of course we're friends," he replies, his hand outstretched, but Alexandra can't help taking a step back, away from his touch. "But we're more than that. Always will be."

"No, we're not! Sure, while we were both single, it was fun to... mess around—"

"We do have fantastic chemistry in bed."

"Not the point," Alexandra says in her firmest voice. "As compatible as we may have been, it's nothing compared to how happy Halina makes me; you have to see it. Can you tell me that you could give me that? A commitment, a relationship, something I could build a future on?"

Various emotions pass in Leo's eyes, ending with pain and bitterness. "What future? She will leave at the end of the season, or did you neatly put that away from your mind?" Leo's snarled words are a knife in Alexandra's heart; she doesn't need to be reminded of the rapidly approaching expiration date stamped on their relationship. "Did you convince yourself that she would leave a world of spotlights and fame to stay here with you and ride into the sunset, happy endings for everybody?"

"No matter how short-lived it will be, it's still a future. Would you rather have me throw away months of possible happiness on the off-chance that you convinced yourself we belong together? After what you did? After, in case you need the reminder, you slept with someone else because you didn't think we were dating because, and I quote, relationships are a scam?"

Leo opens and closes his mouth before bowing his head, eyes closed. "I could not promise you anything," he finally replies, voice cracking in ways Alexandra never imagined from him; dark shadows appear in his usual russet tone. "But I can't lose you."

"You're not," Alexandra replies instinctively before remembering that Leo did try to make her break up with her girlfriend. "Well, it will take me a while to forgive you, but the studio and our friendship mean too much to me to lose them over your stupidity."

Leo smiles sadly at her. He offers his hand as an olive branch of sorts and covers his heart with his other hand, and she slides the tips of her fingers twice against his palm, signaling.

Apology accepted.

"What are you going to do now?" Leo asks timidly, as he returns to work.

Alexandra sighs, pushing a strand of hair from her eyes as she returns to her workstation. "Halina wants to talk to me once the rehearsal is over today, and I really, really want to make it all better," she adds in a slightly whiny tone. "She understands where she went wrong, and I admit I have my own faults in this mess too, and—" She pauses with a sigh. "It shouldn't be so complicated, should it?"

Leo snorts before giving her a pointed look. "Would it truly be love if it wasn't complicated?" Sadness lingers on his face until he shakes it off. "We were always easy, you and me. That's why it didn't last."

"But our friendship is complicated."

"Because it's true."

Alexandra mulls over his words and raises her eyebrows. "Why, Mister Neri, when did you become so wise?"

"It's the beard," Leo replies immediately, petting his precious goatee. "It must have given my brain a boost."

Alexandra rolls her eyes at him. "Su-ure," she comments, elongating the vowel. "Let's go with that."

"Seriously, though," Leo tells her, "as much as I don't want to admit it, you two deserve to work it out." He sighs, loudly, keeping his eyes firmly on his work as he adds foam to a joint to secure it. "She—Halina, she's good for your art. For you."

Alexandra looks down as her cheeks heat up. "You think so?"

Leo picks up the iPad they use to take all their professional pictures. "Lexie," he calls. On the screen is the Philharmonie's central window, inspired by Halina, by her talent shown at the very first encounter between them.

"I know so," Leo says, and Alexandra smiles at him and at the window. "Look at that: Your work is always good, but it never found that balance between movement and stillness before."

Alexandra observes her own work. She conceptualized it, but the physical result, once each panel is sealed and bolted, always differs from her sketches. The truth in Leo's words becomes clearer when she is face to face with a picture.

"She will always be the one who stole you from me, but I can't deny that she's *una vera e propria musa*."

The colors, muted in places and vibrant in others, seem to be alive. The LED highlights it, but it shows more than how Alexandra infused the glass with some of her soul. The fragile material translated the vibration of the place, while also giving the onlooker a sense of peace.

"All right, then," she says, voice hoarse as tears gather at the corner of her eyes.

* * *

THE ORCHESTRA PLAYS UNTIL THE maestro leaves them to their own devices, and Halina turns to her fellow musicians.

"Hey, guys," she says, forcing the words out. "Can you please teach me how not to strangle him when he gets that—eurgh?"

The warmth extended to her when she asks for help is something that's been lacking for a good portion of the past months. Maybe all it takes for the other musicians to warm up to her is her showing that she has flaws and fragilities too. That she is human after all.

Some laugh and shrug, some give her tips about dealing with ego-hungry maestros. Halina stays at the piano to embrace her new appreciation for instinctive playing. She always knew that jazz worked for her, after all.

Ari comes by to check on her and they seem surprised by how drastically her mood has changed.

"I'm sorry," Halina says, stopping her improvisations to face them.

Ari raises one eyebrow and sits next to her. "It's not the first time I've turned into your human stress-relief ball," they finally say, "and I don't mind. If that's my contribution to your greatness..."

"Oh, Ari," Halina whispers as she pulls them into a quick hug, "you're not my emotional punching bag. You're my friend, and I shouldn't have treated you that way."

Ari tentatively returns the hug before they face the other way to avoid her gaze; their ears turn bright pink. "As long as you don't do it too often. Um… anyway, are you—are you ready to go?"

Halina looks back at the keys. "I'm waiting for Alexandra."

Ari starts to roll their eyes, but they quickly cover it when she frowns. "Will you stay at her place tonight?" they ask, and the unspoken "again" is not lost on Halina.

"We need to talk," she replies slowly, "figure things out. But no, I don't believe I'll spend the evening with her. Consider me as free as a bird."

Ari brightens up instantly, and Halina lets a new wave of guilt sweep through her. She has been a bad friend, in addition to a poor excuse for a boss, because of her inability to focus on two things at once. After all, it must have been difficult for them, too, this move to a new country, finding their own bearings, making new friends, and handling all the difficulties that go hand in hand with their responsibilities as Halina's assistant.

"What about dinner tonight, just the two of us?" she offers, spinning around on the bench to sit on it cross-legged. "That is, if you're not too busy with Mr. Green Eyes and Hard Muscles…"

Ari blushes and focuses on putting a strand of hair behind their ear. "Oh. So you noticed him, uh?"

"Pretty hard to miss."

"Pretty, period. But no," they add with a knowing air, "I am not constantly kept busy by a new beau."

"All right. What about the place near the Louvre?"

"The sushi with the conveyor belt?" Ari supplies with a beaming smile and clapping hands. "I loved it, yes, that's awesome!"

Halina gently pats their cheek. "Deal."

"Deal."

"You're more excited about sushi than by your own sexcapades."

"It's sex; it's good, nothing to write home about, though, can you imagine?" they snicker. "Sex is fleeting. Food, on the other hand …"

Ari sighs happily, leaning against on the piano as if the ellipsis contains all the answers. "And what will you do about Alexandra?"

"Fix things," Halina replies, with more confidence in her voice than she feels deep down.

Ari hums, their fingers on a couple of keys. "Playing devil's advocate here," they say carefully, "but why do you want to fix that relationship? It's not as if you can't find someone else to be your playmate."

"I could, but I don't—I don't want that," she says, voice shaking a little with the strength of her emotions. "I tried, but I am sure of what I want—I… I want Alexandra. I want a relationship, a girlfriend, for better or for worse and all that jazz, and Alexandra is the right one for me."

Ari laughs. "All right, all right, boss," they reply, "I just pointed out that you have options."

"Of course I have them," Halina says, shaking her head to free her hair from the messy bun she's kept it in all day, "but I don't want them, I want—"

"I got it, you want Alexandra," Ari cuts her off, this time openly rolling their eyes at her. "Never thought I'd see you lovesick."

"First time for everything."

"Please tell me you're not about to try dicks too."

"Don't be ridiculous."

"One thing at a time?" Ari teases as they stand up. "First love, and maybe…"

"Hmm, it doesn't seem very plausible."

"You didn't say impossible."

Halina can't help but laugh. "Last time I checked, bisexuality is not some transmittable disease."

"No, it isn't."

They both startle, surprised by Alexandra's arrival through the backstage door. She walks in, her head tipped toward Ari. "Mx. Fowler," she greets them, and Ari's eyes widen at the title, their whole attitude softened.

"Miss Graff," they reply, mirroring. "I'll leave you two alone. See you later, boss."

"See you later, Ari," Halina replies, then focuses on Alexandra. "Hey."

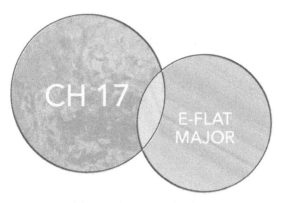

CH 17

E-FLAT MAJOR

Gold, Cranberry, and Glaucous

ALEXANDRA'S OUTFIT IS NOTHING SPECTACULAR—SKINNY jeans and a long, soft sweater—but Halina can tell Alexandra made an effort for her. It reminds Halina of the outfit she wore when she decided to apologize and give her relationship with Alexandra a chance, back in November. Things have come full circle, perhaps? That would be all the more reason to make sure this conversation goes the right way.

"Hey." Alexandra puts her bag on the concertmaster's chair. "How was your day?"

"Trying," Halina replies, "but good, eventually. Yours?"

"Same: lots of work, between the synagogue and the backlog of online orders, lights tests, and a fight with Leo," Alexandra replies in one breath with a tired smile. "We can talk about it all later—if you want, that is."

"I will—I do," Halina says softly, her hands on her lap to calm her nerves.

"I'm sorry."

That tears her eyes from her hands and the shimmer of her dress. "Pardon?"

Alexandra sits on the chair closest to Halina's bench. "I owe you an apology." She adjusts a curl behind her ear. She lets her fingers linger on her neck, then starts again. "I want this," she continues, gesturing between them, "to work, and for that, we need to communicate."

"Yes," Halina says, stunned by this turn of events. She is more than happy, she's ecstatic, to hear that Alexandra wants to keep their relationship going, especially because the little voice of doubt in the back of her head hadn't believed that would happen.

"And for that, I need to let you find your words and express what you mean," Alexandra says with a sad frown. "And I didn't, when—"

"When," Halina cuts her off; she doesn't need the reminder. "But I owe you an apology too."

Alexandra simply sits back in her chair to give Halina the floor.

Halina takes a deep breath and scoots the bench closer until their knees brush. "I let my fears and prejudice blind me, and in the process, I hurt you. And I'm sorry," she says slowly, to give the words she painstakingly put together the impact she aims for. "It was never my intention to hurt you or what we have. But I did. I never want to cause you pain and I can't promise it won't happen again, just like you can't promise me you won't ever say something unintentionally unkind either. But," she adds, holding one hand out, hoping Alexandra will take it, "I promise to try. For us."

Slowly, Alexandra's face lightens, and she quickly, unexpectedly, brushes her fingertips along Halina's palm, twice, before she wraps her hand around it. The gesture must have a deeper meaning, one Halina doesn't get. She doesn't need an exact translation, though: she can read the emotions in Alexandra's eyes. For now, she's relieved to feel Alexandra's warmth around her hand, to bask in Alexandra's happiness, to have Alexandra by her side.

"I wanted—" she starts, her cheeks heating up in, in all likelihood, a blotchy shade of pink, "I want to play you something that reminds me of you, of us, and has for a while. I still, I mean, I still have trouble finding the proper words, but music—music always conveys what I mean more efficiently."

"What if I had said I wanted to stay friends?" Alexandra asks as she lets go of Halina's hand to stand by the piano.

Halina glances at her sideways and shrugs dejectedly. "It would still have been my parting gift," she replies softly. "Just because you wouldn't return my affections, wouldn't make them disappear."

Alexandra rests her chin on the nest of her arms as she leans on the lid of the piano. "Play me your... affections, then," she replies, her tone matching Halina's.

The notes are delicate under her fingers, the way she would translate her mended relationship with Alexandra. She plays around with the original score; the melody is her familiar guilty pleasure. Alexandra might not recognize it, but that's okay. Besides, she has learned never to assume anything when it comes to her girlfriend.

It takes her a moment, but Alexandra can't shake the impression that she should recognize the music Halina plays. It's familiar enough, something half-heard on the radio while she does something else. She listens intently, knowing her synesthesia will help, and that's how she recognizes it; the colors are slightly different than they are for the original song. It takes a lot of control not to launch herself at Halina and kiss the daylights out of her.

"I never thought you would enjoy that musical genre."

Halina sniffs haughtily as she keeps playing the melody, with more variations and harmonies added as she goes. "Just because I'm a world-renowned, classically-trained pianist doesn't mean that I can't appreciate pop music."

Alexandra laughs and leans over the piano, arching her back to showcase her butt. "I didn't say a word, just... One Direction, really?"

A blush spreads on Halina's cheeks and, once again, Alexandra is reminded of her grandmother's porcelain doll, in her white dress, with the two pink spots painted on her flawless face. "I confess," Halina says, taking her eyes from the keys to focus on her, "I find boy bands quite enjoyable."

"All boy bands?"

"Boże, no, just the ones with pretty songs."

"Pretty songs, huh?"

Halina stops playing and frowns at Alexandra, though her affected anger is quickly belied by her smile and the kiss she blows at Alexandra. "Xandra, are you mocking me?"

"Maybe just a bit." Alexandra giggles. "But keep playing; it is pretty."

Halina resumes playing, and the notes turn softer: fewer reds and purples and sharp angles and rounder, more comforting greens with soft lilac and magenta interlaced in the background.

"You switched, didn't you?"

"Mm hmm."

"Which composer is it?" she asks, mumbling against her forearm, but Halina hears her well enough.

"Moritz Moszkowski."

"Hmm?"

Halina takes her eyes off the keys, and Alexandra doesn't look away. She doesn't want to break the moment, surrounded as she is by the echo of Halina's music—of Halina's affections, as she put it so succinctly.

Halina's eyes have a focus that wasn't there before, and she suddenly stops playing. She slides from the bench to the floor, with her hand wrapped around Alexandra's, until she kneels beside her.

"Follow me," she says, letting go to gently put her hands on Alexandra's shoulders and push her under the piano.

"Now who is a potential serial killer?"

Alexandra's eyes adapt to the darkness, but all she sees is Halina on her side under the piano. "What are we doing here?"

"Listening to the music."

Alexandra frowns and scoots closer to Halina until the faint glow from the exit sign outlines her features in the darkness. "What music?"

Halina lightly puts her fingers over Alexandra's mouth. "Just listen."

Alexandra kisses the tips of Halina's fingers, the very fingers she fell in love with in the first place. For once in her life, she tries to stay quiet and still. It's harder than it seems, though—under the piano, every breath makes as much noise as the entire brass section.

"You think too loudly, słoneczna," Halina whispers with laughter in her voice: a deep, vibrant purple on the margins and Halina's usual peach in its center. "Come here."

Halina's hands cup the back of Alexandra's head and pull her closer so her head is nestled against Halina's chest.

The velvet of Halina's black dress makes dull little noises under Alexandra's ear: golden ochre crossing black. She closes her eyes, keeping her hand on the groove of Halina's waist, letting Halina's heartbeat calm her. That sound is the background: strong, deep-blue pulsing in the middle. As the noises from the velvet create lines, the earthy tones fade into the blue.

Alexandra smiles against Halina's chest. Her fingers are tight around the curve of Halina's hip.

"Do you hear it now?"

Halina's voice echoes against Alexandra's face. "I can see it now," she replies, and Halina's fingers plunge deeper into her hair.

She makes an inquisitive noise, and Alexandra tilts her head to rub the tip of her nose against Halina's. "If only I could show you the colors you have brought into my life," she says softly. Her face feels warm. She fears she said too much too soon, but unlike other occasions, when Alexandra expressed her feelings and Halina froze, there is no sudden tension or awkwardness, only comfort and tenderness.

"You've brought new music to my life too," Halina whispers before she gives her a kiss that leaves Alexandra breathless and dizzy with happiness.

*　*　*

THE MOMENT HALINA PULLS OUT a chair next to Ari, they give her a long, sweeping glance and tsk.

"What?"

"It's spooky."

"What?"

"The look on your face," they reply with their chopsticks pointed at her. A piece of pickled ginger dangles from the chopsticks, and Halina bats at it before it can land on her. "It's as if you had plastic surgery, and it's etched there forever."

"Don't I ever smile?"

Ari returns their attention to their plate of spicy calamari salad, and Halina can't resist stealing a piece of it.

"You do," they reply finally, "but not usually so brightly—are you high?"

"No!"

"Sure?"

"Ari!"

"Okay, okay," they say, lifting their hands in surrender—and this time a piece of seaweed does fly. "Good for you; I assume the conversation went in the right direction?"

"It's not perfect yet," Halina replies as she removes the vegetables from her maki roll. "But it's... on track." Her cheeks are tight with the width of her smile.

"It's too much happiness for just one person," Ari comments, trying to appear superior and failing miserably while they pick at the vegetables on Halina's plate.

"You're one to talk," Halina replies, knocking Ari's elbow with her own. "Kettle, the pot called to get its black back. Don't think I haven't caught you strutting around the hotel lobby every other early morning when Mr. Green Eyes drops you off after a night of whatever it is you do with him."

Ari has the decency to blush, and keep from denying this. "It's simply postcoital ecstasy," they reply, sneering, "and I'm not limiting myself to one partner, thank you very much. And please tell me you didn't fuck her on the stage, the idea is just... ugh."

"First of all, I was serious. I need all the PG details of your adventures; it's been too long. Second of all, don't you dare pretend to be so disgusted, Mx. Permanently Banned from La Scala. And third of all, no, but it was even better."

"If you follow that up with 'we didn't fuck, we made love,' I'll throw this very expensive glass of sake at your head, job be damned."

"Wouldn't it be a waste," Halina says with a snort, pouring herself some of the sake from the amber bottle. "No, I'm not so bad just yet; can't wait to fuck her, though, now that you mention it…"

"Ugh."

"What?"

"I want to say 'TMI,'" Ari says with a smirk, "but it would be a bit hypocritical of me."

"Just a bit."

"Anyway—the infamous L word did come up, didn't it. You know what, don't answer, save your dignity."

"My dignity is very much intact. And so is my relationship; look at me go."

Ari dramatically shivers. "I'd rather not. And can you not use that word?"

"Re-la-tion-ship," Halina singsongs as she picks plates from the conveyor belt for them both.

"Ew."

"Commit-ment!"

"Gross."

"Monogamy."

"Oh, come on, Miss Piotrowski, this is not the place for such profanities."

A few patrons turn to glare at them while they laugh and giggle. Though she notices them, Halina can't bring herself to care.

*　　*　　*

THE HOTEL WHERE SARAL SET up their long-awaited appointment exudes luxury and invites her to just relax and enjoy the Parisian way of life, if only for a moment; Halina only sees her manager and the potential in their meeting.

"I got you a white tea," Saral says before she sits. "I remember how much you favor it."

"Thanks," Halina replies, playing with the end of her braid. "Have you spoken with Loupan yet?"

Saral raises his eyebrows and sits back in his chair to consider her. "Straight to business, as usual," he comments, before he pulls a handful of papers from his leather briefcase and slides them on the table toward her. "I did—along with the directors of several other orchestras in Europe and the Middle East."

Halina hums noncommittally as she peruses the different offers.

"They are all very good proposals, Lina," Saral says in a neutral tone. "Both for your reputation and for the environments they would provide."

"Paris isn't in here."

"Do me a favor," Saral insists. "Read them carefully, as objectively as you can."

"Saral, do *me* a favor and give me all the proposals and offers, and I promise to consider their merits before making a decision."

Saral sighs and pulls a sheet from his jacket's breast pocket. "All right."

"Any personal favorite?"

He lets out a deep laugh. "As if I'd tell you before you make your own decision."

"Fair enough."

* * *

TWO DAYS LATER, HALINA IS at Alexandra's door again. She hopes they've resolved the issues that led them to the bitterness of their last date night.

Her knock on the door is answered by the sounds of Punshki's nails against the floor and his owner's footsteps. Halina's smile widens when Alexandra opens the door.

"Where did you find such an apron?" Halina asks once she's out of her coat and had a welcoming peck on the lips.

Alexandra examines herself as if discovering her attire; Halina finds her expression adorable. "What, this?" Alexandra lifts the hem of a vintage red apron, complete with frills and lacy details. "One of my friends gave it to me as a joke, but it's great to keep clean while I'm cooking. Why, don't you like it?"

Halina wants to pull her into a passionate kiss just to show her how much she does like it, but the apron is covered in speckles of sauce she'd rather keep off of her own outfit.

"I adore it." Her fingers brush the ruffles on the sides. "Takes me back to one of those family shows from the fifties."

Alexandra strikes a pinup pose. "Make yourself comfortable, babe," she says, batting her eyelashes at Halina. "Dinner will be on the table in just a jiffy."

Halina follows Alexandra into the kitchen. Spices permeate the air and make her simultaneously hungry and sneezy.

"What did you cook?" she asks, standing behind Alexandra with one hand on her hip.

Alexandra shakes a pan filled with shiny carrots, thin asparagus, and cherry tomatoes, all roasted and caramelized. "I did say I would eventually cook you my famous rack of lamb," she replies with a wink thrown over her shoulder.

Halina opens her mouth to comment—

"Don't you dare mention another type of rack." Alexandra raises her wooden spoon in warning.

"Me? I wouldn't dare. Do you need any help?"

"Not really. But you can open the wine and pour two glasses of it to let it breathe."

Halina makes a jaunty salute before grabbing the bottle, along with the corkscrew that hangs on the wall with all Alexandra's culinary tools.

In the living room, Punshki is in his basket, his own, toy wine bottle between his front paws as he lazily bats his tail. His wag quickens when he sees Halina.

"Hey, *kumpel*," she says softly as she searches for two glasses in the cabinet with pictures stuck all over its doors. The sound of claws behind her doesn't give her sufficient warning, and she's surprised to find him smiling at her from between her feet while his tail hits her calves. "Yeah, I missed you too," she whispers, and puts down the glasses to cup his head and scratch his jaw. Punshki rewards her petting with a faster wag of his tail and a lolling tongue. "You're one of a kind, that's certain," she tells him, then straightens her posture and rolls her shoulders. The movement draws her attention to the dog hair on her hands. "Jesus."

"What?"

"Does Punshki always shed so much?"

"Ah, yeah, sorry about the invasion. Spring arrives, and he starts a fur factory."

Halina freezes at the reminder and tries to keep her conversation with her manager from her mind, to no avail.

"*C'est prêt!*"

Halina blinks, quickly opens the bottle, and pours the Pinot Gris as Alexandra comes into the living room with a large ceramic dish. The spicy aroma seems to expand, filling the room, and Halina focuses on the present.

"Rack of lamb, rubbed with harissa spice and pistachio," Alexandra explains, putting the dish on her coffee table with a flourish, "with roasted tomatoes, carrots, and wild asparagus."

"Oh, wow," Halina whispers. "You're spoiling me."

"Yep."

"Not a complaint, mind you."

"Good—and look," Alexandra points out as she picks up a chop. "You can eat it all with your fingers."

"Hot."

Alexandra waggles her eyebrows. "I know, right."

Halina leans closer, her mouth pressed to the corner of Alexandra's. "Very hot."

"Wait 'til you've tried the harissa."

Halina copies Alexandra and takes a lamb chop by the bone. The meat is covered with a layer of crushed pistachios, and there are red speckles in the crust. The first bite is truly decadent; the meat juice explodes in her mouth, along with the fatty taste of the pistachios. The heat of the spices kicks in, as Alexandra predicted, but slowly.

"Wow," she says, mouth still full.

Alexandra finds a cherry tomato, almost burnt in its caramelization. "Here," she tells Halina, offering it to her.

Halina chews on it. The juice of the fruit, along with the herbs it was cooked in, soothes the burn of the harissa, and she's left with just the kick.

"Delicious," she says once she's swallowed.

"Told you it was special," Alexandra replies proudly. "Here, take some more, and some of that…"

THE PLATES ARE EMPTY BUT for the bones and one lone tomato, and Halina has never been so full. Her belly is bloated, as if she's been impregnated by aliens. "I'm dead."

"Drama queen."

"I ate too much; roll me out of here."

Alexandra giggles as she finishes her glass of wine. "As if," she replies. "No, I'll keep you right here and fatten you up."

Halina gives her a lazy thumb-up. "Sign me the fuck up," she says, before burping loudly. "Oops, sorry."

"It's considered a compliment in the Middle East, so thank you."

Halina straightens up, wincing when her belt digs into her stomach. "I keep forgetting you're not one hundred percent Californian."

Alexandra shrugs. "It's not as if I grew up there, either," she says. "My Middle Eastern-ness is made of habits created during my childhood."

"What a weird mix, though," Halina muses, rubbing her belly contentedly. "American, of Polish decent on your father's side, I got that, and where are you from on your mother's side?"

"Morocco, with a dash of Israel," Alexandra supplies. "Hence the hair, the skin, and the temper."

"Ah."

"The height, too."

Halina scoots closer to Alexandra on the couch. "I like your pocket size."

"Oh, fuck you," Alexandra replies with a laugh and goes into Halina's arms. They get into a more comfortable position on the couch: Alexandra on her back and Halina on top of her. "What else do you like?" Alexandra asks, her arms around Halina's neck.

"Hmm, fishing for compliments, słoneczna? Fine, let's count the ways, shall we," she replies thoughtfully. "I for one have a very deep appreciation for your boobs."

"Wow, shocker. I'm totally surprised, didn't see it coming."

"Can you blame me?" Halina asks, at Alexandra's dry tone. "They're so soft and squishy." Her hand slides over to cup and squeeze one in her hand. "My squishy," she murmurs, bowing her head to kiss the space between Alexandra's breasts.

Alexandra laughs, and it makes her breast jiggle in Halina's hand. "I should have been careful. Watching *Finding Nemo* with you was a bad idea," she says when Halina rubs the tip of her nose around the swell of her left breast.

Halina wiggles until she can rest her head on Alexandra's chest, right under her breasts. "How did you manage to turn me into this... possessive, grabby idiot," she whispers softly.

Alexandra stops laughing with a deep sigh, puts her hands on the back of Halina's head, and caresses her hair soothingly.

"I don't mind it," she replies softly, her lips to Halina's ear "You have the same effect on me."

"I do?"

"You have no idea," Alexandra says with one hand around the back of Halina's neck. "Sometimes, I just want to leave hickeys right here, for everyone to understand that you're mine."

The word sends a thrill down her spine, raising goosebumps in its wake. Her reaction is more visible than she thought. Alexandra's eyes darken as she cups Halina's face with both hands. "*My* babe," she whispers. Halina presses her cheek into Alexandra's touch and tilts her head to extend the caress.

"Hmm, it's nice," Halina says, voice husky. She summons strength to slide back up Alexandra's body to kiss her. The kiss is slow and lazy and languorous and tastes of spices and wine.

"Oh," she sighs, dropping her face to Alexandra's neck and shoulder to kiss it and nibble the skin. "I want…"

Alexandra stretches her neck to offer more of it to Halina's mouth. "Tell me, tell me, Lina…"

As she tries to find the right way to phrase her desire, the memory of a recent conversation with Ari pops up. "I want you to make love to me."

TAKING TO HEART HER EPIPHANY about spontaneity, Halina stops resisting, allows her emotions to participate in the moment, and lets Alexandra break down the last remnants of her walls. Every caress goes deeper than her skin. Every kiss pressed to her cheeks, to her neck, to her breasts, reaches through her entire body and is balm on her emotional wounds. Every touch on her skin, every thrust of the silicon dildo inside of her, becomes the softest of declarations, building a harbor to shelter her.

This embrace is more than another roll in the hay. In many ways completely separate from biology or experience, it feels like a first time.

When she comes, her orgasm doesn't have the urgency Halina usually seeks. The low, building pressure melts away what remained of her fears and doubts, which are pushed out in the form of tears rolling from her closed eyes as her body arches toward Alexandra to get more of what is already too much.

"Babe—" Alexandra starts, voice filled with concern and love, but Halina reaches for Alexandra's neck to tug her into a soft, closed-lipped kiss that's somehow more sensual than the Frenchiest of them.

Alexandra gets rid of the strap-on she had on her hips. Then she lies down, spooning Halina with her arms around her waist and pressing small kisses on her shoulder blades. She pushes Halina's hair away from her neck and back with soft caresses. "You okay?" she whispers, hooking one leg over Halina's thigh.

"Never better," Halina replies as she reclines against her and lazily rocks her hips.

"Whatcha doing?"

"It's your turn."

"Shhh," Alexandra whispers, putting her hand on Halina's hip. "I am good, babe."

Halina relaxes, impossibly pliant in her embrace. The only sound comes from outside: distant cars passing, people coming out of restaurants. Halina, hair spread on the pillow, turns to face Alexandra.

"Will you tell me how you met Leo?"

Alexandra freezes, then mirrors Halina's posture. "You believe me now when I say it was all in his head?"

Halina wiggles, her legs stretched enticingly. "I do."

Alexandra squints, shoulders tense until she relaxes into the pillows. "All right. Once upon a time, we met at our master's workshop. I had just landed from the States and he from Italy. We found a kinship in both being strangers in a new country and we let the chemistry between us turn into something more physical."

"And you didn't introduce him to your parents?"

Alexandra sighs. "I could have, had I been completely blind to how he considered our relationship. But my dad wouldn't have wanted me home by myself. I don't even want to imagine how he would react if I had brought a Catholic with me..."

"You miss them," Halina states, since the pain in Alexandra's voice is easily readable. It's not hard to recognize a pain she must live with every day herself, especially in someone she loves.

"Of course I do. My mother was my model when I was younger, my inspiration. I wanted to be my *ima* when I grew up."

"What did she do for a living?"

"Oh, she stayed at home," Alexandra says. "But she never made it seem to be a burden, managing everything, which included the two of us and my father, and my family in Israel, and the ones in France, *and* the ones in Morocco. Everything felt natural and easy, when she was in charge."

"And you want... to be a stay-at-home mother?"

"Not sure I want to be a mother, period," Alexandra replies truthfully. She looks at the ceiling before she turns to Halina. "Do you?"

"Want to be a mother? Not sure it would be very kind to the child," Halina says with a strand of hair twirled around her finger. "But I suppose it could happen, with the right person... maybe adopt a kid..."

"Huh."

"What?"

"Nothing," Alexandra says with a kiss. "A new side to you is always a nice surprise."

Halina makes a doubtful sound against Alexandra's lips. They both laugh into it; their hold on each other is tighter.

When Alexandra's eyes are closed and soft little snores issue from her parted lips, Halina considers the words still hanging in the air. Never had she considered the possibility of motherhood. She has no idea where that came from. She glances to her left before snuggling against Alexandra, one arm wrapped around her waist.

It's food for thought.

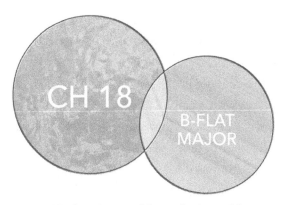

Umber, Periwinkle, and Marigold

THOUGH ALEXANDRA DOESN'T WANT TO say she has a favorite season, she can admit she impatiently waited for spring and the warm weather to finally come back to Paris. As the days get longer, opportunities to have dinner outside with Halina are more frequent, and Alexandra makes it a personal challenge to find fun spots for picnics. The only thing she didn't take into consideration was her own work as an obstacle.

"I hate restoration work," she complains to Leo as she drives the car to their new contract.

He rolls his shoulders in the passenger's seat. "I know."

"It's tiresome, exhausting and—"

"Unrewarding, I know."

"Why did we take it?" She's whining and puts her head against the steering wheel when they stop at a red light.

"Because we need to pay rent."

"Hm."

"And while we wait for the Philharmonie and the synagogue to bring in more clients, it's not enough to make a living. Take a left."

"Yeah, yeah," Alexandra replies without any heat. "It's not my first rodeo. Of course the road is long until we get there. It just..." She blows a raspberry. "It sucks. And on the other side of Paris, too. Transporting the panels will be a nightmare."

"It does, and it will. We can always charge extra. We'll get better jobs soon, just you wait."

"Did you light a candle in church or something?"

"Nah," Leo says with a laugh. "It's just the way things go, the calm before the storm. Soon, we will need to get apprentices to deal with the influx of clients. And take the second exit on the piazza."

"I guess you have a point."

"Course I do. Now stop complaining and get us to the Signora Lagrange."

RIGHT THIS INSTANT, ALEXANDRA COULD kill her new client and feel absolutely no remorse. What possessed the young woman with too much time and money on her hands to plan a veranda for her third-floor apartment? To want it with a stained-glass ceiling is only a rotten cherry on Alexandra's spoiled cake.

Merde, fuck, she already hates this job and everything it entails. Worse, her body hates her for it, and Alexandra begrudgingly admits that, as the saying goes, she may be too old for dealing with irritating, entitled clients under nearly impossible conditions.

The few minutes she wastes finding a parking spot near Halina's hotel are the final push she needs to rush all the way to Halina's door.

"Hey there," Halina welcomes her into the room. She wears a stunning black dress, but her feet are bare.

"You have a concert tonight," Alexandra murmurs, so tired she stumbles. "I forgot, I'm sorry, I'll just—"

"You'll just nothing," Halina says with her arm around Alexandra's waist to help her inside. "Stay here, relax, take a bath, order something from the room service, and wait for me. I'll come back as soon as I'm not needed there."

Alexandra nearly purrs. "Sounds nice," she murmurs; her words are muddled as she fights to keep her eyes opened.

"What about Punshki? Is it safe to leave him alone for the night?"

"He's at a sleepover with his buddies."

"Good," Halina says decisively. "I can even make the order for you, sweetheart, would you like that?"

Alexandra drops her bag and wraps her arms around Halina's neck. "Mmm."

"I'll take that as a yes," Halina says, softly laughing before she kisses her temple. "Come on, let's take you to the chair."

Alexandra lets herself sink into the cushion, toes her shoes off, and tries to shake her pants off her hips. Halina shakes her head. Her bun quivers on her nape while she dials.

"Yes, hi, this is room 1312. Good evening, Jonathan. Would you be able to—"

The rest of Halina's discussion with the concierge blurs into fuzzy peach-color in Alexandra's mind. She would love to listen, if only to figure out what Halina is figuratively cooking up for dinner, but she is just too tired.

It's a battle of wills between Alexandra and her own eyelids to stay awake. She would love to unravel Halina's carefully arranged hair and composure, wrap the soft strands of hair around her fingers, and have her wicked way with her, if she could just stay awake a little bit longer, just one more…

"There you go, honey." Halina kneels next to Alexandra's chair, pulls off her pants, folds them, and puts them on the footrest. "All taken care of."

"'S nice," Alexandra says, valiantly standing to pull off her shirt and waistcoat in one move. "To be taken care of by you."

Halina laughs at her antics and lightly slaps her ass. "Don't make a habit of it."

Alexandra manages to wobble to the bathroom. The bathtub, which has a wall-mounted TV screen installed opposite, seems to call her name. "Oh, this is gonna be good," she whispers. "Will the concert be broadcast, too?"

"Maybe," Halina replies, cocking her hip against the doorframe. In the mirror, Alexandra sees her observing while she takes off her underwear. "Want to catch it?"

"Do you even have to ask?"

Halina steps forward and wraps her arms around Alexandra's shoulders; the sequins on her dress tickle Alexandra's bare skin. "Good. I'll be even better if I know you watch me."

Alexandra drops her head to Halina's shoulder and kisses the side of her neck. "Go," she says. "You'll be late otherwise; traffic is horrible."

Halina sighs, squeezing her one more time before she pulls away. "You're right. I hate how right you are. Your program sounds better than mine," she adds with a pout.

"Liar, you love performing."

"Only half lies, though. I'd love to stay here with you too."

"Shoo!"

Halina blows Alexandra a kiss before stepping out of the bathroom. "Love you."

A pause, and Halina's face appears once again in the doorframe. "Love you too."

Alexandra sighs, opening the faucets to fill the bathtub. Several bottles are lined up near the sink, and she looks for a scent she'll be happy to soak in. At the last minute, she remembers to close the door; she may be exhausted, but she won't flash an innocent bellboy. She slowly slides into the tub.

Alexandra has a very fine shower at home, but this bath is divine. She needs to use it to the fullest and as long as she can. She slides a bit deeper into the water, grabs the remote control, and turns on the TV. Only one channel can broadcast the concert, and she switches to it.

"It's not a concert," Alexandra comments aloud, blinking as images of people on bicycles fill the screen.

"Never mind," Alexandra says aloud as the voice of the narrator lulls her while she lets the oils and bubbles work their magic.

"And after a commercial break, we'll continue this soirée of culture discoveries with the Philharmonie de Paris, for an evening with Sergei Prokofiev..."

Alexandra smiles in satisfaction and closes her eyes as the dual voices of the announcers present the upcoming program.

"That's my girl," she whispers as the camera pans to the orchestra. The audience is a shadow in the foreground.

*   *   *

THE CONCERT IS A SUCCESS, everyone hits their cues, and the public eats it up. Even the maestro has a nice word for her when they take their bow together. Maxime hands Halina a large bouquet of peonies.

"Wasn't too fast for you, was it," he asks with a smirk.

Couldn't resist teasing me, eh, old man?

"Oh, no," she replies, with an answering smile, "if anything, I was worried about you, my dear."

The maestro's expression goes cold before they turn back to the audience. The audience asks for an encore, and she has just the right piece in mind to end the evening on a happy note and shut the maestro's mouth.

Halina sets the flowers down on the bench and exchanges an amused look with Odile. At the piano, she focuses on Alexandra waiting for her in her hotel room to interpret Moszkowski's piece. Her fingers run across the keys to translate its energy. The music is so familiar she hasn't needed a score for it in a long time.

As she follows the slowing rhythm of the piece, she turns to the audience with a smile, including them, but she hopes the camera is on her and that Alexandra sees it, sees *her*, and understands it's all for her.

When her mind is on Alexandra, she feels full of sparks: sparks on her skin, sparks in her stomach, sparks everywhere.

The audience cheers and applauds her when she stands once again with one hand on the piano to bow. When she takes the bouquet from

Odile and leads her and the rest of the orchestra off the stage before the intermission, the concertmaster comes close. "You gave us quite the performance, Hal." Halina lifts her head proudly. "The old man is going to eat his baton."

"It would serve him well for even doubting my ability to follow him."

"He didn't!"

"Oh, he sure did. Even asked me if he was not too fast for me."

"Pff, what an idiot." Odile takes off one heeled shoe to massage her foot. "At least we got to do the last piece together. Want to hang out in the foyer for the break?"

"Of course," Halina replies. "But I gotta go home afterward."

"Right, no piano for 'Pierre et le Loup.'"

"Nope."

"*Veinarde*," Odile comments with an eye-roll as they pass the maestro on their way out. "She is waiting for you, yes?"

Halina takes her eyes off the illuminated glass panels to face the woman who has become her friend. "Yes, she should be."

Odile puffs on her electronic cigarette as she nods. "Good, that's good."

"What is?"

"For you to have some… incentive, to stay in Paris."

"I'm still weighing my options."

"Oh, I don't want you to refuse formidable opportunities," Odile says, lightly touching her forearm. "But I would be sad to have to say goodbye. You're good, Piotrowski."

"You too, Moineau."

"Thanks, but I meant for us, for the orchestra," she adds with a pointed look over the rim of her glasses.

Halina nods back. "I promise you'll be the first person I tell about my decision when I reach it."

"You do that," Odile replies, squaring her shoulders. "Hey, if you do leave, we'll celebrate it properly."

"With more lukewarm beer?"

"Non! With wine!"

Halina laughs at Odile's offended tone. "Good to know. All you needed was the proper incentive."

"To stay?"

"Only if we celebrate it with wine too."

"Duly noted, Halina," Odile replies with a wink, before shooing her away. "Now go home, before they make you stay!"

THE PICTURE ALEXANDRA MAKES IN her bed is adorable and too funny for Halina not to be amused, but she manages to keep her laughter silent. Alexandra clearly sleeps where she fell; damp curls frame her face and cover the pillow, while the darkness of her skin is showcased by the white sheets wrapped around her like a toga. The whole scene becomes irresistible when Halina catches its soundtrack of sleepy mumbles and soft snores.

As silently as she can, Halina undresses, lies behind Alexandra, and pulls her into a cuddle. She kisses the side of Alexandra's neck and brushes her hand through the mess that is Alexandra's hair.

Still asleep, Alexandra leans into her touch and scoots closer to her with a satisfied smack of her lips. Her snoring smooths into peaceful breathing.

Halina waits for sleep to find her while Odile's words turn as a carousel of ideas she cannot stop.

* * *

"WHAT'S THIS?"

Judging by their tone of voice, one would think Halina brought Ari to this restaurant in order to fight bare-handed with tarantulas.

"Dinner," she says, deadpan. "Surely you've heard of it."

"Har, har." Ari's shoulders don't relax one iota. "As if that's what I meant. Why did you bring me here to have dinner with her?"

They stand at the entrance. Halina grimaces as she follows Ari's gaze toward Alexandra, who is not alone. The tall man who is the biggest pain in Halina's ass sits at a table with her.

"She's here so you two can get along…" Ari lets out a long, suffering sigh. "…and to give me the opportunity to get along with her best friend, too."

The rushed words stop Ari's antics in their tracks. "I'm your best friend?"

"Of course you are; how dare you doubt it."

Halina steps back to let a waiter pass with a heavily loaded tray and observes the pair, who haven't noticed them yet. Alexandra's hands are folded on the table while she quietly talks to Leo. He pouts, and if she didn't want to slap him, Halina might be able to accept that his could be an endearing face.

"Any tips on the best friend?"

"Hmm?"

"Very yummy. Gimme some ammunition, Halina. Be a good wingwoman for your bestie."

"I won't help you seduce Alexandra's partner."

Dark amusement takes over Ari's features. "Partner? As in, *the* infamous mustache-twirling asshole?"

Halina sniffs disdainfully. "*That* is a goatee. He doesn't have the refinement necessary to rock a moustache."

"A villainous goatee doesn't have the same ring to it." Ari tilts their head and appraises Leo. "Not too shabby for a villain. I wouldn't kick him out of bed."

"Ugh, come on, Ari."

"Hey, I have eyes—and needs, too."

"Humph."

Ari bumps lightly into her, forcing her forward. "Maybe I can fuck his bad attitude out of him."

"Ari Fowler, sexorcist extraordinaire?"

"The power of my ass compels you!"

They're still laughing when they reach the table. Alexandra raises an eyebrow. "Hi," she says as she pecks Halina's cheek. "Good to see you in such a good mood."

"Seeing you always puts me in a good mood, słoneczna," Halina replies and moves her chair closer to Alexandra's.

Leo and Ari roll their eyes at them. They can mock all they want. She wouldn't want Ari to build a friendship with Alexandra if she wasn't serious about her, and vice versa. Meeting Ari outside of their professional persona is her version of meeting the parents.

"We are gathered here today," Alexandra says, with Halina's hand squeezed in hers, "because you are the most important people in our lives in Paris—"

"Thanks for the precision." Leo cuts her off; his tone alone grates on Halina's nerves. "Makes me all warm inside."

Before she can tell him where exactly he can shove his ego, Alexandra moves her leg. Leo's wince of pain is a balm to Halina's feelings.

That's my girl.

"Don't be stupid," Alexandra says sternly. "We live in Paris; presenting you as our most important persons here is a compliment, and you know it, so zip it."

Leo does clam up. *Unbelievable.*

"All right, so we are your BFFs," Ari intervenes, leaning forward on their elbows, body twisted toward Leo in one sinuous line. "And if I got this right, you want us all to get along as a big, queer family."

"Gay-mbaya," Leo comments with a smirk, and Ari reluctantly responds to his proffered hand in a high-five.

Halina glances at Alexandra, who shrugs. If the pair uses mocking them as a bonding tool, it's as good as any other solution.

"Before we all braid each other's hair in a big, rainbow circle, let's eat and we'll take it from here?" Halina suggests as she unfolds the menu.

Ari sighs and then nods in agreement. "I guess—let's unite the two coasts," they add, offering their fist for Alexandra until she bumps it.

Halina focuses on Leo, who shrugs. "Let's work on the European Union?"

They shake hands, and Halina squeezes his hand just a bit too tightly.

Ari returns their attention to Leo with a hunger entirely unrelated to the menu. "What about working on the bond between the US and the EU?" they ask sweetly, with their chin cupped in their palm.

"Should we leave them alone?" Alexandra whispers, and Halina shakes her head.

"Ari is always better with an audience."

"Oh my."

"Exactly."

"Leo is going to be eaten alive, isn't he?"

"One can hope."

"Lina..."

"Sorry, sorry," Halina says, barely suppressing a laugh as she lifts Alexandra's hand to kiss her knuckles. "Old habits. It should be interesting," she adds, observing Leo and Ari.

"Mm hmm."

Leo mirrors Ari's posture; his arms are crossed over the table as he flexes his biceps. "I'm all for intercontinental friendships," he purrs. "Besides, isn't your side of the US home to Little Italy? This was fate."

"*Little* Italy?"

"Maybe yours. Mine is *Italia grandissima.*"

"You don't say?"

"Oh, yeah."

Alexandra claps her hands. "If you're done with this preliminary pissing contest, maybe we can move on? Or just wait for us to be gone to continue?"

"Sure, *principessa,*" Leo replies, beaming at her.

"Whatever, Cali," is Ari's response, and Alexandra squints at them.

"Bite me, East Coast."

"Do I need to turn this car around?" Halina cuts in.

"Funny to have you play the mom-friend," Ari says mirthfully from behind their menu. "So responsible, all of a sudden…"

"It's called growing up, maybe you can try it sometime." The smile Alexandra gives her is well worth the second eye-roll from Ari.

"You didn't always sing such a tune, is all I'm saying."

Alexandra leans forward, an ominous glint in her eyes. "You don't say."

"Ari…"

"Hey, now come on, boss; you want us to bond, you said so yourself."

"I don't want you to bond over dirt on me!"

Both Ari and Alexandra give her epic puppy looks: dangerous alone, fatal in tandem.

O, Boże, what have I done.

While Ari starts telling a tale of one of her less-glowing moments, Halina smiles at Leo, and he replies with a fond smile of his own.

Maybe this won't be so hard after all.

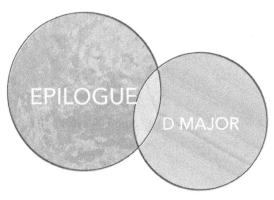

EPILOGUE

D MAJOR

Blues and Silvers

"I HAVE A KEY TO your hotel room. It's only fair to give you a way to surprise me, too, now that you have fewer rehearsals."

Halina enjoys the domesticity of being able to wait for Alexandra to come home. How Alexandra's apartment has become her home is a constant bewilderment, but she has learned to live with it. Her life has two parts: Before and After Alexandra. BA, domesticity was a nightmare, the epitome of surrender to a routine bound to be Halina's downfall, a fear she could only respond to with flight. She never thought she could fall in love, let alone with such a woman as Alexandra, with her complex blend of restraint and passion.

After Alexandra, domesticity became a harbor, an anchor in the storm to keep her afloat and at peace.

Halina's fingers curl in Punshki's fur, and he tips his head back to grace her with one of his doggy smiles. His tongue lolls as his tail thumps against the couch. The door opens slowly, and Punshki jumps from her lap to trot to his rightful owner. Halina instantly misses his weight on her lap.

O, Boże, her past partners would have a field day if they could see her now, settled in a relationship, and not only that, craving displays of affection such as cuddles and other snuggles. She may have rejected it all in the past, but she now craves it.

Love changes a person in remarkable ways.

"Welcome home, słoneczna." She stands, gathers the two glasses of wine she had prepared for Alexandra's return in one hand and buries her free hand in Alexandra hair. Smooth jazz plays in the background.

"Good evening, ba—hey!" The pet name dissolves into an exclamation as she takes in Halina's appearance. "Wow!"

Halina flushes at the open praise. She runs her hand through her hair; the longer strands are barely long enough to reach the nape of her neck now. "Ta-da?"

Alexandra remains silent, slowly stroking Punshki's fur. Her dark eyes are locked onto Halina.

"You hate it," Halina laments. "It will grow back quickly, and I'll have Rapunzel's hair all over again before you—"

"Don't you dare." Alexandra's voice is close to the purr Halina loves so much. Letting Punshki go down, she cups Halina's face in her hands. Her fingertips caress the short strands. "You were magical, always have been, but this—it frees you."

Halina's chest almost hurts with relief. "Rea-really?"

Alexandra pulls her toward her to give her a kiss. "It suits you," she says as she folds herself into Halina's arms and dips her head to nestle it under Halina's chin. "Ah, it's good to be home."

Halina pets her hair and shoulders. Alexandra's warmth seeps through her clothes and she takes comfort in this bubble of love she never thought she would be allowed to enjoy. "Shower, wine, and sushi?" she suggests.

The vibrations of Alexandra's purr resonate between their chests. "Switch sushi with burgers, and I'm in," Alexandra replies, mock-drunkenly.

Halina smothers a laugh in Alexandra's hair and presses a kiss to her forehead. "All right, słoneczna," she says. "Come on, I am not carrying you into the shower."

"Even if I beg?"

"I would definitely enjoy it, but no."

"Even if I promise to do anything you want?"

"Anything?"

"Any—" Alexandra is cut off by a yawn. "Anything."

"We'll revisit my darkest, most nefarious plans some other time, when you can actually do something. Let's go, słoneczna."

The walk to the bathroom is a lazy affair. Alexandra's state of fatigue is even more obvious once she starts undressing. As she drops her shirt and jeans haphazardly on the floor, a grimace of pain crosses her face before a deep yawn makes her throw her head backward. She stretches her back, rolls her shoulders, and lifts one hand toward Halina. "Join me?"

Halina's heart quickens with excitement. If she had a tail, she would be powerless to stop its frenetic wag. "B-but what about the burgers?"

Alexandra wiggles her fingers impatiently, beckoning Halina to her. "They can wait."

Halina's dress is off before Alexandra can finish her sentence. Once they are both in the shower, she puts her hands on Alexandra's hips and kisses the tattoo at the base of her neck.

"Love you," she whispers against the rainbow cardiogram pattern, and Alexandra bends her head back to look at her upside down.

"*Je t'aime aussi,*" she replies before stepping away from her to modulate the temperature of the water and the various sprays. "Now, serious talk: warm-warm or boiling-warm?"

"You're the one who needs the shower the most, you decide."

Alexandra turns the knobs until the temperature suits her. Then she gives Halina a sly, sideways glance. "I love this side of you," she says, with a raised eyebrow. "I'll have to remember to appeal to it more often."

Her eyes cloud for a split second. The unspoken "while I can" rings between them with the strength of a bum note on a piano, and Halina bites her lower lip to keep the words in. She has a plan, a plan she intends to stick to.

"You would abuse your power and knowledge so ruthlessly?" she asks, her body fitted behind Alexandra in the shower. "I am appalled."

The clouds in Alexandra's eyes disappear, and she pokes Halina's nose. "Without a shred of hesitation."

"Ruthless." Halina makes a mock attempt to bite Alexandra's finger before she finds a bottle of shampoo from the shelf. She squirts some of it into her hand and massages it into Alexandra's curls. "Maybe I love *this* side of you."

Alexandra's answering giggle dissolves into a moan as Halina presses her fingertips into her scalp. Halina was already on hot coals while she waited for Alexandra to come home, but the sounds coming from Alexandra's mouth turn those feelings into white-hot arousal.

With one hand on Alexandra's hip, Halina makes her turn to face her and tilts her head under the water to rinse away the shampoo. Taking advantage of her stretched neck, she kisses and kitten-licks the wet skin of her throat in abstract patterns. Her hands slide down to palm Alexandra's full breasts, and she brushes her thumbs against the hardening nubs.

How she ever judged this woman to be anything but spectacular is beyond her.

"Lina," Alexandra mumbles, her hands on Halina's shoulders, "babe, I, uh—love where this is going, don't get me wrong, but I can't—"

"Shh." Halina removes her hands from Alexandra's breasts to pull her close. "It's okay, just wanted to make you all relaxed and happy."

Alexandra's expression is the epitome of contentment. "I am."

"Achievement, then."

"You fucking dork."

Halina is not about to correct her, and they manage to wash themselves without too many incidents. Alexandra nearly jabs her elbow in Halina's ribs, and Halina almost hits Alexandra with the showerhead, but the would-be injuries are avoided with laughter and pecks on cheeks.

"One day we will have shower sex," Halina says as they emerge from the stall.

Alexandra raises an eyebrow before giving her one of her fluffiest towels.

"What?"

"Oh, we theoretically can," Alexandra replies while she shakes her hair and sprays an anti-frizz conditioner on it. "I just think we need some practice to make sure we don't injure ourselves, and I'll be so busy the next couple of weeks before—"

"Before you leave" goes unsaid; Halina's departure once again comes between them. Halina can't put Alexandra through this torture any longer. Alexandra's smile is too painful, her demeanor too compliant, to endure any longer.

"Yeah, about that…" Halina starts.

"Yes?"

Alexandra's tone doesn't leave any room for delay. Her whole demeanor demands answers fast.

"What if I were to tell you I don't have to leave in two weeks?"

A quick succession of emotions crosses Alexandra's face: hope, excitement, and confusion.

"You're taking a holiday? The first one in, what, ten years? Good for you, babe."

Try again, my little słoneczna.

"Well, yes and no."

Alexandra braces herself on the sink and frowns at Halina. "What do you mean?"

"I will take a month of holidays," Halina replies slowly, "but I won't have to leave afterward."

From Halina's point of view, her meaning is more than obvious. Either Alexandra refuses to believe what she hears, or she is more tired than Halina thought. Alexandra's frown deepens into three lines on her forehead. "Explain."

Halina drops her towel and stands facing Alexandra, so close Alexandra has to tilt her head up to maintain eye contact.

"May I introduce you to the new *pianiste en résidence* for the Philharmonie de Paris," she says softly, cupping Alexandra's face with her thumb on the hinge of her jaw.

Alexandra's eyes open wide and her mouth drops open.

"Wha—" She makes a weird sound, somewhere between a giggle and a sob, and puts her arms around Halina's neck. Halina keeps them from toppling against the sink.

"You are now the soloist for the Philharmonie," she repeats, waiting for Halina's nod to press an enthusiastic kiss to her lips. "For—for how long?"

Halina's smile widens, and she kisses the tip of Alexandra's nose. "Five years, for starters."

Alexandra barks a tearful laugh. "For starters, she says," she mumbles before pulling Halina to her for a deeper, more passionate kiss. "So you're staying?"

"For as long as you'll have me."

In the second Alexandra takes to reply, her expression is the most open Halina has ever faced. Her girlfriend is usually easy to read, but never so much as she is now. Her eyes are wide and wet, and now a lighter hue. The color, such an important part of what drew Halina into her orbit, makes Alexandra appear younger, more vulnerable with this added light, in a way that's directly connected to Halina's heartstrings. Her lips are parted in a disbelieving smile, and Halina wants to kiss them again and again.

Alexandra pulls Halina impossibly closer, so Halina's hipbone digs into Alexandra's soft belly.

"I'm not letting you go anytime soon," she says softly, and claims Halina's lips in a deep kiss while she twists her fingers in the short hair on Halina's nape.

As she lets herself be swept away in the kiss, Halina already thinks of the music and colors they'll inspire each other to create.

Concertos of colors, canvases of music… as far as she can see.

THE END

GLOSSARY

FRENCH

Au contraire: On the contrary

Bienvenu(s): Welcome

Bonsoir: Good evening

C'est prêt: It's ready

Cœur d'artichaut: Literally, artichoke heart. Figuratively, someone who falls in love easily

Comme d'habitude: As usual

Corps d'orchestre: Orchestra

Crétin: Moron

Je t'aime aussi: I love you too

Merde: Shit

Moelleux au chocolat: Chocolate fondant

Non: No

Oui: Yes

Passage du désir: Literally, desire's way. In the story, the name of a Parisian adult "lovestore"

Pianiste en résidence: Official pianist

Pièce à quatre mains: A piece played by two people, hence, four hands

Pièce de résistance: Centerpiece

Pierre et le Loup: Peter and the Wolf. Russian musical tale written and composed by Prokofiev in 1936

Premier violon: First violin, Concertmaster

Putain: Fuck (in French, can take many meanings, from pure rage to extreme satisfaction)

Que sera, sera: Whatever will be, will be
Réservation: Booking
Tire, tire l'aiguille: Pull, pull the thread. French version of a traditional Yiddish song
Veinarde: Lucky girl

HEBREW
Gett: Divorce in accordance to Jewish religious laws
Hag sameah: Happy holiday
Hanukkah: Jewish holiday commemorating the rededication of the Second Holy Temple in Jerusalem. It occurs between late November and late December in the Gregorian calendar
Ima: Mother
Ma'oz t'zur: Jewish liturgical poem sung for Hanukkah in the Ashkenazi tradition since the 13th century. The poem is quite long, but the part in the novel is translated as:

> *O mighty stronghold of my salvation,*
> *To praise You is a delight.*
> *Restore my House of Prayer*
> *And there we will bring a thanksgiving—*

Mehitsa: Separating wall between men and women in a synagogue (temple)
Meshuga: Crazy
Motek: Sweetie, darling
Nessya tova: Safe trip

ITALIAN
Cara mia: My dear
Carissima: Dearest
Certo: Of course

Italia grandissima: Greatest Italy
Principessa : Princess
Signora : Madam
Une vera e propria musa: A genuine source of inspiration

POLISH
Anioł: Angel
Barszcz: Polish beet soup
Bombka / Bombki: Handmade glass baubles
Buhaj: Bull
Cześć: Bye
Diabełek: Devil
Drań: Scoundrel, villain
Dzidzia: Baby
Gówno: Shit
Idioto: Stupid
Ja pierdolę: Fuck
Kumpel: Buddy
Kurde: Fuck, damn it
Lulajze jezuniu: Traditional Polish Christmas hymn
Makowiec: Poppy seed pastry
Miód pitny: Mead
Na szczęście: Good luck
O, boże / O, mój boże: Oh, God; Oh, my God
O, cholera: Oh, Hell
Pączek / Pączi: Doughnut(s)
Perun: Slavic god of thunder and lightning
Placki: Potato pancakes
Psiakrew: Hell, shit
Psotnica: Playful
Rosół: Chicken soup
Słoneczna: Sunny

YIDDISH

Bubbeleh / bubby: Term of endearment for a younger relative

Gelt: Money

Krupnik: Barley soup

Latkes: Potato pancakes

Mamuschka: Term of endearment for a mother; derived from Russian

Oy vey: Short for "Oy Vey iz mir," Woe is me

Ponshkes: Jelly-filled doughnuts. A Hanukkah treat

Schmuck: Literally, penis. Figuratively, jerk

Tuches: Buttocks

ACKNOWLEDGMENTS

First, I want to thank the whole Interlude Press family for cheering me on when I didn't think I could work on this novel any longer and for making it happen. You all rock my admittedly impressive collection of socks!

Annie, Candy, Choi, from the bottom of my heart, thank you so much for believing in this story when I did not—you made it all possible, and I owe you. Annie, for your positivity and support through it all. Candy, for your love for this story and your priceless advice. Choi, for the incredible talent and insight you displayed in order to create this masterpiece of a cover. I don't think this sight will ever fail to make me smile.

To Nicki: I am so grateful for your dedication to push me in the right direction, to make this book what it deserved to be, and to make me the author I can grow to be. To Zoe: what you call "nitpicking" is what the French call "travail de dentelle," as in, the finishing details that will change a piece into a masterpiece. So, please, by all means, nitpick away, because my *Concerto* would not be the same without you.

To Kate: thank you for being my writing companion from start to finish (and for checking my Polish!). To Heidi: the gift you gave me is one I can only hope to repay some day. To Sam, my partner in crime and ever-present cheerleader--we did it, my friend!

To Kim and Brittney: thank you for being sensitivity readers on this story—it's important to make sure all the representations featured in the book are accurate, and sensitivity readers are essential to this goal.

Thank you for being my first readers and for giving me the tools to improve as a writer.

Moune, thank you for believing in me and for never making me feel like my oddities were negative traits. Thank you for showing me that there is nothing I can't do. Thank you for letting me ramble at you whenever I was blocked and thank you for your patience and your never-ending supply of love. Thank you for making me a nerd. Thank you for Asimov. Thank you for all the books. Thank you for your strength and the example you set for Yael and me.

Yayuschka, ma puce, thank you so much for having an unwavering faith in me. For keeping me on track. For kicking my butt whenever it needs a good kick. For loving me, in spite of how weird I am sometimes (or maybe because of it?). For being the best sister a woman can have and above all for being my friend. Thank you, thank you, thank you.

Papa... how I wish you could have been here to see it. Many first drafts of this book happened between the two of us, in the kitchen while preparing a meal, with the bubbling of a dish as background music. I will cherish those moments until we meet again. Thank you for making me passionate. Thank you for making me believe in love and romance. Thank you for the music—you are in every note Halina plays through the story. I hope you are proud of me, wherever you are (even if you stole every singer and actor you loved to keep you company. Not cool, Dad).

To my very own Scooby Gang, for being so supportive and for renewing my motivation whenever I faltered: Gabby, Ben, Caroline, Agnès, Morgane, Cécilia—never underestimate how much of your love I poured into this story. It is irreplaceable.

And to my Israeli Powerpuff Girls: distance doesn't mean a thing when love and encouragements can cross seas and mountains.

To the composers and musicians referenced in the story: thank you for creating such important pieces. You have no idea how many colors you brought into my life.

To the owners and chefs of the many restaurants I used as "research" for my girls, particularly Tutti Amici, Flesh, Privé de Dessert—you have given me more than fantastic meals; you have inspired me, and that's priceless.

To the PR team at the Pavillon de la Reine: thank you for humoring me and for giving me information about staying in your hotel (still on my bucket list, but you never know!).

Finally, to you, the readers who took a chance on me and my words: thank you for taking that leap. I hope reading it was as entertaining for you as writing it has been for me.

See you on the next adventure!

ABOUT THE AUTHOR

BORN AND RAISED IN PARIS, France, Naomi Tajedler learned to love art from the womb when her father played guitar to her pregnant mother. Her love of books led her to a Bachelor of Arts in Book Restoration and Conservation, followed by a Master's Degree in art market management. Her first short story, "What The Heart Wants," was published in *Summer Love* (2015), an LGBTQ Young Adult collection by Duet Books. In 2017, one of her flash fiction stories was published by Queer Fiction Press. She also contributed to the Cassandra Project, a collection of works sold for the benefit of Rrain. When not writing, Naomi can be found sharing body positivity tips on social media and trying recipes out on her loved ones.

interlude**press**™

 interludepress.com
 @InterludePress
 interludepress
 store.interludepress.com

interlude  press
you may also like…

"What the Heart Wants" by Naomi Tajedler
Short story published in Summer Love: An LGBTQ Collection

A young student discovers attraction and desire through her experience drawing figures in her summer art class. What the Heart Wants is a short story originally published in *Summer Love*, an LGBTQ young adult collection published by Duet, an imprint of Interlude Press.

ISBN (short story eBook) 978-1-941530-93-1 | (Summer Love print) 978-1-941530-36-8 | (Summer Love eBook) 978-1-941530-44-3

Storm Season by Pene Henson

When Sydney It-Girl Lien Hong finds herself stranded and alone in the stormy New South Wales outback, her rescue comes in the form of wilderness ranger Claudia Sokolov, whose isolated cabin and soulful singing voice bely a complicated history. While they wait out the weather, the women find an undeniable connection that long outlasts the storm.

ISBN (print) 978-1-945053-16-0 | (eBook) 978-1-945053-29-0

Burning Tracks by Lilah Suzanne
The Spotlight series, Book Two

In the sequel to *Broken Records*, Gwen Pasternak has a job she loves and a beautiful wife, Flora. But as she grows closer to country music superstar Clementine Campbell, Gwen second-guesses her quiet life at home. Meanwhile, her business partner Nico Takahashi and his partner, reformed bad-boy musician Grady Dawson, face uncertainties of their own.

ISBN (print) 978-1-941530-99-3 | (eBook) 978-1-945053-00-9

CPSIA information can be obtained
at www.ICGtesting.com
Printed in the USA
FSHW02n0511040718
49891FS